LIFE IS ABOUT LOSING EVERYTHING

LIFE IS ABOUT LOSING EVERYTHING

LYNN CROSBIE

ANANSI

This edition published in 2012 by
House of Anansi Press Inc.
110 Spadina Avenue, Suite 801
Toronto, ON, M5V 2K4
Tel. 416-363-4343
Fax 416-363-1017
www.houseofanansi.com

Distributed in Canada by
HarperCollins Canada Ltd.
1995 Markham Road
Scarborough, ON, M1B 5M8
Toll-free tel. 1-800-387-0117

House of Anansi Press is committed to protecting our natural environment.
As part of our efforts, the interior of this book is printed on paper that contains
100% post-consumer recycled fibres, is acid-free, and is processed chlorine-free.

16 15 14 13 12   1 2 3 4 5

Crosbie, Lynn, 1963–
Life is about losing everything / Lynn Crosbie.

Also issued in electronic format.
ISBN 978-1-77089-003-9

I. Title.

PS8555.R61166L53 2012   C813'.54   C2011-908582-8

Text design and typesetting: Alysia Shewchuk

We acknowledge for their financial support of our publishing program
the Canada Council for the Arts, the Ontario Arts Council, and the Government of
Canada through the Canada Book Fund.

Printed and bound in Canada

For David

But life isn't about what you acquire. Life is about losing everything.
— Mike Tyson, to Michael Jackson

In memory of Stephen McDougall, 1961–1981, and Steve Banks, 1958–2006:

Lux et umbra vicissim, sed semper amor.

The names of actual people in this book have been changed, as have the actual people. Its chronology is impossible to follow: for example, I did not finish the book on April 14. That is my mother's birthday, and that fabrication is for her. Other fabrications are for the reader to consider, but as to the way in which I go back and forth about people here, I cite my friend Daniel Jones's suicide note. Largely estranged from everyone, he wrote, "I love you all."

I started writing this book, fitfully, and according to my notebook, on December 7, 2007. I finished it, more or less, the year I quit drinking (and everything else), and the year that Michael Jackson died.

Stephen McDougall was a boy I loved in high school, who died many years ago; Steve Banks was my first boyfriend. They are the way and the truth.

The book follows a period of trauma, excess, then morbid solitude. Having lost everything, I found my way back to writing and a great deal more. Good or bad, I am most grateful to God, for all of these words, for this story of much of my sickening and beautiful life.

Rarely visible but evident everywhere is my adored family.

My foster pig, Stormy.

Blaze Starr (named after the great showgirl) and Jack (named after the slasher who once haunted Whitechapel), my beloved cats.

Jack died as I finished this book: Thank you for your love; I will see you again.

And there is Francis, who is, as my grandmother Mary said, "the dear, dear friend of friends."

THE WRETCHED LIFE OF A LONELY HEART

I have entered middle age.

I am overweight, and I live with a little dog and two cats. I have been alone for more than seven years.

I keep a journal, as Jenny Craig suggests, about what I eat and how I feel about the things I eat: it is emotionally exhausting.

The entries include the following sad arcana:

— The delicious white border of a bad steak, what the sea leaves when it drags its waves back.

— Fat, as yellow as custard, but sweeter than that. I touch and caramelize my glowing flesh.

— The livid red marks that jag like lightning below my stomach are a fire I cannot extinguish.

I have let myself go.

My hair is mouse and silver; my eyes look like small pastry decorations. If I were being sold on The Shopping Channel as a piece of Joan Rivers's jewellery, I would be described as a "chunky, hammered comfort bracelet" or "faux-python teardrop necklace."

I am a teacher, whose students rate me as approximately average or lower and claim that I do not "treat, or speak to, them like human beings."

I used to write a great deal of poetry about criminals and heroin addicts, things I thought were sexy.

I wrote what follows during a few years, off and on, after Steve's death.

He died of a heart attack, and he died alone.

I always return to him, and to a time when we were together and very young.

Every single thing I have written is for him, and I hope that he likes it.

He once broke up with me for a while. I am like Shane, he said.

I read that book until he returned to me. In the time in between, I thought of him racing away on a dark horse.

Of the horse kicking up dust and sage as I called out, Come back!

THE MOON

The moon is a woman, veiling her face, a poet said to me once, quoting someone French.

In my new book, I said, I call it a wheel of cheese. That's terrible, he said.

I cannot see the moon from any of my windows although I once could, long ago, with another man, the despicable pirate Lafitte. It was too beautiful to describe, how it metallized the room in knife-cuts of light.

There are so many characters in this book. They are staring at the moon: the moon is a cell mutation, irradiated with illness.

As for me, I am huge and indolent. I live in my mind, but not the way a writer does. I make lists there, and invent sandwiches. Occasionally, I remind myself that Joan Crawford felt women should constantly look in the mirror and say, Yes.

I am afraid of having dry hands and feet. I cannot wait to go to bed every night, where my dog, Francis, simmers.

I was almost beautiful once, and am the trash of that now.

People are more audacious and more kind.

At meetings, I draw myself trudging in the snow, holding heavy bags.

I see the moon in my fat, waxing face.

I often go days without hearing from anyone. There are the usual concerns about the cats and dog starving if I die, choking on a handful of cheese bunnies, then bloating into a ball of noxious gas.

Loneliness has attached itself to me with suction cups. I do not know what to do. I have tried to tell it, politely, I am just not interested.

Despair's involvement is also torrid.

I watch a great deal of television, and sometimes I see a commercial about a worm that wraps itself up then roars out, all gorgeous.

A commercial for dental floss, I think.

I call out to my mother. I do this often. Or, to no one at all: I'm dying here.

There are days I find a whole potato on the street or, once, in my yard in the moonlight, and those are very good days.

THE CAPTAIN

Love comes to me in a dream, exhausted. She is former Playboy Bunny Dorothy Stratten, dressed in a dirty white slip. Move over, she seethes.

Several of her red Velcro curlers pop off and roll between us: she sleeps fitfully, starting at loud noises.

Most nights, the dead appear and disgust me with their ardour. Alternatively, I throw up filth, and start cleaning, ineffectually, with a sponge.

One night, The Captain calls. He is a giant bear of a man who makes dates off the Internet using a picture I took of him pawing salmon out of a glacier pool.

He takes a rowdy bong hit and says, Lynn, you need something to care about in your life besides cheese sliders and liquor.

He is feeling helpful and wise. He has forgotten about the black squirrel that keeps darting off his balcony and into his apartment, that squats on his coffee table, filling cups with seeds and nuts.

. The squirrel I call Blackness — what he and I feel, most days.

I called this guy, he tells me. He's like the hottest guy in L.A. And I told him the sad guy story, and he blew me off.

I love that story, I say.

I mean, I didn't even finish it! he bellows.

I ask him to tell me the story again.

The Captain was at a variety store, standing in line behind a tense, florid guy who took forever finding exact change, asking for directions and moist towelettes.

When he finally slid his wallet back into his pocket and left, he forgot his purchase: a package of razor blades and a rainbow candle that said I Love You.

The Captain is a great raconteur, and often punctuates his vile stories about log-sized dildos or incontinence by yelling about how amazing he is.

I tell him I have let everything go, and would like to write something besides sonnets that end with this kind of envoi: Bourbon distilled from God's brown eyes / Sandwiches, crustless, of miniature size.

That I had gone to the staff Christmas party.

I was there early so I had a grilled cheese and coffee at Bellwood. It tasted the way it always did, and I sat there thinking of Steve, who The Captain knew. That he and I would go to Bellwood loaded up on Valium and could only talk by writing on napkins, passing them back and forth. I still have one that says, HOW R U? With his answer underneath, a blacked-out box.

When things were good between us, so long ago, it was like this Tantra: *O Beauteous one! She who holds a book in her hands can never attain Siddhi even if she persists for countless millions of years.*

Captain, I say, I would wake from nightmares and he would hold me. He wore an orange robe that was the soft heart of the sun!

I remember you, the Bellwood waitress said, as Jesus quietly bussed the table, His hands moving slowly.

At the party I sat with two women who worked in the office. One had twin daughters, a small and big one. The other had a hamster named Snowball.

The president of the arts and crafts college where I work walked in and looked as slinky as a fly-strip; everyone moiled around her.

I saw people I knew, but they never said a thing.

I can't even cry about it, I tell The Captain. I am walking through my life like a ghost.

Do something creative, he says.

That was always tied up, for me, with love, I tell him.

Write about THAT, he says. I feel like he has just told me to make lemonade from the lemons life has handed me.

Make a movie about Blackness, I say. Splice orange into every frame — The Captain hates this idea, and cuts me off by dialling up *Axis: Bold as Love.*

I want to tell him more about the grilled cheese, how soft it was, then sparkly.

How I had lingered over the coffee, giving it sugar dandruff, then stirring into it a storm.

They were so mean to me, is what I want to say.

THE MYSTERY

I am staring into a mirror, the only time I remember doing this.

I have long, light brown hair and large blue eyes. A handful of freckles. I am wearing a blue boat-neck sweater and a white blouse. I have hidden the tangles in my hair, and I look beautiful.

I am ten years old.

I will think of this image for the rest of my life, and think of what I have done to this girl.

Of her own rage, when she looks back at me and asks, Why are you doing this to me?

My childhood is otherwise only a sensation, lacking details. It is *A Mystery*.

My best friend, Kissa Museveni, was aware of the mystery, of what the strange man in the bandages, hat, and dark glasses had done.

What happened later was the product of Kissa's own fertile devices: the map she showed me with an X over where he had taken me; a red car she once saw following us; a note, left on my family's stairs, made of pasted, cut-out letters: YOU BETTER WATCH OUT.

And then how she turned my friends against me, and walked to school and back with them, always ten feet ahead.

Kissa had so many Barbies, and a mansion for them filled with Victorian furniture, including a thimble-sized stuffed peacock and purple velvet chairs.

There was a butler, extending a tray of chilly martinis; a pair of satin tap panties, in a square of white tissue; a toreador and gored bull.

Mine were a handful of dirty whores, dressed in Kleenex.

I remember playing outside and some fat woman with a cigarette adhered to her lower lip muttering, She's got the goddamned things in toilet paper. Then exhaling like a dragon.

One day Kissa and I stood on either side of an intersection and saw a grey cat get hit by a car.

I looked at the cat, then her, and she called out, I wish it was you!

I don't know what happened next, or when my life severed from the small thing dying.

Only that I took a flower and left it in a note, apologizing.

She agreed to be friends again: *She fills my heart!*

HAVE YOU SEEN THIS CAT?

The summer all the cats went missing was relentlessly hot: the grass was scorched, the flowers beheaded.

These were sick cats, requiring medication; cats with long and short hair; cats who performed unusual tricks with tinfoil and felt mice. One who could not "open his mout."

Their eyes invariably sad and worried.

I stopped looking when I knew they were not missing but dead.

When he has been gone a week, I buy an X-Acto knife and a glue gun and start postering. Above a photograph of a listless tabby, I have written the following:

> De-afara, picuri mari si grei/Din ploaia ce-anceput de-aseara,
> S-au strecurat in ochii mei/Si sufletul mi-l infioara.
> — Daniel Branzai, "Melancolie"

I am learning Romanian, and how to draw cats in a variety of poses. Sleeping, batting at insects. Crouching, packing their clothes into small valises and waiting by the door.

I helped him wedge his new shirts and slacks into the suitcase's plastic-bagged hanger compartment; filled a bag with fruit and diagonal-cut sandwiches, a selection of sleeping pills.

He was going to teach English in Korea, for one year: the deaf man who had hired him thought that he was born and raised here.

He is wearing a pale blue shirt, his one wide, textured tie. Faking all the things he does not know.

He used to follow me around and ask, Lying down, laying down, what is the difference? What is subjunctive? Why is it that? The gerund—

I would eventually plead with him to leave me alone.

The packing dragged into the early morning.

He left his friend waiting in his car and seized me. I will come back, he said.

I rested my face against his shirt's stiff placket and sighed.

He writes me when he arrives: he is very tired. He tells me how the mountains looked, as he passed overhead, like the arched back of a green brachiosaurus.

It is very hot and the air is heavy with moisture; he lives close to a forest and a bar.

In the bar, he draws objects and names them, in English, for the waiter with a teased blond beehive.

Plate! he says. Ship, hat, fork, dragon.

He stays until he is drunk enough to sleep and dream of an alphabet ejecting its assonance in pieces.

Of my "soft otherness": my dog, who slept between us making compounds and phrases.

I offer a reward. Walk through the park and see a hawk, looking back from the black branches of a slender tree. Below, a mass of feathers, enclosing a bloody heart.

The hawk flees as I gingerly pick up the heart. I go home and wrap it in cellophane, freeze it.

This is the first reward and no one collects. I see it now and then, tumbling between macaroni dinners and ice-furred tubs of soup.

We scared each other, and fought like maniacs.

I am still here and violence retains its history: tangibly, at first, then in changing currents.

HE IS NOT TAME! I write in block letters.

When we argued he would count to ten, outside. He learned this the second time he tried to choke his wife.

I was not afraid of him. Write that in asperous letters that take up, that strangle, the page.

One day, we sat on the couch and he put his arms around me and I fell asleep.

He stayed awake, it turned out, watching me, incredulously.

You make noises and thrash, he said. It is like holding a little monster.

He is stripping to his socks, then flinging them into the air. There is a single mole on his abdomen, and he admires it.

If you were a mole, he asks, wouldn't you know this was the place to be?

He slides between the sheets like a flyer in a mail slot, lazily advertising his beauty.

Don't touch me, he says and rolls toward the wall.

I look at his shoulder, at the freckles he says fell from his face. They are ants rolling in sugar, a small armada, anchoring at shore.

Where he is and where I want to be will become as resolute as points on a map that never meet.

Paper folded into flaps, octagons, triangles. How I have tried to mangle the space between us, how adamantly it retains its shape.

Like anything extraordinary, there is no accounting for the sum of his parts.

His hair is styled like Andy Gibb's. He wears tinted sunglasses and a brown puffy leather coat, tight Alpine shorts and brown loafers, striped acrylic sweaters and pleated corduroy pants.

He is blind in one eye, his tongue is partially amputated, the top of his right ear is torn off and looks like melted wax.

He tells bad jokes and laughs and laughs; he surprises me by making horns from the ends of cucumbers.

He will run madly up my stairs, having heard that I was sick; stand by the bedpost, smiling, and say, Troublemaker.

He will stand there and I will feel as though I am being smothered by the sweet weight of stars, deferring their meaning.

NO LOVE

I got no love, Christopher says. He is my boyfriend and crack dealer.

He is beautiful in a saintly way, a saint fasting on Freezies and having knife fights.

He rambles on about the things he has: a bayonet, a satin Lady Diana pillow, a chair made out of deer skin and antlers.

My uncle used to say he liked the way I talk, he tells me.

A selection of ladies' jewellery, boots made out of a cobra. Movies, I got movies. Oh, and this ant farm. Cactus flowers. Dead baby.

I have stopped listening. It is always the first hit, then chasing it like a hoop. That hit is when the Peace That Passeth All Understanding breathes for you.

The rest is all scorching panic, and it still frightens me to talk about it.

I get jumpy around the mere mechanics of baking soda, rubber bands, and tinfoil. Something I used to love: We are making a rocket!

Hold it in, hold it in, he says. I want to let go; the hit is God and I am George Herbert, pulling back.

Christopher always asks who would win in a fight between a grizzly bear and a gorilla. He insists, preposterously, that the gorilla would.

He pulls his hair back with a piece of string and lays a track of Armani cologne when he comes in.

He starts unpacking his pockets, then makes, finally, a miracle of snow roiling in blue fire.

AMERICAN PIE

It is my father's favourite song. I keep asking him why. No idea, he says. I explain the meaning of each coded line to him; he listens politely.

At one point, he did drive a huge Chevrolet Impala that he called the Boat. I am not sure he even likes the music of Buddy Holly.

There is a lonely teenage boy in the song.

My father's brother tells me my dad used to stay out very late and come downstairs, to his room, with a stack of peanut butter sandwiches; that he was a hellraiser who was always in trouble.

I once found him alone in the middle of the night listening to music on the box stereo, turned low. A drink in his hand.

There is this loneliness that never goes away.

The loneliness that is a hole that wants to be filled by anything dark and terminal.

We sit side by side, our hands behind our backs, and sometimes he tells me stories about people he has known.

Never answers questions.

He holds his privacy as fiercely as a glass tumbler.

That holds a galaxy of fire.

E.G.U.

This meant "Ecstasy's Gone Underground."

One of Ministry of Love's songs, one of Steve's, who is dead now. He was my first boyfriend. There was another, technically, but Steve and I, many years after we had split up, vowed to revise our stories and call each other the first people we ever loved.

It is winter and I am walking through Trinity Bellwoods Park, looking for the plaque his friends told me they had paid to nail to a tree. It isn't there.

I can't find him.

He came to me a year before the stroke, his head shaved, and in pain. He begged me to let him live with me, and I said no. I found him an apartment, and lent him money and, one day, shopped with him for toothpaste and shaving cream and other little things.

I asked for the money back, I became angry at him when he kept dropping by. I did not help him move, even though his legs were deformed with arthritis.

When he stopped speaking to me I was angry and relieved. His shaved head made me think of cancer; his obvious distress felt like an attack.

I was lonely too, I wanted to tell him.

I am standing in the slush, listening to him sing so sweetly, and his voice is dirty and low, and he is holding me there. We are both very young, and we have just fallen, hard, for each other.

I am falling hard now, as I feel what my life once was, and who we were. I feel all of the anguish of everything beyond me, and hold my heart; I hold him in my heart and, unsteadily, move along.

EIGHT HARMS

I need eight harms, the beleaguered VIA Rail steward says, as he tongs little plates of sole onto the tray tables.

The train is coursing west, past snow-larded trees and wild mustangs.

I think of offering him the following, in the brown bag that affixes to the nail beside me:

1. A tin box with a wind-up mechanism that plays "Someday My Prince Will Come."
2. The mirror beside my parents' bathtub, filled with a huge, pinkening pig.
3. My mother's small hands, holding mine.
4. My father in a bear hat, its eyes wobbling as he reaches for my bag.
5. A sign saying QUINTE like a poem.
6. My sister's eyes pooled with tears, two fish darting.
7. My Poppy, on the corner of the sofa, like an admiral; my grandmother in pale blue, starboard.
8. Killer and I at the Gentlemen's Choice, Sandra's rough leg on my lap, telling us her mother worked at Nick's

Sex Aquarium, a bar I liked, then asking me to buy
her a 50.

We are rushing past what appears to be time itself. When I go home,
I retrieve a distressed letter from my pocket.

It is an old Tan Hong Pastry & Shoppe menu, where, beneath
a delicious red list that includes Ananas Glacé, Donut Frit aux
Haricots Rouges, and Gâteau aux Noix, Neil has written, Please
write me back and tell me something and ask me something too.

Neil and I were friends, when I was seventeen and he was
twenty-one: I would write in my diary about the way his black hair
fell into his cow eyes; about his sweet, red lips.

He has included a series of directions to his apartment on Pine
Street, to the metal fire escape where we will stand, at last, in sheets
of rain, and kiss until sparks and tiny pieces of metal machinery fall,
crashing, on the living street below.

BEST DATE EVER

In the postcard from Cyril, sent from New York, the word EVER is underlined.

We had just gone out for the first time in several years. When he saw me, he looked fleetingly shocked, then pleased.

We went to the Cadillac Lounge where I promptly became ill and drunk. I leaned on, then fell on top of, him. I am in love, I told the waitress.

I don't blame you, she said.

Cyril is the subject of thousands of pages of what I now realize was graphomania, ten years ago, most of which detailed how he looked and smelled, as if I were a mentally ill botanist.

These diaries are named after a postcard I bought the day I met him: DESIRE. Every page is Thirty-Six Views of Mount Fuji, cresting into The Great Wave Off Kanagawa.

His eyes are takoyaki, a complicated gift from a grandparent: sakura ebi and flour folded into small bowls. His lips are a velvet sofa, tufted with teeth; his skin not like, but is, the masses of cherry blossoms that were falling in drifts, some suspended —

The sensation of falling in love, still.

1. Petals as heavy as snow.
2. Vancouver in the dark rain, lit with amber.
3. The fire escape by his office, curving away from sight.
4. What it is to see, and to know.
5. My earring in his mouth.
6. His mouth that is signally gentle, leaving marks.
7. He would call this some kind of energy that may occupy music.
8. *Phantom energy.*
9. How it was that he would let me go.
10. And return, in anger: "It is the idea of me that you like."
11. An idea about living underwater.
12. Each occasion spectacular.
13. Stay with me; you sleep there.
14. He is as cool as the ice protecting a fossil.
15. Get in the car.
16. You are bigger than me, and stronger.
17. An embarrassment of roses.
18. The time I almost drowned reminds me of him.
19. What I would have done, if he loved me too.
20. Calm knowing more about fate and abject also.
21. Disgusted by his turtlenecks and sport coats, his critical view of everything primary.
22. His affectation, singing T. Rex.
23. His hairline receding like malignant exhaustion.
24. His *cloak full of eagles.*
25. The name of an angel; the way that he speaks.
26. You have to tilt your head.
27. Sexual mutilation, a memory of bites that draw blood.
28. A picture of me and Carol, sweet and tangled.
29. Other things I have sent him, chalk letters that I saw

chalked on the street.

30. Grey pantyhose he files under ADVENTURE.
31. *I want to come and come a lot.* Here, he means, and
    doesn't.
32. He is the pearl, undiscovered, that each oyster infers.
33. I have learned to take pleasure in each inference.
34. He was very ill when he was young, and he fished and
    read Gray's elegies.
35. This all turned into poems.
36. Poems like scorched highways, all the places he has
    been burned black.

How the waves swell with each gush of my heart, then ravish the shore. What language is left there is his.

A story of bones and claws and bright arcana: on the best date, ever, I listened to him breathe the way shells do; I listened to him speak about the sea.

GOO GOO MUCK

I have not been with anyone for almost two years. Eighteen months, seven days, and four hours.

My friend Jeremy calls and asks to come over. He brings a two-four and a bottle of Wild Turkey; he looks deranged.

His hair is standing on end, and he sits and we drink and drink and he tells me about a letter his girlfriend left for him, asking him to seek help, or else.

I look better after every beer it seems, and soon he is saying I love you and smacking me around, leaving bruises.

He is out the door in the morning, immediately, and I don't hear from him for a month. When he does call, he asks, Can we please talk?

Okay, I say. What are your periods like?

He gets mad, and I stop hearing from him for a while.

Then I have to have a D&C because of some disgusting uterine problem.

I decide that I am pregnant, and have taken care of it.

In the morphine shadow, I think of my friend Mauve, of the night we went out on Halloween in Montreal and took acid.

She was pregnant, and scheduled for an abortion. There were

four of us and we drove along St. Catherine Street, watching. There was a man dressed in a straitjacket, on a leash. The man leading him was carrying a boom box playing "Super Freak."

There was a pastel Rubik's cube, and a filthy bum in the restaurant we stopped at, who had covered his face with burnt cork. *Carrie* was on the little TV and the waitress was vacuuming, insistently, as the filthy bum kept saying, "I spilled some beer on the table, man. Gimme a rag, I'll wipe it up."

Back in the car, we heard the Cramps for the first time. This moment returns as a streak of serrated buildings and curves, as a mass of cells, pinging to a new sensation.

It is this sensation I tell Jeremy about when I write to tell him I have aborted "Lyon," our unborn child.

I swear that I never did drugs! I add in a swollen postscript.

Jeremy's girlfriend, Del-Ray, finds the letter and loses her mind. He tries to call, and I refuse to answer. On my answering machine: the tiniest ghost noise you can imagine.

You need to know that I skinned a Pro-Life man's hand one time.

Because no one knows unless they have had to say, No. No, thank you; I will simply tell this grey peanut of all the wonders of the world it will never see.

Mauve is a young grandmother now.

Like the man in green with the filth and the rags, I am certain I can clean things up without disgusting or hurting a soul.

I WANNA BE CREMATED

I am so afraid of being buried, Lafitte tells me, typically morbid.

I hold my big, lanky baby and swear to him I will tell everyone!

Lafitte will leave me, and burn my heart into a hard, shining sliver.

When he is killed in a freak accident — involving an actual Pinhead, in a tulle skirt — his mother calls me.

It has been seven years, but she is drunk and nostalgic.

You KNEW him, she slurs.

Yes I did, Effi, I say. And I feel obliged to insist that his wishes be carried out, as I still love him. He wanted to be buried in a simple pine box, preferably lidless, I tell her. He was always going on about Nature devouring him and making him its bitch. I do not say "bitch," actually, but she gets the point.

They bury him naked in a long paper bag.

When I visit his grave, I say, Worm-meal, or Maggot-face, before falling down. Why did you leave me? I say, and I laugh and I laugh.

SO SCARED!

My sister Mary and I stay at the Chelsea Hotel and drink bourbon all night, talking about the building where she lives.

The lady upstairs, she tells me, is so scared!

She came up to Mary and said, The floors go CRACK CRACK, all the time! And the landlord is so stupid, so stupid!

What will happen? she asked, running her hand over her mushroom of scorched black hair. My mother could go crashing through the floor while your husband is in the bathtub, or the shower, or going pee!

I am so scared! she said. And I love you.

She loves me! Mary didn't say anything. She was uneasy with the woman's fantasies about her naked husband's activities; with the pattern of her sweater — a fawn, eating doughnuts; with her rank, feral smell.

So Scared occasionally helps people with their parcels. The super tells them to leave a tip under the lip of the carpet on the stairs.

So Scared takes her change and goes to Barcade, where the blackboard says, Tonight Only! Good Times.

And plays Centipede, so scared! of the spider, of the festering mushrooms.

Isssss like my mother, falling, she says.

So Scared wants to buy a shirt that says YOU ARE STUPID and wear it over a red lace bra and tap panties.

She wants to stand on 4th Street as the Brooklyn sun falls and the moon rises against the stop lights, spelling out Slow, Stop, Slow. To stand by a rust-stained mattress and two derelict umbrellas, actually stopping traffic.

She leans over and tastes the garbage as the garbage tastes the moon.

IMAGINE

Imagine how the parents of the American Idols feel!

The old man yells this as I stand outside of the food court on St. Patrick Street, waiting to go back inside and try not to have my students catch on that I have not and will never read *Don Quixote*.

It's a funny book, one of my reserved students said. But you were just fake-laughing, weren't you? I replied, approaching her desk with my hand raised.

The old man is wearing a feathered hat and is parked on the curb: it is twenty below and he is furious.

I see it, he says. They show it to me. I see that the shame and the joy is worse.

It is intolerable!

I told them last night to turn it off, he says. A fat grandma in a flowered dress told Ryan Seacrest that her child always sings to her. Then she whispered, I love it.

What would you sing? I ask him.

Wearrre an American Bannnd, he sings. We come to party your town, we gonna party you clowns —

Your parents are dead, I say.

Turning in their graves! he says.

His face is as red as Mars, and for one moment, we party it down, and pride is a monster, we feel.

REMEMBERING, IN PARAPHRASE, *THE LOVE MACHINE* AS A SHORT, SCINTILLANT MYSTERY

— What is it, Robin? It looks like a white hot dog!
— Where he proceeds to have an explosive bowel movement, that pig!
— No tits!
— How do you know it was still alive last night?
— You are clean and strong and beautiful.
— I don't need anyone, baby.
— You're all faggots!
— If you play like an alley cat ...
— You're just some bastard named Conrad!
— I take it back, you are a nut!
— Cigarettes smudged with orange lipstick.
— Lancer Bar at five?
— He doesn't know you exist.
— O to be born beautiful!
— A black eye, an eyepatch.
— Her eyes became huge, she said I love you.
— I NEED YOU.

HE KEEPS CALLING ME

This is the only place in the house I haven't kissed you, he says, in one of the dreams where his hair is growing back in, light brown and soft.

There is a blue-feathered cat toy on the floor of the only place, and he kisses me with lips that are coming in full and unlined at either side with chevrons: how you would draw a bird among many in the sky and far away.

I own so many things, small, beautiful —

Parisian soap, white Hermès scarf, spiked silver band, pear compote, Chanel pearls, mink brushes, a tiny basket of dolls' clothes, love letters, snail tape, an Amish pig pillow, jars and jars of olives in vermouth —

All these things that will leave with me; the idea of leaving, of having nothing.

Early into our relationship, Steve had stopped wanting to see me and I didn't know why.

He would not come to the phone. I got to know William very well this way, his pretty, bookish roommate.

William always had a girl at the door and another sleeping at the foot of his bed, begging him to love her.

His and Steve's bands jammed in the space called Ministry of Love. I would sleep through all this and worse.

He must be out looking for a job, William would say kindly.

Oh, come on now, he would say indulgently, as I cried.

Sometimes Steve would answer and let me come over.

If anything happened, he would say: This doesn't change anything.

We would have breakfast at Bellwood, stoned on Valium, and he would be remote, wearing a pale blue suit.

He had hair on his chest. My girlfriends and I only liked hairless men, but he smelled like musk and something else — he smelled so good.

One day — and it is impossible to remember why, or how — I came over, and he had bought me two old Weebles, a fireman and a baker, and I looked up in his cool, filthy kitchen and he smiled and I knew he loved me again.

He wouldn't answer when I asked if there had been someone else. What does it matter, he said, when you're the one I love?

The look he gave me. That belongs to me.

SIXTEEN BITES AND SCRATCHES; SIXTEEN
SLAPS AND SCREAMS

The wide hips and wasp waist, scrolls of hair: someone I used to be, among the vines and mangos.

The embrace of a tall man; folding into it like a dove.

An amorous dog's fierce bite.

A golden foot, braceleted and descending the temple stairs.

The partial body of the "helper" as she, as I, fall off the side of the bed and hang there, like a bat.

The man who talked like Floyd the Barber and made blender drinks = "The Congress of a Crow." Yakshi in a leopard shift and leopard slides.

Excavated from the ruins of Pompeii: a bullwhip and a bottle of Hap-Penis.

Frozen on Khajuraho: Lana's nervous kiss.

The retention of semen, in labelled envelopes: DNA, Date, Name.

The petals of the mandala, Billy's bouquet, signed, *I would die for you*.

The erotic, comic, sympathetic, furious or angry, heroic, terrible, odious, wondrous or marvellous, peaceful. All of this.

Birds *feeding on dirt*, again.

You come home and I am climbing a vine.
What is lost is *some sense of being alive.*

MORE THAN WE CAN BEAR

Where you going? To CHURCH?

Our upstairs neighbour, Clarice, liked to hang off her balcony and scream this at me and Lafitte, if we happened to be walking together, wearing black.

I would soon learn this was her only endearing quality.

When he and I moved into the house in Little Italy, we had already had a fight with her.

Through our aggressively friendly landlord, she had demanded full access to our little backyard: I like to have a glass of wine under a tree, is that a problem!?

We won that fight, but it was a pyrrhic victory, as she would go out of her way to make us, more specifically me, miserable for the four years I lived beneath her.

She yelled in the hall about me, sat in her kitchen idiotically stamping her feet for hours, told the landlord my dog should be kept in the basement as his barking was "interfering with my cellular telephone calls!"

She kicked my door if Frank rushed towards it, took up bongos, and slipped into the backyard to practice her Tarzan yell.

I heard her whispering about me — She wears a beard of

bees! — and one night, her friends called down, asking me to show them my "curly vestigial tail."

When Lafitte left I got all skinny and coke-jittery. She asked me what was going on the day his moving van appeared and left with everything in the place.

He left me, I told her, and wandered back to my empty room with the marks on the wall where his things had been.

The next morning, I found a little azalea outside my door with a note.

It said, God never gives us more than we can bear.

I turned it over in my hands, wondering at how people so often surprise you.

I knocked on her door, and when she answered, I smashed the plant in her face.

He just did! I said.

BAROLO

Is the name of the wine that Don Ho ordered on our date.

A distinguished member of the paleontology panel interjects as follows: Are you able offer us a temporal marker, Dr. Criswell?

Which is what my colleagues call me; occasionally, Mrs. Frosty.

To which I respond, This happened when some of my massive bulk had started to shift, at the outset of one of the interglacials.

Using a chisel and hammer, I was able to free myself quite easily from enough hard blubber that I could be seated without having to ride my chair sidesaddle, and I felt pretty.

The waiter brought me a number of fortifications: he was sweet the way that beautiful young men are at that vital stage in their dressage when they have mastered so much and are easy in their classical grace and power.

Don Ho was very late. He was an old acquaintance who had recently ended a long-term relationship with another singer — one who had written a badly attended yet quietly respected opera about her fibromyalgia — and when he asked me to Spazzatura, I assumed that it was a date.

Who needs to listen to the shingles aria again? he asked. Not me!

I had asked Carrie Bradshaw for advice. She suggested that I wear Spanx tights under Spanx underpants *and* a Spanx slip. Over that, a black velvet dress and a stunning white wrap. I wore a white fabric camellia in my hair.

I must have looked like an orphaned whale who thought she was Billie Holiday (in the plot of an animated film that ends with a spear and a vast, soulful ghost).

The waiter raised his eyebrow at Don Ho when he arrived: his hair was dirty and large; he wore checked pants and a Billy Squier T-shirt.

Well. Look at you, he said nauseously. He had walked right by me and actually snarled when I touched his arm to get his attention.

He knew me when I looked good, and was obviously distraught.

I am totally hung up on my girlfriend! he shouted.

I said that was nice and asked about his work. I ordered a little meal and a beer, and he made a huge, pompous show of ordering a tiny bottle of wine.

He told the waiter about the grapes, how firm and sweet they were, then winked.

Is it good? I asked, and the waiter said, No. No it isn't.

Don Ho ignored him and, as we waited, told me about every single song on his new record.

I'm having a blast! he said as the Barolo arrived, then he smelled the cork and swished a taste in his mouth.

You don't even have to do that! the waiter snapped.

I sat staring at my lap as Don Ho talked, chewed, and drained his glass.

Give me the bottle, he ordered, and wrote a song lyric on it. I still have the bottle because I had to pick up the check: he had forgotten his wallet.

He wrote, There is so much more to me / Than "Tiny Bubbles" and the shell that is "Pearly." / I live my life with fire and style / Me ke aloha pumehana, baby! / Aren't you glad you had me for a little while?

Yes, I said. Yes, of course. His cell phone was sitting on the table, turned off, and he picked it up and pretended someone was on the other end.

No, not his legs! he gasped. His thick, athletic legs! I'll be right there!

Mahalo, he said, bowing a bit, and headed out.

I saw the waiter speaking to him at the door. He came to the table with a complimentary bowl of gelato, his eyes dark with anger.

I drank coffee with my creamy dessert because I wanted to stay up late and think about Don Ho and how I might protect myself better. I would stay home every night and watch movies with Frank, who really does watch them. I would tell old friends, directly, that I was unrecognizable.

I would think of the waiter, my gallant, like this: *Sometimes there is God. So quickly!*

MANIAC

I took driving lessons in the summer, many years after I had received, then lost, my first licence.

That was in Montreal, and even though I ran a stop sign, forgot to wear a seatbelt, and ran over Bigfoot, the guy testing me — a cool, fat Frenchman who had a black pompadour with sideburns the size of beavers' tails — passed me.

I ran over Bigfoot!

Now get out of here before I change my mind, he said, while passing a little comb through his wet locks.

My parents congratulated me, then said I was not allowed to use the car.

Your father and I love that car, my mother said. The Cavalier is like a child to us.

As if I don't know that! I sulked. At night, my mother spooned applesauce into its gas tank while my father revved the engine and recited *Goodnight Moon*.

I could not afford to renew the licence, and my father, in any event, kept stealing and disposing of the paperwork.

My brother and sister, fraternal twins named Chang and Eng, were allowed to drive, of course. They were given summer jobs making sombreros in Mexico and baguettes in Paris!

Whenever we planned a family trip I would go to get into the car and my mother would observe, histrionically, that they had filled the space in the back seat beside Chang and Eng with boxes of packaged gags — "Stinko" wet napkins, squirting flowers, detachable bloody fingers, and plastic "Bunny Teeth," advertised as having an "E-Z COMF'TBL FIT."

We ran out of room again! everyone lamented before my father — usually wearing a jaunty tam-o'-shanter or dashing scarf — fired up the car and drove off.

One time there was no room because of Chang's invisible friend, Wang. Another time, my dad wore comically high-heeled shoes and needed "elegant leg room."

Now I was determined to become independent. I saw myself driving on a beach, with the cats bunched together, hissing, in the back window; with Frank beside me, in a smart tartan scarf.

I saw us racing the night as it slammed shut and breathed stars, and I signed up for driving lessons.

I enrolled at a Portuguese school called Dirija Como Jesus!

For six Saturdays in a row, I sat in a tiny classroom with twenty enervated teenagers, watching Humberto teach, looking at the signs on the walls.

An old Children Crossing sign, for one, which I drew as Rat Crossing around my useless notes: Here comes the school bus. What you gonna do?

Humberto had a magnetic chalkboard and six coloured, pointed rectangles that he gave names. Now, here is Tony, he's a real leadfoot! He's coming fast to the four-way stop. And here is — oh, Mike, approaching. Who has the right of way?

Humberto was mesmerizing in his ability to be boring: I could feel the class clenching, like a single, cocked fist.

Oh no, Tony, too fast! As the rectangles collided, he called a break.

I would go to stores that sold Loteria sets, a marbled spa, a butcher shop filled with dripping chunks of meat. Drag my ass back and sit down again for movies made in the 1960s about how it's "Just not groovy to drive drunk!"

Whenever you are depressed a friend will say, "Take a class!"

I took this class, and aced it. Then Humberto and I started to drive together.

Maniac! he was given to screeching. Or, in his manner, "Maaaah-niac."

He spent all of his time mumbling, holding on to the wheel and braking, sometimes when we were stopped.

I'd pretend he was talking about his collection of women's panties, and I'd drive up and down hills until it was time to collect his next student.

It all went pear-shaped. By the last lesson, Humberto had tried to teach me parallel parking by sobbing, Look at the little tree-angle! The building! The Big Picture! Signal, signal, Oh, no, Maniac.

If you don't want extra lessons, go see some Paki, he said.

In Portugal, we say "Negre," he explained, when I objected. He then showed me a page of drawings of kittens and told me I had failed.

I had failed, and this was his gift as an instructor. To pass along his hatred and exhaustion; to know that we would always fail in a world populated by geometry and maniacs, in a world where Tony has no respect for the rule of right of way.

Where his hair grew from his ears like seaweed; the seaweed of the Mediterranean he seldom visited but dreamed of, in dreams that were a fried egg on something savoury.

When his wife wouldn't answer the phone during class, he would lose his composure and yell, Dolores!, then mumble, I hate this.

In the summer I took a driving class.

Every Saturday, young couples would be gathered on the steps of the adjacent church, nervously posing for photographs.

You have no idea, I would think, as the bride's dress rose like a memory of what it is to be young and billowing with dreams.

ONE CRULLER

We were fifteen and stoned at a doughnut store, five of us, mocking a fat man showing some crack. "Monsieur, ton derrière!" French was hateful, also hilarious to us.

We heard him start to order before we turned to see him.

One. Strawberry. Jelly.

One. Chocolate. Glazed.

We knew about this guy: he had tried to kill himself with a shot-gun and ended up just blowing off part of his face and rearranging his features. He had one tiny eye and one huge, flat eye; a wedge of nose; and a tiny slitted mouth, halfway across his chin.

One. Maple.

We all started to laugh, in sort of quiet seizures.

Shut up, Jill hissed. What if he turns around and kills us?

This was a sobering thought.

One. Hawaiian.

One. Cruller.

It seemed to take the whole night for him to fill the box. We sat pressed together like bullets in a box, empty and cool to the touch.

EXPERIMENT 44

HOW TO GET THROUGH ANOTHER DAY.

The days are long and difficult to fill. There are only so many times you can walk your dog or lurch around in chaps and a tube top, making pancakes. Using the following tinctures, you can occupy time the way a fat ass fills a chair.

THE THINGS NEEDED

Percocet, Valium

Vodka

Mortifying phone call to aloof man

Ice

Thin Lizzy

Heavy drapes

WHAT TO DO

Swallow three Percocet with one Valium (for racing heart). Wash down with vodka on the rocks. Dial blindly and leave an unintelligible message, hang up tremulously. Play a song as you draw the curtains against the obtuse rays of the sun that are making everything come to life — the noxious lilacs and bluebells; the green shoots; the long, tanned legs of young women and ardent, simian prowlers.

Lie in your crumb-covered sheets, taking vital notes on the *First Chemistry Book for Boys and Girls* you have prised from the trash of the old woman who yells at you, often, "I no speak to you!"

Bookmark an experiment called "How to make coke."

Wait until the moon starts bleeding and try to focus closely on the terrible misunderstanding Jack, Chrissy, and Janet will have when it appears that Janet is auditioning male prostitutes.

Add one more half a Perc and feel your thoughts try to assemble, then implode.

Track the thoughts, then enter the tracks and just stand there, your left eye twitching as it tries to ascertain the sound of what is coming, its size and strength.

Think of the old woman then, cutting her roses back, and her garden filling her days and yours, all blurry peonies and pale, orderly heaven.

SNOOPY

This Jack Russell I am telling you about was a bad dog, Jean tells me as she pours bread crumbs and two muffins from a bag.

The pigeons scramble over, flashing their purple tails.

This dog would bark at people and bite them, she says. Once, I saw it bite the head off a bird!

She tells me this last part very quietly, so the pigeons cannot hear.

Anyways, so you see up there? she asks, pointing to the upper floors of the twenty-storey building that overlooks the park like a monstrous piece of beige Lego.

Well, one day, she got so mad, the lady who owned the dog, that she just threw him from her window.

Then she jumped out right after him! They both died, of course.

Frank and I have met most of the people who walk in the park, and some of them scare us. Especially Cheryl, a vast stump of a woman with a pit bull who likes to let it off leash and laugh when I protest, shakily, that my dog is not very good with other animals.

Yeah, well, this'll learn him! she yells as I scoop up Frank and start walking backwards.

Some are harmless, crazy women, like the one who says the rosary all day while pacing the park, her eyes milky with love.

Or the pantless woman who likes to stand and flex her ruddy ass cheeks and tease her bush with an Afro pick.

Or Dusty, who is having pieces of her internal organs removed, bit by bit. Shortly before she dies, she tells me that this is no kind of life. I'd rather pick fly shit out of pepper! she snaps.

And there is Alva, an old woman with a mangy poodle she calls Snoopy. She has been apprehensive about letting Frank near him, but after we talk a few times, the two dogs play a bit, and I feel happy for my strange dog and his secret reasons for hating many things.

One day, Snoopy comes barrelling over with Alva in hot pursuit. He begins sniffing Frank, spending a fraction too long at his butt.

SNOOPY, Alva screams, her face wild. YOU'RE NOT THAT WAY! YOU'RE NOT THAT WAY!

And she yanks her dog away from mine and streaks off, panting and still crying, No, Snoopy, no!

And then I walk my gay dog home, past the path of clover, violets, and buttercups.

MORE DEAD THAN ALIVE

My neighbour Tanya is greeting her visitors, guests for a long-weekend barbecue. Her dogs are howling; a tiny pair of her shredded jeans is drying on the line.

All around me, lawnmowers charging, tinny music playing, girls whizzing past on bikes, their long hair following them like yellow Doppler.

I've just spent the night doing "summer coke," fat, misshapen rails, while becoming increasingly ill, and nearer to the heart attack I will surely have any day now.

I was with a friend I cannot name. He has a small, recurring role on a Canadian TV show. He plays Glorius, a sheaf of wheat. His lines are all gestures and noises:

> Alistair: Comes a wet, dark night!
> Milady: Indeed!
> Glorius: Shudder.
> Alistair: The crop had better be hardy!
> Glorius: Squeak!

My friend acted out the best scene he ever did, which was when he was on fire, then stamped on.

He left when he got a text that said, COME FUCK ALL MY HOLES. I stayed up, terrified. Then flushed what was left and said, That is the last time.

The last time! I whispered to Frankie when he brought me Mr. Pinky, Puff, and Private Gomez.

It was the last time. It has been eighteen months.

I wanted to write about what it feels like, those hangovers like beds of nails, the filth and the shame.

But it is too disgusting to think about.

I wrote this, trembling: I want to have long hair and a prairie dress; to be riding somewhere with a bag of flowers and wine slung over my shoulder as the sun torches my face and I ride past the dark, quiet places where people like me sit like mushrooms, easing deeper into the shit and the shade.

In smaller, shaky letters: Someone to love?

Love is a habit I can't shake. Except now, it is like those people who have the odd couple of cigarettes at a party and otherwise never think of them.

Today, for example, I lost my wallet and was stranded, and there was no one to call so I walked home, and it was very cold and I had quite a party in my head!

You aren't dead! I exclaimed to Steve. It was all... a terrible... nightmare!

When I got home, I held the little doll I have of him and breathed hotly into his plastic hair, crying, and he said, Are you okay? Are you okay, Lynn?

IT GETS A BIT LONELY

Seeking good times! You: Sexy lady. Age/race not important. RBT

This was what Robert's advertisement said, not that I ever look at classified ads.

What happened was I was sitting at the computer one night, drunk off my ass, trolling discussion forums through one slitted eye.

I went on the Haiku site and wrote, *Please, I try hard! Grammpa donut hurt / ME! I love you old white hairs, TRAINs / No vazeleen, I stab!*

I added the following to the Kink board: *Run a train on my fat ass fo the fawklift cums!*

Then I looked at Casual Encounters. This guy I knew was getting laid after composing such ads as "Vibrating Tongue Seeks Quivering Legs" and "Are You Still on Your Period and Feel Like Gettin Some Man-Tampax?"

I wanted something approximately that serious, and was about to write "SWF Seeks Man w/ Forceps, Lesions, and Good Sense of Humour" when I saw Robert's austere ad. I wrote him and pretty soon we were writing back and forth.

He was a good listener in that my letters were long and rambling and usually had an attachment from a play I am writing called

Sex and the City, which is about a gigantic woman who fucks skyscrapers and uses waterfalls for a douche.

Excellent, he would always say.

I have to meet you, I said. I am not pretty but could be sexy for the right man.

He agreed, and said, It had better not rain! And that seemed angry and weird, but I let it go and I took forever, dressing like Carole King on the cover of *Tapestry*.

I was waiting at the bar, this bar called NIGHT, which was of course very dark, and sort of rancid, and the bartender had thalidomide arms, which, after a while, started to look like shooting stars.

And then this robot came in. Tall as my waist, with a square head and hinged jaw, rotating middle, and jointed legs.

Yes, this was "RBT," and he crawled onto a stool and the bartender made a fuss, and he kissed me and shoved his metal tongue in my mouth and we drank motor oil and grenadine all night long.

And yes, I did sleep with him and it was incredible. Me, him, and Maurice — the bartender — and in the morning, a piece of paper shot out of RBT's mouth that said, I will be slammed at work for the next few weeks. Leave me your number?

Maurice was in the kitchen and he waved at me — those stars!

I waited for RBT to call.

I took the blender to bed one night, set to "Liquefy."

Weeks later, I read that he had been arrested. CRAIGSLIST ROBOT KILLER NABBED IN CHIC DISCOTHEQUE! the headline read.

I was badly shaken.

It could have been me, I said, to the trash bag of tin cans that I sleep with.

Why wasn't it me?

CYCLOPS

I started teaching with Georgette after the college where I work added "Appalling Deformity" to its diversity criteria.

Georgette was tall and plain. She wore tan sweaters, pleated slacks, and enormous Earth Shoes. Between her fierce brown eyes was one tiny, milky blue eye that rolled uncontrollably and cried much of the time.

She was the only other sessional, a medieval historian who insisted, in our team-taught workshop, on making a marshmallow soft sculpture of Usamah Ibn-Munqidh.

I tried to get to know Georgette better. She was always telling dire stories about her twenty-five-year-old dog and her efforts to carry it up and down ten flights of stairs so it could weakly urinate.

You have seen a lot of pain, I said soulfully.

No, she said.

You desire love!

She then opened up a bit about her boyfriend, her former Ricardian Poetry prof, who I assumed was a known sex offender with a walrus moustache.

Her tiny eye sparkled when she told me they dressed as the Great Vowel Shift on Halloween.

That was the last time we spoke civilly.

I wrote an anonymous note to our dean, stating I was a "student of colour" and that Georgette had written, in the margins of my final essay, "Obvious rapist."

I saw her the day she left with her dirty coffee mug and pile of stupid maps and books. I tried to say goodbye, but she grunted at me.

So I said *bitch*, in a voice as small as a tear, and as grotesque.

EDDIE

I met Eddie when he came over to photograph me for the back cover of a book I wrote called *Them Panties Too*, about the bizarre rape and murder of a piano teacher by his imbecilic students.

Eddie was small and muscular, with big brown eyes and black hair with white ticking. He had me stand in a field of goldenrod, then rushed me.

His mother, an alcoholic who broke her empty bottles and sucked on the glass, named him after a dog she had when she was a little girl.

My daddy kilt him for soiling on the chesterfield, she told Eddie. He was looking right at me when the rifle went off! She would often cry about the dog or, on other occasions, beat her son with wood and a blackjack she made out of a sock and a handful of pennies.

He was born in the Year of the Dog, and on our first date he licked my face while we were parked by the gigantic metal bucket of KFC that towers over the lakeshore.

We smoked a lot of this hairy purple pot he liked that incapacitated me. That's God's Value Meal, I said as he scratched my back and felt between my legs as if looking for ticks.

He was so nice in the beginning.

He shovelled my walkway and brought me over strange little gifts: a rawhide shoe; a branch; flowers, still attached to their roots.

He started to get snappy and mean and bit me one day for rubbing his neck where it was sunburned. Some days, it was better, and we would go to the park or watch movies as he lay flat on his back, his legs twitching, breath heavy.

When he started pissing on my floors, then bed, I didn't know what to do. Then he started biting strangers and chewing my things to shreds.

Let's visit a nice farm, I said. He loved driving around, so he was happy to go.

He started to panic when we got to the clinic, and I told him the doctor just needed to look at him for a minute.

I hate needles, he said, his eyes filling with tears. I hate them! he screamed, in the waiting room, before bolting wildly down the hall where the doctor was waiting.

I stroked his head after they got him into the crush cage and sedated him.

I reminded him of the time we were lying on his red velvet chaise and he told me, You're so alive. Of all the things I loved about him: how he smelled, and sounded; how tenderly he trusted me; how I knew he could be mean, but it wasn't his fault.

You're a good boy, I said, as the doctor slipped in the needle and Eddie sighed and it sounded like a bird, and his eyes stayed staring open as if we were looking for the farm, for a red barn in a field where horses go racing past.

DENTIST IN THE MIST

She is seventy years old or so; her long, jagged teeth are the colour of mahogany.

She is a large heavy smoker who likes to garden, and has a piranha named Chewy. She tells me that Chewy could skeletonize me in two minutes. She has forgotten the gloves again, and her bare fingers ping my teeth like a mallet on a xylophone.

She hates fear and any expression of pain. I have been seeing her for twenty years and have learned never to yelp.

One day, she is staring at an X-ray she has just got back from the lab, her eyes floating blindly. She insists something is there. What, she does not know.

She calls in her sister, who jams her hand in my mouth. The hand tastes like beeswax.

My dentist pulls out a Black & Decker drill and starts boring into the mystery tooth.

She gives up after a while, as blood fills the plastic vacuum tube she likes me to hold.

She keeps clay models of dentists in action poses by the chair, and old, furled cartoons about dentistry.

Her hands shake as she retrieves her metal instruments and

starts to rub them together. Now you can smile in front of people, she always says when we're done.

She develops a limp, then her spine erodes.

She has started to walk on her knuckles, and the hair under her smock is wild and silver.

Nothing can explain my devotion to her but love.

When she shakes, I hold her hand to steady it and say, Queen, we still have a long way to go.

WHAT IT FELT LIKE

When Rick and I met he was hotter than hell.

Long, golden hair, chiselled features, muscles popping in a racer-back tank, and his huge dick and balls nicely outlined in skin-tight jeans.

I am foxy, but I always thought he was too good-looking for me. Girls would get all up in my face, saying, HE'S your boyfriend? Or, He's YOUR boyfriend? and pretty soon I was screaming, Back off, skank! 24/7.

We were tight, but I got jealous. And jealousy is bad, it's like that eczema my mother has that is always flaking and she is holding her disgusting arms over the food, and where I sit, all the time.

I'd say, Who's the whore that called? even if I answered and it was clearly his elderly aunt. Or, You better fire that receptionist at the shop, slut's staring at your ass behind my back.

I got mean, and he got sad, and started eating all the time.

At first it was just junk food like a bag of burgers and fries and whole, deep-fried chickens and day-old bakery cakes that said, Happy Birthday, Fuckface, or sometimes just DIE in red icing.

Then he started eating old candy canes, and crumbs off the counter with his tongue and jars of pickled beets and cans of haggis, whatever he could find, and cut his hair short with one rat-tail, and started wearing silver track suits.

I tried to get him to stop, but he would get furious and my man is strong, so I knew to let it go.

He ate nails and Brillo pads, he grazed on the lawn, he ate a push-mower and two tubs of Vaseline, he chewed the paint off the fence and emptied out Roach Motels.

He was so big he had to wear two sheets stapled together, and I slept on the floor beside him. We stopped being intimate because I was scared he would kill me, and I know it's mean to say, but he looked bad. He was grey and swollen, and stank from stuff lost in the folds of his belly.

I took up with a skinny guy, a dealer who liked to fuck me up the ass and call me Buster. I felt guilty, and I told my man what I was doing.

He stabbed out the number for the ambulance and they took him away and he came back home a few months later, quite a bit smaller, and said, We need to talk.

He told me he was only eating because I was so jealous of all the girls chasing him. He thought if he was gross, they would stop and I would be happy.

I was so blown away I just grabbed him and held on tight, and then he told me he missed what it felt like. When you eat so much, he said, your stomach feels like a gourd of sweet milk spilling over.

You're jonesing, I said, and when I kissed him I gave him a crack stinger and he said, Ahhhhhhh.

We are on the pipe all day, and the streets too. Chasing that dragon, the first hit that makes your knees go weak, how I sometimes feel when he punches me in the face for starting all this.

WHAT FRANCIS HAS FOUND

Piss clam
Tiny teapot
Blue shoe
Acorn
Dwarf pine
Hypodermic needle
Yellow barf
13 chicken heads in a circle
5 combs, different colours
Squashed squirrel
Pigeon wing
King of Diamonds
Broken action figure
Balled-up pants
Violet (from Tanzi)
Potato
Teddy bear diaper
White Medea wrapper
Bag of burgers
Silver key

Prague pin
Red suitcase
White nightgown
Five dollars
Brown rat
Cookie
Glassine bag
Plaid change purse
Forked stick
Tennis ball
Buttercups
Orange leaf
Pacifier
Black shadow
This note —

> Where you at for the support we need
> Where da food for the family
> Where you at for the support we need
> On alcohol there goes the money
> Where you at for the support we need
> Where you at?
>
> — Livin in da low Pain

THE ACORN

Jamie drew the menu illustration: a wispy tree with an enormous squirrel crouching in its branches. He also wrote the text, relying on a variation of the following claim: "Jumbo Burger. And Do We Mean Jumbo!" or "Curly Fries. And Do We Mean Curly!"

I worked at the Acorn for a year. Jamie's girlfriend, Darcy, hired me. Darcy was very emphatic about her likes and dislikes.

I will have a tea in the evening, but never in the morning. I like my tea without milk. Black. I like a mug, not a cup and saucer, and if you put sugar in my tea I will throw it right down the drain. Even saccharin. I don't like a biscuit with it either.

She would go on this way, but spoke so precisely, she was nice to listen to.

The regulars included a very old man named Leo, who waited to the second we served beer, then started stamping if I was not standing *right there* with a Molson Ex. There were three or four older Portuguese men, the only guys who tipped, who drank a lethal combination they called "Whisscoffs." There was Marla, who would get angry if her ice cubes looked "yellowy," and a changing group of mostly guys, one who asked me if I "sprung a tit leak" when I spilled water on my shirt, and another who liked to put his glass eye in his mug and whine for a free beer.

There was the wiry redhead who made skull rings for Satan's Choice who drove me home on his bike one rainy day, and there was Alex, who took me out and blew all his money on a stuffed polar bear for me.

Ho-cake, who convinced me to take a tole-painting class with him and then told me, on the way home, My girlfriend got rough with me last night and hurt my testes — I mean, my testes are *all blue.*

Darcy — when I think of her now, I see a thin girl, with light brown hair, and nothing else. Nothing but her desire to be remembered. As someone who liked things a certain way, who possibly preferred the smell of coconut air freshener to lemon air freshener, who watched five minutes of *Casablanca* and was "bored out of her mind."

Who had a man send her a clay burro from Tijuana once, who was afraid of loud rain and liked pancakes shaped like cats' heads and cried every time she heard "More Than a Feeling."

I am alone and have been for so long, I think of her as though we are friends.

I like my own tea milky, no sugar. Francis is the only thing that has ever made me happy; I collect bars of soap and never use them. I feel sick listening to Joy Division, sick and religious. I have never pulled the wings off a fly.

It's not spelled that way, I told Jamie, shyly.

He had typed "Tall Frosty Cock."

I was wringing my hands on my black apron, by the dish cart. I was nineteen years old and in love.

ALL THINGS ARE ALIVE

When Marty started coming home later and later from work, I started to worry.

While he was sleeping, I looked in his pants pockets and found a little notebook, pale blue with a puffy yellow chick on the cover.

I finished Maranatha tonight, he wrote, somewhere near the middle. And he is glorious.

The other pages looked like schematics, followed by words and phrases that made no sense: A sense of pizzazz! Something like Richard Nixon? And, Sweetly.

He smiled in his sleep, snoring gently and moving his hands like lobster claws. I slipped the notebook back and slept beside him, my hand stuffed in the crack of his hairy ass.

In the morning, he would go off to his job as a collections officer, where he would spend all day on the phone, hissing *I know where you live.*

This used to make him very depressed, making people cry and having to invent even more vile tactics every day. Now he came home with bags of warm, greasy food, singing, and calling me Cowgirl.

I would get at the notebook when I could. Sometimes it was

in his pocket, sometimes not. He started writing what looked like little plays:

> Goober: I do not wish to be dishonourable!
> The Tsar: I shall then issue the Emancipation Edict!
> Goober: And I shall inform the Duma.

There was also a list of names, including Skippy, Tralala, O.D. Skelton, Doobie, Messiah, Suzen, Phaedra, Baby Dayliner, and Jiff.

I found the first peanut when I was vacuuming.

It was perched under the couch on little black licorice legs and arms and had a mop of cotton-batting hair. Eyes, nose, and mouth drawn on with a marker; a gauze-pad toga and toothpick sword.

I stood up and started to notice them everywhere. Peanut beatnik on the DVD player, with wild yellow yarn hair and candlewax bongos. Peanut scholar, with a grommet-monocle; peanut cavalry, charging the flanks of dust under the bed. Peanut movie starlet in shimmering glass beads.

I never mentioned them. I just kept screwing Marty's best friend, Umesh, and when Umesh tried to look at the *Ziegfeld Follies* diorama on the nightstand, or at the pendant peanut Esther Williams swimming in a coral reef of starfish, anemones, and tongue-depressor polyps, I steered him back into my arms.

The notebook started to take on a dark edge. PNTS. HATE ME? read one entry. Another drew plans for making small, octagonal caskets out of balsa wood.

One night I saw the funeral cortège approaching our bed like black ants. Marty was dead when I woke up, his eyes open and wet.

I threw all the peanuts away and shredded the notebook. With the insurance money, Umesh and I were able to get a nice little place in Sarnia Forest, and sometimes he would say he felt bad about Marty and I would sigh that Yes, I did too.

Sadness: I am not sure if we are real!
Marty II: I still wish—
The Choir Invisible: Why? ♫♪♪♪♫
Marty II: I wish all things were alive.

Marty said that to me once when we were young and fooling around with a couple of toys we'd found in the park.

He said it and cried. He cried most of the night and I covered my ears.

The razor beside him glittered hard, as if it were trying to tell me, Look. Look what happened.

THESE DAYS

I went back to see you again. The blood appeared in a map of the park, and your song shuffled into place, so we walked together. Your smooth voice, feeling *closer than we've ever been.*

You told me you wrote this song for me, which may not be true. Still. It is a lotus blooming from the fire of your hundreds of notebooks, all kept with a green marker: verse, chorus ×2, verse.

This day, these days —

I cleaned the plaque where dirt had covered the word FRIEND and left you a pink gerbera daisy, wound into the wood shavings, over one sunflower seed.

You and I, these days, are no longer friends.

I have been reading the diaries about separating from you, and getting back and getting back.

Something sexy about you grabbing your crotch and saying, *This* belongs to you. Some terrible fights, a night spent in bed with a pizza.

These days. How can I have one back?

I come home and there is a pigeon leg on my path, stripped bare, beside its bloody torso. Two crows are screaming in the tree.

I pick up the pieces and look again. There is another leg, flung on the sidewalk, loose and sticky.

Two complicated little burials. That is, two bags, hidden in other bags and dreaded.

This reminds me of terrible things. The headless pigeon in the snow, the newborn gerbil I dropped, then watched, helplessly, as it staggered around the floor.

How much you repulsed me, sometimes. You, your head shaved, a few years ago, taking a bath and coming out in the pink terry robe I lent you and you looked like an egg hatching.

This fragrant image is cherished by me now.

Your hand reaches from the earth, in crayon colours, Mulberry and Thistle. Reminding me of a toy we liked, called the Chicken Baby.

All I do is cry and think of you. This is the happiest summer of my life.

SO MUCH LOVE

Think of it, Otto says.

Stretch limos, red carpets, festivals in Marrakesh and Bucharest, parties below the Black Sea with Neriedes in coral waistcoats serving kale and salty potables!

Otto is a film producer. We are at a restaurant celebrating my completed first draft of *Sylvia Rising*, a horror movie about Sylvia Plath crawling out of her grave and going on a killing spree.

He asks me to tell him the story again and says, My dear, it gives me shivers!

I sit beside him on the banquette and he covers my hand with his warm, plump hand and I sigh contentedly.

I will give you the general idea, I say.

The new poems will crawl across the bottom of the screen like hurricane warnings. Her brain is mostly liquid: the poems are terrible.

In the sequel to "Daddy" she calls her father "Dad," in order to use new rhymes, and is only able to come up with "rad," "plaid," and "really, really mad."

And "Lady Lazurus" becomes "Lady Lentil," after one of Christ's minor miracles, known among Biblical scholars as "one of His simple, spicy recipes."

"Out of the pot I come with piping hot flair / I serve four, and thrive in Tupperware," goes the envoi.

I will use the kind of writing one sees on summer produce stands, Otto muses.

I want Plath to be frightening, I say, but still pretty. Her rosy, necrotized flesh will cling to her tall, graceful skeleton.

Her long, dark-blond hair will cascade over the shoulders of her pink wedding suit.

Otto reminds me of the Ted Hughes poem about their wedding and we agree that when she is stalking her victims, her eyes will be great, sparkling jewels.

We pass a glass of cassis back and forth. I tell him that Sylvia is intent on killing the writer Erica Jong, but there are many other casualties as she makes her way from the English countryside to the streets of Jamaica Plain, where Jong keeps a pied-à-terre.

The street will be alive with police cars and helicopters! Otto says.

And SWAT teams, I say. She will bat at them with her large, verdigris-green hands.

I tell him that as Plath makes her way, at night, feasting on girls stealing rhododendrons or, once, a woman highlighting passages in, or raping, a library book, Jong is being interviewed by a college student at her vast Connecticut estate.

Otto puts his head on my shoulder, and I smell musk and copper fused together like an estuary: he is a river and my heart is the sea, I think, happily.

Jong is wearing pink mules and a roomy caftan covered in hot-pink azaleas. Her lips are painted to match; her tiny, expressive eyes are heavy with blue powder. She scrunches her blond curls and speaks: When I wrote *Sexual Vegetables*, no one had ever heard of a liberated lady with a soft, juicy, slippery cunt writing of having such womanly, powerfully intellectual feelings toward zucchini and cucumber!

I have been compared to James Joyce, she declares, now sitting on the sad college student's lap and yelling into his tape recorder.

I am a genius like Plath but I chose life! I chose to ride all sorts of rootlike, tuberish cocks, to take them deep into the sticky chthonic mysteries of my being.

Sylvia Plath's husband flirted with me once! Jong continues. He drew a penile serpent in my copy of his book.

I was aroused but I resisted his vampiric allure! For I would not die for poetry, not like Sylvia!

Otto squeezes my hand. This is the good part.

Jong and the student hear a tap at the window. Night has fallen, the wind howls. The student dislodges her, and she smoothes her hair and outfit as he pulls open the pink drapes.

And there she is! Otto says.

There indeed is Sylvia, her beautiful bones gleaming in the moonlight! Beside her is a new grave. There is the flash of a scythe, and suddenly, there lies Erica Jong, headless beside her new manuscript of poetry, the title of which contains seven ampersands, two obscenities, and the words *Cooter Jam*.

The young student says, None of them ever came close to you, Sylvia, no one ever could.

The house catches fire, and Sylvia is a golden lotus, she is a golden lotus amid the fierce flames.

We should end it there, Otto says sleepily.

I can't sacrifice the monster movie ending, I say.

When Lafitte leaves me, I go to Otto immediately. Love me, I say. His girlfriend, Gemma, overhears me: she is a tall, Slavic performance artist who uses knives and cyanide in her work.

The next day I am informed by Otto's secretary that I am never to speak of love to him again.

We never make the movie, and when we do meet, years later,

his son Fabergé is always there, crawling under the table and sawing at my Achilles tendon with plastic cutlery or lighting matches on my shoe.

One night Fabergé screams at me, I hate you, you're ugly!

I am sitting on the loveseat, my legs drawn up under my loose white caftan with the gazania print, my fingers tousling my short, red hair.

He is just tired, Otto says, and takes him to bed, whispering stories to him until I leave, two hours later.

How dare you? I fume to him later in a strongly worded email. I had many other places I could have been!

In truth there was nowhere else to go and nothing to do. I had looked at myself in Otto's black windowpane and remembered reading that in bright light, the petals of the gazania seem to be "on fire."

I could only see the lines in my face, my vast bulk.

I still flinch, remembering the look of shock on Otto's face when he saw me. It had been a long time.

Call Dr. _____ , I write on the memo pad by the door and go outside and stand in traffic until the police are able to coax me into the cruiser and home.

After several more years have passed, I see Gemma at a boutique on College Street. I am holding a stack of cards.

It is my mother's seventieth birthday, I tell her. I want to send her seventy cards.

She writes me a little note later. She says she is sorry Otto and I do not speak and hopes that changes. That Fabergé still wears the cowboy vest I bought him years ago, and that she is pleased to remember me buying the cards.

So many cards! she writes. So much love.

At the restaurant that night, they were playing "The Blue Danube" and I remember the notes leaping and falling as I bowed my head like a dying flower, as Otto and I shared a dream of Sylvia living and dead.

Of Sylvia as the warm, beating pulse between us, of our heavy, misspent love.

BABY-FACE

Billy married a woman with a baby face, by which I mean damp and fractious.

He promised we could still be friends, then stopped talking to me when Baby-Face became convinced we were still seeing each other. You go get a blow job from her! she would shriek, of me.

Billy was doing commercials back then. He was stuck reprising the same ad for pulp-filled orange juice for years. Juice you can eat with a spoon! he yelled, while rubbing his round, leaf-sprouting belly. Yeah wiss spoons! people would yell sometimes.

I got pregnant by him, and the ultrasound revealed a piglet with no legs and a white Afro.

Start up the vacuum, I told the doctor. Its syncopated heartbeat means nothing to me.

Baby-Face ended up having quintuplets, and was photographed for the *Toronto Sun* under the headline KNUCKLEBALL! In the picture she looks dirty and angry, and is actually slapping one of the tiny quints.

Mother is decked out like a gorgeous sow, Billy told me from the hospital payphone. Just baring her sweet, pink teats.

He started to cry and I did too.

I was thinking of what I like to call the world's tenderloin district, filled with things like men raping goats and children covered in scars; that is, the fat on the meat we do not consider to be edible.

And the baby, also. Nursing in garbage. My own sweet pig-child, who would have been twenty-one this year and maybe cruising along on prosthetic hooves.

Yes, it was a real baby, shaped like a cashew nut and filled with warm blood.

The pregnancy stick developed into a happy face. I think of it also, buried under two decades of trash, still trying to say, This is good news!

COCK FOOT

This is the amazing story of Cock Foot.

My mother took me out for a pedicure in Pointe-Claire, where she lives. We kept having the appointment cancelled, then reinstated. By the time we did get there, I was expecting, at least, a pool of the "hungry fish!" I have seen on cutting-edge infomercials.

But it was just some mini-mall dump: five women, including us, lined up in moaning shiatsu chairs.

This thing is aggressively nubby, I complained, until they placed a beach towel behind my back, then another on my legs.

My mom said this was because the young Vietnamese girls were trained to guard against accusations of looking up their clients' skirts. Like these girls are interested! she said.

They showed a video that my mom says they show every time. It features package lunches of Asian Sno Balls, in pink and yellow, and at its climax, a hog is slaughtered and rammed into a pole.

She was sitting beside a white woman with brown hooves who declared, I have never had a pedicure! The bark shaved off her feet could have made twenty canoes. The woman beside her was old and aloof, and kept making cellphone calls about "Debbie's absurd decision."

And beside me, a tall, large woman with a small, frosted crest of hair and the biggest feet I have ever seen. They were tanned and long as loaves of bread: each toe was at least five inches long and four inches in diameter.

One thing they did at this place was airbrush designs on your nails. The girl slaving over my feet drew — maliciously, I thought — upside-down hearts on mine.

I looked over and Cock Foot was having a variety of master artworks, including *Guernica,* painted on hers, with extra room left for the odd dying horse or battle spear.

I only wear running shoes, she grunted at me. But they seem to like doing this.

That woman could satisfy ten men, I told my mom later. Or one man, ten times, she said.

When one of my two hearts chipped off I remembered Cock Foot and imagined her peeling off her sneakers and feeling something new before the lilies, the blue-green dreams, slipped below the water and fell away.

SCREECHING IN

We are SO fucking Newfies, Veronica Lodge and I said to each other in the months leading up to our trip.

We were both going to look for men this time. She was newly single; I was, as always, sexually desperate.

At night, in the hotel, I invented two dream men for us, Clyde and Bo, who ran a meth lab in Witless Bay and carried firearms.

We talked about their violent sexual techniques and missing teeth as we made our way to the bars, three days in.

There is a thing in Newfoundland, a ceremony, where you, "'aving drunk aye shot ou rum — staide straite — an' kissed de provincial bird," become "nited" and "n onirary member of the province."

I am pretty sure I stood straight and kissed a rubber puffin as well, but nothing in my certificate explains the father-son rapists.

Veronica and I went to Trapper John's to get Screeched In, and we were so nervous. We were worried they would make us sing, or wear hats.

But this was the thing to do in St. John's, a criminally boring city.

But beautiful! It should have its own version of the Hollywood sign that says NATURE. They should pass out tissues at the airport:

Ye will cry on the clapper on Bell Island, Miss.

At night, I would look at the parking lot through our window and remember all that nature. The mist around Signal Hill, or even the displays at The House of Stoyles Ltd., which feature doll brides surrounded by crocheted slippers, and ornamental flensing knives tricked up in pink and green beads.

The old man who makes tiny ships and tugboats and sails them on a rivulet by the highway.

The Sacred Grotto in the woods, where a dwarf Jesus presides over an incomplete and lustful series of renderings of the Stations of the Cross. In the most inept, Veronica seems to be using her veil as a dust rag; another shows a centurion beating Our Lord and Saviour with a fan belt.

Trees and rocks and the wild sea.

It's all good! I toasted Veronica, the Screech night, after a brief, monotonous pub crawl.

We waited forever until two guys hovered by our table, and we asked them to sit down.

The son and I'd thought we'd Screech In, the older one, with a snarl of red hair and a stitched-over harelip, said, gesturing to the son himself, an idiotically muscular kid in glasses and a polo shirt.

Veronica and I drank everything the bar had, including apple jacks, as the men started, earnestly, to love us.

You are merely a child, I told the kid, Alex, as he followed me to the washroom, panting about older, big women.

I am a decent Christian man, the father — Peter — told me as he cornered me by the bar and massaged my back. My cock is real hard, he added.

A few shots later Alex inflated his chest and told me I just needed a good fuck, and I said, You're telling me.

Finally there were eleven of us gathered at the bar to be Screeched In. The ceremony was mortifying, and Alex had started to run between Veronica and me, insisting that he had never left a woman unsatisfied.

I made out with the bartender and stole all the spangled tooth-picks from behind the bar.

We left abruptly and went to Signal Hill, which had clouded over. I hate the father-and-son rapists, I said, somewhere near the place Marconi first sent his dot-dot-dots.

Still, there was something romantic about being there in the shadows of their bad intentions, intentions that followed us the next day as we laboured up the steps of Cape Spear and saw them, and they said, We are feeling up for another night on George Street!

I started to feel sick from the drinking and disgusting slashes of memory.

I slowed down and watched a fat woman sweating on her way down.

Hard climb? I asked.

No, she said. I was up at the gift shop and it's boiling in there!

She kept turtling along, gasping. When we reached the gift shop, we noticed it was quite chilly, and Veronica seemed mystified by the lie the woman had told; by her having worked so hard to go such a small distance, and been ravaged by her desire to get somewhere.

BLOOD WHERE IT SHOULDN'T BE

And then and then she had to take off her shoes —

I wondered when he would get to it. Roy, the foot fetishist with a case file as thick as a platform heel.

I made jerking-off motions to Simon, my colleague at the Distress Centre, and performed a small pantomime with my stilettos. After I told Roy I was on to him, Simon and I robbed the emergency cash box for beer money and left the phones unattended.

I am not sure why I started working for a Distress Centre after high school. I just want to help, I told the head volunteer at the orientation meeting. At this same meeting, she asked the group about the happiest day of our lives.

The sad man remembered paddling his canoe towards a Tango-orange sunset; the housewife recounted meeting a "handsome and affluent merman" at Marine World. Simon started to tell a story about "a well-developed girl," blushed, and changed her into his sister with cerebral palsy. I said, "This moment. Right now."

The calls were pathetic, and I found it hard to care. "I ... am ... a ... hundred. And ... get ... lonely." Or "I want to cut more octagons into my legs."

DO IT, Simon would hiss, listening in.

Simon had developed a crush, and had started leaving me trashy magazines and papers he knew I loved, like *Allô Police*.

He was also very hostile about his affection: once, he said I looked like Jack Klugman. But on *Quincy*, on *Quincy*, he said.

Another time, he asked me to have a "nice, possibly candlelit dinner" with him. But don't wear that, he said, gesturing to my vintage dress. It smells like cat, or something —

I waved him off because I was interrogating an elderly man.

During our orientation, we were told to ask, politely and firmly, whether a given caller was pleasuring himself.

Are you masturbating? I asked the panting man, after he made several not-too-veiled references to my alleged cold and how nicely an "ahhhhhhh" "big thermometer" might "uhn" fit in my mouth.

How dare you? he said. I am a grandfather! I apologized and made small talk until he said in a mean, little voice, Do you remember when you asked if I was masturbating? Well I was! And I just cummed!"

I hung up as if the phone was on fire and Simon and I screamed.

So, Swiss Chalet? Simon suggested. I told him I had work to do for school, a paper about Erasmus, and then kept writing in my diary and reading him the spicy bits about a punk I was in love with who slept in a cage, fortified with electrical wiring and surrounded by attack dogs.

Please stop, Simon pleaded.

I would find chunky troll dolls in my purse when I got home, cans of Silly Putty, licorice whips.

The phone would ring at home and I would hear long, hissing sighs or plaintive squeaks.

Was that you? I would ask.

I finally agreed to go out for coffee with him, and he dressed up in a tight T-shirt and torn acid-washed jeans. I took him to the Acorn, and he leaned in as I absent-mindedly started marrying the ketchups I snagged from the other tables.

I have to go to the doctor, he said. His lank, thin hair fell into his eyes, obscuring a new, livid series of boils.

Why? I asked, signalling for the bill.

He lowered his voice even more. Because, he said. I have blood...in my pants. You know. *Blood where it shouldn't be.*

When Darcy brought over the bill, Simon turned red and got angry. This is a waste of my time, he said. I thought we were doing something! I took two GO Trains!

But we are doing something, I said miserably.

I bought *Phantom* tickets! he yelled and burst into tears, laying his head on the table.

I hear the phantom is tremendously disfigured, I ventured, as his shoulders jerked up and down.

But he wears some kind of a mask, or a maskette?

Simon quit the Distress Centre, but I stayed on for a few months, talking to teenagers holding cans of Drano, to perverts, and to lonely people.

I remember my last call. A woman who said her adult son never phoned or wrote. She sent him cards and money, but he wouldn't respond, except to say how busy he was, if she managed to catch him.

Blood where it shouldn't be, I told her.

Honey, she said.

Everything's coming up roses for me and for you!

WAS THAT NECESSARY?

I came home to find a notice on the door. An envelope waiting at the post office.

I was feeling a particular misery that day. Something like prison, without the upside of having wilded someone or just gone off, guns blazing.

It was a letter from Korea. I was stunned and wary.

I opened it on my way back home, at Wong Variety, where they were selling dirty stuffed animals "For Tammy's College." Tammy Wong is a little girl whose parents work at two variety stores, twenty hours a day, and shy away from customers as if afraid of being pistol-whipped.

Beside the cans of turkey gravy and bags of cat litter, I slit open the envelope.

No note. A religious medal, which had belonged to my dead grandmother's sister.

A thorn-strapped flaming heart that read, Cease! The Heart of Jesus is with me!

I was grateful to have it back. I had given it to him for a safe trip: it had been five years. But it was in a torn glassine envelope that also contained two antique white buttons. I had written, mawkishly, on the paper holding them: *YOU AND ME XO.*

I had no memory of giving this to him.

I wrote back, *Was that necessary?*

I was thinking of my friend's birthday party, that summer, at the Skyline. The waitress was a thin, fractious marmalade blonde, and the menu was filled with beautiful drawings of strong men extending milkshakes or plates of steaming, boiled potatoes.

I dare you to use the washroom, I said to a guy at our table. He went down and came back. Someone is taking the shit of the world in there, he said.

We kept looking to see the guy come up until we realized it was our friend's awkward new young boyfriend, whose seat was vacant.

But when he came up the guy yelled, There he is! And we all stared.

Was that necessary? another guy asked.

The night went badly, and I minced home in too-tight shoes and a dress, railing at the stars.

I am standing by Tammy Fong's makeshift desk, holding a bag of pork rinds I will never eat, feeling responsible for having loved him.

Somewhere in Seoul, he is pointing, lazily, at an old picture, and saying, That's her. That's her!

TELL MY FATHER I LOVE HIM

One day, toward the end, Lafitte was walking up the shag-carpeted stairs and he doubled over.

What's the matter? I asked.

He gasped and crawled to the chair on his belly like a soldier. Collapsed and said, I am dying.

What? I asked, incredulous.

I. Need. You. To — tell my family I am sorry, and to tell my father I love him.

Come again? I said.

He started clutching his heart and panting.

What, do you want me to call an *ambulance*? I asked.

HURRY! He screamed. Heart. Attack.

I called 911 and told them some guy claimed to be having a heart attack in my house and could they come. I tried to sound like a neutral observer, like someone watching a student production of *Death of a Salesman*.

The EMTs arrived and rolled him onto the stretcher. He reached out a feeble hand to me, and said, Don't. Forget —

I followed him in a cab. By the time I got there, his stretcher had been abandoned by the vending machines, and he was sitting up eating a bag of Doritos.

I have a quite serious headache, he huffed, and I took him home.

They billed him the full ambulance freight, the fee they reserve for people who call because of mosquito bites or "oddly shaped moles."

Veronica said, a long time later, that it was probably his guilty conscience, and I was mystified. What conscience?

Maybe it was the stress of lying to so many people and in such detail: Which girl did I tell I worked for CSIS? Did I really say I would like that other one's adult son to call me Daddy?

In any event, I am writing this to tell his father.

I am telling you that he loved you and his last thoughts were for you, and that they were honest.

That's right, Arliss. Your son almost died of a headache. And, in the middle of all that, he longed for you to hold him and tell him, I love you too.

There. Done!

YOU BROKE IT

Lafitte developed Peyronie's disease, a year or so before we broke up.

This disease affects the connective tissues of the penis, and involves the formation of fibrous plaques in its soft tissues.

There is no known cause for the disorder, which may result in penile deformity, and lead to its painful abbreviation.

He was mortified, then angry. This is your fault, he said.

The doctor told him that extreme pressure could cause the condition.

Broke it? I asked indignantly. I never even touched the thing.

It was at this time he started shaving his balls, acquiring surveillance apparatus, and growing a soul patch.

He left me for an event planner who gives me dirty looks when I see her at parties, and I cannot blame her.

At a book launch I looked up and saw her angrily folding a plate of cheese straws into a familiar shape.

She is an attractive woman, thin and athletic. Above the boatneck of her sailor blouse is a necklace of skin tags. Some plain, like small tonsils, others as huge and succulent as grapes.

Her ex, a good-looking sculptor with a dynamic facelift, tried to befriend me by telling me actual horror stories about her that ended, And then the cop said, You'd better run like hell, buddy, she's in the house! Or, The writing on the mirror said, LOOK UNDER THE BED. *She* had been licking my hand all night!

But I am tired of talking about her and them.

I don't even react when someone mentions buying milk or 6/49 tickets at their convenience store.

If you ask him a question, one friend tells me, he always says: Ask the boss!

The boss — his wife — will scowl from her station at the register as he sweeps and whistles Jerry Vale songs.

Pretend you don't see her, my love —

The first time I saw him was in High Park. He had several parts in a series of musical adaptations of classic plays. I saw *Disco Othello*: Lafitte gestured to Iago with a coke spoon and a choir sang "Moor, Moor, Moor."

He was wearing a billowing white shirt and his dreadlocks tumbled over his shoulders; his face was illuminated by a rainbow.

The director had spoken sternly to us about race before the curtain. People, she had seethed. Are people. Black, white, yellow, purple, or green.

Still, you have to watch those Purples, I whispered to my friend. They are congenital crooks.

My friend said, Shhhh. He was desperate to have sex with the director, who was on the cover of *NOW Magazine* that week, applying rouge and lipstick to a bust of Shakespeare.

We went backstage after, and Lafitte was holding hands with the director.

That was funny, when Desdemona sang "Stayin' Alive," I said. No one said anything: I had made a terrible gaffe.

But Lafitte liked me. He took my hand and wrote his number on it as his girlfriend told her admirers about *Mall for Love*, a tragic love story taking place in an exotic pet store.

He told me, later, that he had looked out into the audience and everyone had disappeared but me.

Your face was a china cup, taking in the darkness, he said.

All too soon, I was just another version of the director. The day he left, I entered the hold of the WABAC Machine, and Mister Peabody and I travelled to the future. This is a radical change of events, he said, but I wish to take you away from your pain.

He panted on his small glasses and cleaned them, saying, Seven years forward should do the trick!

We land in a darkened room, where a middle-aged woman lies on the left side of a big bed.

She is heavy-set, with short brown hair. Tears fall steadily from her closed eyes, past her ears. They form lakes on the pillowcase: Mites, invisible to our naked eyes, are capering there, Mister Peabody says.

I watch the woman's lips moving: *Laugh and pretend you are gay.*

This is deplorable, I say. Quite, says Mister Peabody, and adjusts the date.

We land in the variety store. And what do you feel now?

Nothing, I say.

I used to be devastated, Mister Peabody tells me, when little Sherman was killed, in our travels, by Mongols, Aztecs, or David Berkowitz. Yet, this morning, when he was torn apart by Apaches, I felt only a heavy sense of dismay, at the needless carnage.

I understand, I say, and squeeze his paw. Let's watch a movie, I suggest.

I should like an ahistorical fiction for a change, he says brightly.

We travel to the store and ask Lafitte where *Showgirls* is shelved.

Ask the boss! he says.

She jerks her thumb to its location on the metal rack and grunts.

How thrilling, Mister Peabody says, when he locates the film. One day we shall speak with Gianni Versace himself about this!

Sherman and I call shotgun at the exact same time, and Mister Peabody pats his red bow tie.

The door is stuck, he frets. Sir, he calls out to Lafitte, May we use your penis as an Allen key?

I know, I know, Mister Peabody adds, motioning Lafitte to be quiet.

I shall ask your boss!

BUB

He and I moved in together a week ago, and I am still blown away by my feelings for him.

I had given up, after my last date ended on the roof, with hostage negotiators yelling through a megaphone, PUT THE MACHETE DOWN, SIR! at the shirtless, sweating maniac holding the blade to my throat.

A friend suggested I try a dating service, Perfect Love, and I spent one long day posting a picture of myself dressed as a Halloween pumpkin and answering question after question.

I was so honest, it took weeks for the service to return with three candidates. My friend, in the interim, had met a guy who ran a B&B out of his mansion in Collingwood. He had a mouthful of veneers and called everyone "Bro."

My first date was with a man suffering, agonizingly, from necrotizing fasciitis, and I spent the day at his bedside, in a gown and mask, listening to him talk deliriously about the time he was a roadie for Tiny KISS while the doctors amputated his legs.

So that guy died.

The next date was at the Kingston Penitentiary, with a pretty famous murderer. He and I talked through Plexiglas, and he was cuffed and shackled the whole time. He said I was too old for him, but would I put on a dirty puppet show involving girl-puppet-on-girl-puppet action?

I did the show, and he and I were so close to something special. I loved the way his eyes narrowed and turned into black, flat buttons when he directed me: Now have the one girl shoot the other one! No, choke! Choke her!

But he lost his visiting privileges that day when a guard walked in while I was holding the puppet's bare chest to the glass for him to kiss.

Finally, I met Bub.

Yes, Bub is a zombie, one of the legion of the undead. And yes, it is hard to keep him from trying to attack and eat me — or it was, until I got a zombie-taser and turned him on to Thai food.

He lives in a room in the back I secure every night with whatever wood is around. In the day, he likes to lie in an elongated box filled with dirt while I throw him chicken heads and canned haggis.

Love! Is the first word he learned, a word he also uses to refer to the neighbourhood animals he kills.

Bub was obviously a handsome man once, and his black suit, white shirt, and floral tie look *fine*.

He gets tired easily, so I tend to go to bed early, taser him into his room, toss in a pile of white rats, and start nailing the door shut.

He loves the Discovery Channel, dancing to good tunes, and working out by running really fast with his arms outstretched.

Some nights when he is screaming and swiping at the door, I swell, like those days when God fills the sky with falling feathers and white spores, and the warm sun adores you and you are moved enough to write *I LOVE BUB* in sidewalk chalk everywhere.

This is what I do now, mostly. This is my man.

A STINK FOR THE AGES

My neighbour's husband Joey died, and I didn't hear about it for some time.

When I found out, I began spending time with Anna, drinking in her filthy apartment, listening to her talk.

I had been over there before when he was alive, listening to them yell over each other about art and science and politics while gesturing to their stacks of bloated, yellow books.

The place was disgusting: when a neighbourhood woman's headless torso was discovered in an alley, the police searched everyone's houses, several times.

But when they got to Anna and Joey's, they declined.

It is not the mess, which is astonishing. Or the halo of flies around the black dish rack and random piles of plates.

It is not the many overspilling ashtrays, the dripping walls, or unlaundered sheets and single pillow on the yellow mattress.

It is the rank stench of cat piss that originates in the beige, crate-sized litter box in the centre of the apartment; that spreads, beyond its point of origin, into every crevice, every scrap of fabric or upholstery, every dirty, black inch of the place.

After I'd spent a good deal of time there, breathing through my mouth, Anna asked me to cat-sit for cats I had never seen.

I went over with a scarf around my face and tried to clean what I could. I emptied the whole cat box, finding stratum after stratum of ossified waste. I wiped down the plastic mat where the cats ate, making one white space in the lightless kitchen.

I lured one oily, striped cat out. The other stayed under the couch, its eyes glowing.

The striped cat alternated between sitting in my lap eating scraps of turkey breast and running to the window I had opened and squashing its body against the screen.

I felt like a saint.

I love animals, I thought smugly. I would never let *myself* fall apart this way!

The day Anna was to return, I bought her a bottle of Cat's Pee on a Gooseberry Bush, a nice Sauvignon Blanc.

She called me, wasted, the next day. I have to go get *litter*, she said, infuriated by my wastefulness. There were other complaints about an excessive use of the bottle of Tresemmé she keeps in the bathroom as hand soap, about the accusatory new and clean cat bowls, the bottle of Evian I left for them in the refrigerator, and the sink filled with soapy bubbles and all of her flatware.

What a bitch, I thought.

I told everyone I knew about how disgusting her place was, how I would need a suit of armour if I ever went there again.

I imitated her drunken stumbling and the cat flattening itself against the window, sucking clean air like a trapped miner.

Total bitch.

Right after Joey died, I'd brought her some seeds in a bag to plant and asked what I could do.

Can you bring my baby back? she asked, and all of the light in the world lurched.

I THOUGHT IT WAS YOU

A shot of yellow gingham, pink face: Mary, I thought it was you.

It was an old, fat woman trudging across the street, her mouth like a horseshoe.

Bald man in a pink STYLE T-shirt, carrying pink dry cleaning.

Girl in a hat crocheted into a rainbow.

Slovenly man bent over on a bench, smoking.

Crazy girl yelling, This is what I will not do with you!

Mother in a green smock, on a hill of wildflowers.

Worm undulating below the train tracks on its purple belly.

Furry brown dog, off its leash, eating a toasted bun.

Five crisply curled wigs in a WHAT-A-MELON box.

A bolt of blue sky, seducing a black cloud.

Scuffed tap shoes; a baby-pool's curved centre; something funny you said, written as scripture on the church's bulletin board.

I saw a woman putting her suitcases into the trunk of her sister's car. She was sad and beautiful; her sister hung back, trying to say goodbye.

Not you.

This morning I thought of your angry, flushed face as you stormed out, dragging your bags behind you; how things invariably ended with us.

Unanswered messages: *I am sorry, I am so sorry.*

Every aspect of you still here, like the pulp of a fruity drink or the blue of your terrible blue eyes and veins, and your little knitted hat, making horizons.

Everything will be all right this time, you said.

I thought it was you.

PARADISE CITY

When I was fucking Axl, years ago, he would indicate that he was good to go by blowing sharply into the whistle he wore around his neck.

Okay, he was not Axl *Rose*, but the lead singer of Paradise City, a G N' R cover band that kicked ass every Friday night at the Mount Royal Tavern in Owen Sound.

I would try to get up there most weekends: I sat in the back sewing synthetic cornrowed hair to a red bandanna and mending the splits in his latex tiger pants.

This one! Is for. MY LADEE! he always called out before "Sweet Child O' Mine." The girls in the pink cashmere sweater sets and white shorts, the limpets against the stage, would scan the room, their eyes narrowed.

After the set, after the hauling and lifting and getaway in his pea-green Parisienne, William Bailey, his real name, would shrink a little, like an unwrapped piece of marzipan, and sigh.

Babe, he would say. I wish I could do my own tunes.

He always said that, and I always said, I know, I know, before coaxing him to some wharf or canoe or patch of emerald woods, sliding Trojan XL on him, and riding him like a rodeo bull.

I prayed he would never perform his own songs. He had played them for me: they were contemplations of everyday life, including "The Potato":

> Did you ever forget to wash off their eyes?
> Did you? (×3)
>
> That hot wet potato just cries and cries.
> Wouldn't you? (×3)

He was bald under his bandanna, and his stomach soared out of his pants like a Kayapó Indian's lip.

I left him the night he stopped in the middle of "November Rain," folded up his wig, and sang, without accompaniment, "Wonder-Thighs," a repulsive and entirely too personal song.

He had put on a small pair of glasses to read from a sheet of looseleaf, and when he smiled at me, it was a big, pink smile: his dentures were at the bottom of a glass of water on the amp, shining limpidly.

I met the local coke dealer, Brandon, that same night. He was a young, beefy hockey player with a shock of dyed red hair.

Veronica went off into the woods with his friend Rick. Brandon and I saw the flash of his huge white shoes; heard the skitter of her feet, trying to escape him.

Oh the beauty of the misty grass is parallel to yours, Brandon said, in aid of some action. I fell backwards, flat on my back, and he laughed and fell down too.

I would fall again, the next time we met, the last time, climbing down a rock path behind the Glennburnie Inn, a motel filled with moose heads and damp desperation.

"A telephone!?" the proprietor would ask, incredulously. "Coffee!?"

A marina had opened beside the place, and the water around the docks was slick with motor oil. Getting to a pay phone to call Brandon and beg him to meet me involved wading through waist-high water, picking off fish skeletons and leeches.

You have to meet me at the Royal tonight, I said, knowing William Bailey was touring other Sounds.

He did meet us at the Royal, and we watched Klaus shred "Crazy Train." I met a guy, Danny, whose sister was an artist, and he asked me to come by some time and buy one of her painted rocks after I admired his complicated pebble.

Brandon, Veronica, and I drove to his place, leaving Rick behind to make Rohypnol moonshine or whatever his hobbies were. Hang on, Danny said when we got there, barrelling upstairs.

We looked around.

A single room comprised the main floor, completely empty of anything but two chairs and a card table.

The older of the old men, passed out on the chairs in front of hands of cards, reared up and moaned.

The walls were yellow, the floor was darker yellow; there was nothing else.

I love what you've done with the place, Brandon said as Danny returned with a large rock signed Lynda Pitwamakwat.

I gave him twenty dollars, and we went back to the Glennburnie and hooked up while Veronica hid on the balcony.

In the morning I said, I will never see you again.

Never say never, he said.

It has been six years since that night, since William Bailey and Brandon.

The rock says, LOVE, HARMONY, FAITH, RESPECT, below two painted herons whose bellies are filled with pink maps.

It never did bring me luck, but it is always beside me when I write, reminding me what is out there.

The surface of the rock is Brandon's lap, which I lie in, my feet out the window, tasting the night.

It is William Bailey's throat swelling, an artifact of saying never. *Take me home.*

A RIDICULOUS PLACE

Lil and I were having our palms read at the Ex, in the Professor Orlando tent.

She did two Percs beforehand, and ate them like a wolf, baring her teeth and everything.

When you was born, her psychic said, you was born under a lucky star. Don't tell nobody.

When you was born, you knew ya brother would make a video with Denny Terrio called "Jive Walkin'." Is this true?

When you was a teenager, a bug bit you in the eye and you was outta ya mind with fear; ya fatha ate tha body of Christ and it turned out it wasn't Christ I'm gettin' *Chris*, whaddid he say?

My psychic was named Mrs. Calderhead, and she just kept apologizing to me. O, your family! I'm so sorry. Your life! Your face! I am very sorry.

She did say something I liked. She said, You are leaving a ridiculous place. *Ridiculous.*

I bought a heart amulet from Jerusalem that two days later I would tear off angrily and throw against the wall.

This night, all of our swerving was lined up perfectly with the star in the fist of the princess at the gates.

Through the obviously mentally ill adolescent singing "Sorry Seems to Be the Hardest Word." The ride that soaked us with black water; the enormous carnie giving us ten free balls and practically placing the last one in the barrel. The plush, club-footed Appaloosa I won.

At one point, Lil left me by the inflated black dog in the Pavilions of the World building, to look at discount T-shirts. You have five minutes! I yelled, easing off my shoes, looking up and realizing I was five feet away from an old woman's hard, swollen gunt in grey sweats.

I told Lil about it after, passing her a slash of morphine on the Ferris wheel. You are making me sick, she said.

Then she said it to the world, as she curved into the sky as the morphine rushed and her pale red hair glowed like a fire in the sky.

BIG HAIRY BUSH

Estevez was the name of my friend Ella's one and only online date.

He showed up at the bar late, and high.

I need to get stoned for my work, he told her. I am a major record executive!

Ella looked into his cognac-coloured eyes, took in his red shark-skin suit and mane of tawny hair, and went Rasta.

They smoked hash all night and made out, then almost fucked.

This is happening too quickly, she said, buttoning her blouse and pocketing her laddered stockings.

That's cool, he said. He introduced her to his white rat, Tessio, played "Butterfly" on his Gibson, and complimented her "ginormous baps." Breasts, I mean, he said, holding them and squeezing.

She was surprised to realize she was waiting, excitedly, for him to call over the next few days.

He never did. So she wrote him a note and asked, Can we meet again?

He wrote back, Regretfully, no.

Ella went crazy. She met with all of her friends and outlined the outrage in detail.

He told me he could really talk to me! That in another life, I was a goalie and he was a puck!

Son of a bitch bastard, they all said.

She called him and asked what had happened.

I'm not into delaying pleasure, he said. He coughed, thickly, and a girl in the background started whining, Put on Duffy, put on the Duffy!

Ella was furious and said, Be honest, you said you were honest!

She was entirely there in that moment, in that moment of the script when a woman pounces and the man shrinks to mouse-size.

Okay, he said. I am not into your big, hairy bush.

She was mortified and hung up. She spent months following him on the Web, and is still doing so, as far as I know.

She talks about him all the time. The faggot, she calls him. His family's coat of arms is the Village People!

I told my brother this story, and he now calls Estevez his idol.

Do not ever ask a question you don't want the answer to, is the main thing.

Like, Is my ass gelatinous; Do I smell like Funyuns; Do you love me?

Do you love me?

Someone I loved once answered, Not exactly; it's more like "love-ish."

I still pine for him. Like one of Tom Thomson's Jack pines, bending to the ground in grief.

We once studied Canadian poems about trees. This man was my student, and he got an A.

BLOOD ON THE GIZMO

Often, I am just standing there.

And I move into the past as if making a gesture as simple as a wave.

There is a loss of oxygen, stars raging in my eyes.

My mind is like a key-operated gizmo that shoots sparks. Moving slowly through a puddle, tilting back and forth.

A sheet of paper folded in to a hat, sailing across Shiloh Pond: that is my memory. All I remember is a constellation of injuries also issuing blood.

A camellia in a bowl of pink water, *a deliberate form of frenzy*, a squeezed tomato: Don't leave me.

After our first date I wrote about walking with you in the park. A yellow flower.

I am standing in front of the quivering maple planted with your cremains. In the same park, where we were.

The ashes are in a concrete canister, with a metal plate screwed to the top that calls you an artist, a friend, and inspiration. I leave a fat green apple in the dirt and clover.

Stand up and sigh. It is difficult.

I can't imagine not holding you like this again, you said. The night, this moment, you are standing behind me, squeezing me like a king cobra.

The sun turns white and blooms black lakes; the clouds ruffle into deep purple cats'-paws before the light returns like a knife, and more becomes fluid, and more is lost.

THE GUY FROM THE BEER STORE

Just before Christmas, two years ago, I was invited to a party at the house of friends who live in Cabbagetown.

I headed out in a tight dress and heels, carrying a huge, wrapped bunch of holly branches.

I had been afraid to go to chic parties after gaining so much weight, and I thought about how I would deal with the ill-concealed gasping and sibilant whispers.

A week before that, I had met a guy in the Beer Store who I ended up having drinks with. At the end of the night, he told me it was his birthday and kissed me goodbye. We had spent the whole night talking about what a bitch his neighbour was, a woman who would come over *only* when he had just made a nice lemon bread or black-and-white cookies, then eat them all.

She also left bobby pins all up and down the stairs and once brought a criminal, still in handcuffs, over, who yelled, "Ride it, bitch!" while he was trying to sleep.

I didn't have enough money to cover the cab to Cabbagetown so I had the driver pull up to an ATM, and after I finished, someone grabbed me from behind and shoved a gun in my throat.

Some dirty base-head.

I was scared, but I talked him down by telling him that I was a fan of crack, and happy to help him out. That he smelled like Axe cologne; that his gun felt super-smooth, Do you oil it a lot?

He let me go and I called the cops, who left me waiting in the lobby listening to "Santa Baby," still clutching my stupid, festive sticks.

I called the guy from the Beer Store and he met me at my place. I told him what had happened and he was shocked.

I just feel numb, I said.

He slept over.

He told me, pointedly, that a close girlfriend of his had come over in the morning. They ate Bananas Foster and talked about his inability to commit to anyone. She was wearing a see-through blouse! he said.

I think we should be friends, he said in the morning as I stared at him with hollow eyes.

Why? I asked. What for?

After the base-head robbed me, the police drove me past a crack bar and went inside, leaving me locked in the patrol car.

A bunch of people came out, and joined others on the street in screaming at me for being a narc.

That felt bad, but the guy from the Beer Store was worse. Worse than the mugger, who held me so tightly it felt like he never wanted to let me go.

IF YOU FIND THEM YOU CAN KEEP THEM

I had heard of him and you would know his name, if I told you.

He was in an 80s hair band that played what they called "Sexy Metal."

Friends of mine knew him, and long ago I would be introduced, repeatedly, to him, by one awestruck person or another.

Ivan Van Ivan, yeah, nice to meet you, he would always say as his eyes roamed the room.

A few years ago, I ran into him at a club, and he had changed, of course. His hair was short and thin; he dressed casually except for a bright pink scarf, and wasn't wearing makeup. I liked the last part. I hate men in mascara, I told him, as he started winding his scarf between us, eventually using it to pull me into a loud kiss.

He came home with me, and we sat on the couch while he told stories about his band's heyday. I met them all, man. Bachman! Fucking, Peart *and* Geddy, Geddy's cool, Offenbach, and —

I had to interrupt and tell him I had never listened to his band, and no, I did not know the tune "Pussy 666" or "My Soul Was Made for Tits and Metal."

He was stunned. He was working at a dry cleaner's at the time, and was convinced everyone recognized him as they handed him their balled-up, hircine party dresses.

But I have heard of you! I kept telling him. All the time, even now, I hear about you, I continued, until he said, Let's go upstairs and finesse that bra off.

We slept together and it was not memorable, except for some metal grunting and one "Hello, Toronto!" screamed in the middle.

In the morning I felt contempt, as always, for the snoring, long pig in my bed.

You have to go, you have to go, I kept urging, as he hopped around, finding his clothes.

I, ah, lost my tighty whities, he said at the door. If you find them, you can keep them, he leered.

I found them.

Pooled around my bedpost in a grey puddle. I ran downstairs and got plastic bags, gloves, and a pair of pliers.

Lifted them with the pliers only to see two skid marks: one tawny-coloured, the other, a more burnt sienna colour, probably from two days earlier.

I manipulated them into a bag, then another and another, then buried this bag in my trash.

Ivan called me and called me until I relented and let him come over. He gave me a leather band that closed with a snap, and called me his Tight Jam.

And this is the sick part. I went away for the holidays shortly after, and told my family that I was seeing someone I liked. I wore the bracelet to dinner, and I thought about him. I had not been fair, or kind, I thought.

I would change.

When I got home I called him, and said, Ivan, I am feeling it. He had told me, that first night, that he always knows things will work out if he's *feelin' it* with a chick.

He didn't call back.

I called him and asked what was happening.

He hedged, then said, I'm steaming and bagging clothes until two, three in the morning.

Everyone's so busy, he said.

He sounded exhausted.

I understand, I said.

When I was little, I brought home a field mouse and tried to feed it Velveeta cheese until it bit me. You can't keep that, my mother said.

The valiant garbage-men arrived the next morning.

You're too kind, I told them, and they bowed, deeply, in return.

TEENY TINY MAN

When I was a child, my mother would tell me a story she made up about Teeny Tiny, a girl with one green and one blue eye, whose accessories amazed me.

She washes with two dots of powdered soap; she sleeps on a ball of cotton and drinks from an eyedropper.

Shortly after Lafitte left me, I made a date with a tiny, perfect version of him who was much younger, a PhD who wrote complicated poems involving physics and pornography, such as "Quasicrystal Gunns."

His name was Michael, and he was an inch big.

This was adorable, and difficult.

Our first date started abruptly after he crawled under my door holding a *Pseudolithos migiurtinus*.

It's beautiful, I said, examining it with a magnifying glass.

I held him in my hand and took him for a walk. Look at the leaves! I would yell, or Watch out for that hornet!

I gave him a saucer of bourbon when we got home and he lapped from it until he started rolling around like a dog in piss-grass.

Let's move this into the bedroom, I said, and carefully situated him in my navel. Where he navigated from there and what kind of disarming pleasure he gave me, I am unable to reveal.

I slept with him, and woke up every five minutes, terrified he was squashed.

In the morning he was gone, but had managed to write XO on the pillow with a matchstick. Later I would find a bottle cap filled with water, a wet sliver of paper towel, and the knotted-up tissues he'd used to slide off the bed.

He sent me, on the slips from fortune cookies, poems and poems, about love and electrons, S&M and Absolute Magnitude.

And then he started writing about his ex, a relationship he could not get over. She is tall — taller than me, he wrote.

A salt shaker is taller than you! I wrote.

Now that's just mean, he wrote, enclosing a lipogram that excluded the letters of my name.

That's pretty clever, Tiny, I thought. I still think so, as I imagine him working hard to write with an insect-feeler; to teach after rappelling the sheer face of the lectern.

I remember him best in bed, sliding down my belly and going Wheeeee! as I confided that Lafitte was truly a small man; as I closed my eyes and wondered at what would happen, now that I was free.

DOES ANYBODY REMEMBER LAUGHTER?

We were at the Lisbon Plate, before it became the mysteriously apostrophied Amadeu's, drinking pitchers beside two long-haired dudes in jean jackets and faded Wranglers.

They looked pissed off, and we edged away from them.

Veronica was telling us about a man with a tiny dick she'd just screwed, and we were all thinking of things to compare it to for complete accuracy.

Song's ledger included a shell casing and a marshmallow chick.

Farrah mounted a scientific analysis of a "negative genital."

Veronica decided that it was like a slightly elongated thimble, yet more narrow.

"Stairway to Heaven" was playing. We listened, and I was thinking about this hot guy I went to high school with who, the year after we graduated, found out I had never slow-danced at any of the school dances and grabbed me outside a bar where this song was playing and danced me to its end.

My head on his flannel shirt and —

DOES ANYONE REMEMBER LAUGHTER? one of the angry dudes yelled.

Then he flushed, realizing he was listening to the studio, not the live version of the song. His friend spat on the ground.

We all tried to keep straight faces, but we would tell this story for years and fall apart.

I don't speak to any of these women anymore.

This morning, a strange man on the street frowned at me and said, What happened to you?

I really can't remember, I said.

ANGEL

Girl, you are wearing the hell out of that!

This is what a transvestite screamed at me the other day as I walked toward the Beer Store.

You too, I said, and she and her companion gestured me over. We don't bite, baby. I am wearing Chanel, for Christ's sake.

You like silver? she asked.

Then sold me a ring off her finger, saying, We're hungry. Oh God, I cannot believe I am selling this.

A silver-plated ring with paste brilliants.

I gave her more than she asked, and bantered with her until her face slipped and I saw her hunger, and her rage.

Across the street, a little machine blew bubbles and they attached to me like leeches. A man and woman were singing karaoke from a makeshift booth, "Kiss" and "Voodoo."

The rain breathed in and out, asthmatically, making sexy mist.

By the automatic doors, someone was mumbling, My daughter.

It was Mark, the hot street guy I call "Handsome."

What? I asked him finally.

My daughter is Daniellynn, he said.

Her name had been all over the news that morning. I lifted my sunglasses and stared at his·shattered eyes.

My baby, he said.

The white spores have fallen all summer; soon, the monarchs will cluster at the end of my street in a rush of gold.

There are black hearts painted on the sidewalks.

Mark and his girlfriend left their daughter with a crack dealer for "personal reasons."

They left her sleeping on the floor in what may have been a terrarium of rocks and insects and earth.

The dealer and his girlfriend beat the child viciously; they tore off her scalp and killed her.

I have seen Mark again, since, hustling, always smiling, always obsequious.

His eyes —

There are times someone looks at you and you think of passing a truck filled with pigs on the road, and you are imagining their terror, the raw and dirty sound of pain's prelude.

I don't want to think about it and I won't.

I won't remember that her middle name was Angel, and that her hair came off like a pop-top. That no one cared about her, but her mother was on the news and said, She's happy now. She's safe.

No one can hurt her anymore, she said and smiled.

HERE COMES YOUR MAN

Brian and I met at Steve's funeral, though I do not remember. He told me how we reached for the same limp slice of cheese, and retreated, as if the cheese were an explosive. He told me he sang a song there too, and read a poem.

I don't remember anything that happened after laying flowers on the coffin. I had stood there for a long time, fretting about the Y-incision on Steve's chest that was a meadow of flowers; about his green eyes, spooned from their sockets.

These disgusting thoughts are fused with my memories of Brian.

I spent the days before he visited cleaning and having panic attacks.

I am grotesque, I warned him. I have Kuato growing out of my stomach. Kuato, the leader of the rebel army in *Total Recall*!

When he finally showed up, I saw him through the window and fell to the floor and told my dog it had all been a terrible mistake.

I got up and said hello. How can someone have acne on their teeth? I thought. Then, later, after too much bourbon: He is made of wax. And, why is he walking around in his enormous underpants?

Let's leave Steve, you know, in his *grave*, man, he said, then asked for pizza money. And, cupping his tiny genitals in his hand, he ordered an extra-large Hawaiian, later rolling each slice into a juicy pineapply cone.

I ended up throwing his plate against the wall, which enraged him, and as he stampeded, it occurred to me to try to change my life.

He called me the next day and said, Never a dull moment with you!

I called back from the Value Village while tossing a black rayon skirt on the counter and said, I feel we are too different. You live in your mother's basement, I do not. I have a job, you take anti-psychotics. I mean, I could go on and on, I said.

The week we met he text-messaged me every morning and called me "Babies." Then, "Angels angels angels!"

The thought of someone loving me is freaking me out right now, he said.

As if my isolation were a footnote to his.

I took a pair of scissors and cut him off, like a price tag: "AS IS!"

He snored like an aging dog dreaming of grey, stunned squirrels, and it is hard not to miss him when I think of him almost here in a taxi and the Pixies playing and hope, that charlatan, blooming like an illness inside me.

THE PERSISTENCE OF LIGHT

Marlene was a switchboard operator, and so was I. We worked at a big hotel, and our training sessions involved a thin blond martinet telling us always to enter through the service doors.

Imagine walking by a guest, reeking of onions! she despaired, of the kitchen workers.

Those people keep themselves cleaner than her, Queen T. said

The hotel had the last cord-board in the city, which meant stuffing holes all day and trying to memorize the key extensions, especially the one for the executive manager, an abrupt, pint-sized Belgian we had to wake up each morning, our voices cracking with counterfeit goodwill.

Sank you, he would say. Sanks ess so mush.

Everyone who worked there was a borderline personality; our boss, a sad and, in retrospect, misguided socialist, went out of her way to hire the most unfit people imaginable.

There was Babe, the wizened alcoholic, who shook her way through each shift, rasping vile responses to polite questions. If a guest called down to ask about "that big space needle," she would suggest that they might know what it was if they stuffed it up their fat ass. What? people were always saying. Did you just tell me to find the pool by using my "filthy privates" as a forked stick?

Did you actually call the Barry Manilow Fan Club Conference Centre the "Shootin' Retards in a Barrel Room?"

Babe would deny everything, and was too fearsome to laugh *with*. Unlike Queen T., who encouraged calls from the persistent pervert who phoned every day for the two years I worked there, asking tremulously, What colour panties are you wearing?

While the rest of us hung up, Queen T. would draw him out. None, baby, she would say. What you got on?

Swivelling in her chair, she would tell us, I never wear no panties. You got to let the animal breathe.

Jemal, the self-professed "high fashion model," and Maddie, who claimed only to work there for kicks and wore mangy fur stoles, would sigh at Queen T.'s vulgarity, and the younger girls would keep their heads down.

Divine, the aspiring opera singer, would call her boyfriend at Larry's Hideaway, where they lived, and cry, and Shelby, the Fiorinal addict, would clinically describe her husband's "radish-sized" balls, and then there was Marlene.

Marlene's husband had left after she had a double mastectomy. She had lived through the war, and was still damaged enough to buy ten-cent hard-boiled eggs from the cafeteria and stack them in a honeycomb in her purse.

She wore blazing diamonds on every finger and fluttered, interminably.

She took me under her wing when I started, which unsettled me, since everyone hated her.

She would shrink when yelled at and stare straight ahead.

I began to find her sickening.

I started going to Holt Renfrew with Maddie during breaks to watch her buy hundred-dollar face creams as she twitched her furs; I drank codeine cough syrup on ice with Jemal and started midnight shifts with Divine, where we took turns sleeping and demanding entire roasts from room service.

Steve came to meet me once when I was in the middle of screaming at Marlene. You idiot! You never get anything right!

She was flushing and speaking in broken Polish as I flounced off.

Why are you so mean? he asked.

He would ask the same thing when I started making dates with a legendary guy I met at the Cameron House, who slept with a machete and wore pink socks and Fagin gloves — on our first date, we walked the length of Queen Street, and he was stopped every five minutes by his admirers.

Then he beat a man to a bloody pulp for staring at me.

I have no other memories of Marlene. She is the yellow scar the light leaves, the shadow that creeps after all of my bad will.

She is presenting her mutilated body to her husband.

She is every act of surgical cruelty I have ever performed; she is closing her robe because he is nauseated and, impossibly, angry.

She rushes through me like shame, frequently, and I think of her as an animal that is taken in and whipped.

Cruelty has got me only so far.

YOU TOUCHED MY ART!

There he is, screaming at me, fat tears rolling over his plump red cheeks.

Yelling as I, five years later, walk Frank over a sidewalk where someone has written *MAMA* over and over.

Manny and I were going to be roommates. We were both coming out of relationships, and wanting more room.

My friend Nora found us this place, and when Manny and I saw it, we were sold before we got through the tiny foyer.

Are you sure? I asked him when we went out to celebrate after signing the lease with a man who looked like a perfectly formed eleven-year-old in a Hugo Boss suit.

Okay, I have a girlfriend, he said. But she knows I need some time for me and she is not jealous.

We got drunk and he reminisced about having been a foundling child.

They left me in a Count Chocula carton, he says. They rang my parents' door and ran.

It was Halloween, he tells me. They were dressed as Steve and Eydie Gormé.

We moved in in haste and confusion: my crew, hired via a

drunken glance at the Yellow Pages, consisted of an outspoken felon on parole, his shiftless son, and a hundred-year-old man who kept napping, fitfully, in the emptied boxes.

Shut up or I'll tear your larnix out! the crew leader yelled at my new neighbour, who had asked him to move the van off of his lawn.

That is, I believe, pronounced *larynx*, the old man said, primly, before drifting off again.

Manny moved in quickly, with his girlfriend's assistance, then the two of them spent the rest of the day watching me and my skeleton crew heaving and swearing, from two chaise longues they had set up on the lawn.

His girlfriend was a pretty-ish fat ass.

She and Manny holed up in his room, and my father came and helped me hang curtain rods, assemble shelves, and unpack.

My father was going through a hard time and began throwing hammers.

Lafitte was watching my dog, and after three sleepless days and nights, I briefly considered letting him keep him.

Luckily, Lafitte was too lazy. BABY, I often say, chalk-speaking to him. MAMA was so lucky.

My father hung curtains, emptied jars of nails on the floor, and left. Frank, my dog, came back. I slept for five hours, a miracle.

In the middle of the night, I grabbed a slab of canvas in the dark, to block off the stairwell so Frank couldn't run out the door.

Feeling something like refreshed I went into the kitchen and saw Manny, who had spent the morning picnicking with his girlfriend in the backyard and putting photographs on his corkboard with bright yellow push-pins.

You sleep okay? he asked.

Yes, I answered nervously, noticing his eyes were red piss-holes in his distressed snow-face.

WELL, I DID NOT! he screamed. YOU TOOK MY PAINTING,

YOU TOUCHED MY ART, AND USED IT AS, AS A GATE OR SOMETHING! THAT ART IS MEANINGFUL TO ME! THAT ART IS MY LIFE, THAT ART! IT IS ART ABOUT ME!

This was about the thing I had wedged on the stairs, a raw canvas depicting pulsating brown orbs, smeared through with beige.

Manny was projectile-crying. I backed away, citing my need to "focus" with coffee.

I am, ah. Sorry, I finally said.

But I wasn't, and two days later, after the plumber had torn the ceiling open because Manny left a tap running all night, he would ask for another sit-down talk.

My girlfriend is convinced we are sleeping together, he said. I have to move.

We had signed a lease with a dagger-shaped lawyer; the rent was very high.

Well, if you gotta go, you gotta go, I said, relieved to be free of his art, his love of art, and his shrill, pointlessly jealous girlfriend.

So many years have passed.

I want to say that I miss him and cannot.

But I will say this: I knew he loved that painting and I put it there on purpose. I rigged the taps and also called him "sex candy" to his girlfriend.

It was going to cost me a fortune to live alone, but it was a bargain.

Years later he sent me a Christmas card and I sent him one back. Nice kids, I wrote, of the five chimps in reindeer sweaters.

Hey Manny, I added. Manny, how's that goddamned art?

THE COOLER

He came to my house to clean the eavestroughs, and when Frank started barking he threatened to "fire him down the stairs."

He was cleaning his fingernails with a switchblade; he had black handprints on his T-shirt and a lightning bolt of hair.

You seem like a lonely broad, he said, after I brought out his sixth beer. And he smiled, revealing sharp grey incisors.

A man could do a lot for you, he added. I mean, like bulldozing and roofing, heavy lifting, he said. Maybe more.

Yes, I live in a trip-wire triggered bomb site, with extensive surveillance equipment and starved, vicious animals! he snarled, apropos of nothing.

You don't need to know about that. All you need to do is clean my clothes and make me chicken pot pies.

By then, we were sitting outside, watching huge bees lunge at the grapevines.

Aren't you being paranoid? I asked. I wanted to add, What are you, Public Enemy Number One? But there was something in his eyes that suggested a homicidal aversion to sarcasm.

He catcalled at a girl walking by the house with shiny black hair and a silver dress. Don't worry about it, Chunky, he said.

Man's got to look, is all.

That's a compliment, he added, when I flushed. A compliment he emphasized with a sharp pinch.

I am not making this up.

He comes to see me in the middle of the night and commits felonies against me that I love. This morning when I woke up he was gone.

Someone had posted a cruel picture of me online. There were many corresponding comments.

I know where they live, The Cooler carved into the bathroom wall, spitting blood into the sink.

Loneliness is the Devil and tortures you in its name.

He uses a rake to lift up arson after arson, leaves me snakes and bats and ferocious rats for company and it rains black; I scratch his back to remind him I was there.

Alive and unwell, wandering into love, the beauty of his crimes.

ROMANTIC POETRY

I remember him saying, I am a lonely man.

I live alone, he said. He then began reading from his soft, yarn-bound book, *Aureole*:

> White masts on blue midnight
> The ship saws at the isthmus
> Whirl of pearly ejaculate.

Childe Harold was my Romantic poetry professor. He wore his grey hair in a pageboy and combed his eyebrows straight up.

He wore distressed velvet suits, and stalked around the seminar table as he spoke, occasionally alighting on its corner and making small, complicated adjustments to his accessories.

He was given to violent philippics about the writers we studied. I cannot think of a more despicable beast than Dorothy Wordsworth, he told us. Filthy-minded shrew! he railed as if he'd known her.

I thought he may have. He looked like a sexy fossil, pieced together by a forlorn paleontologist.

Having just recently looked him up online — his website declares he is working on a poem that will make all who behold it fall to the floor "paralyzed by its grace" — I see he would have been in his late forties when I knew him; my age now, more or less.

As my erratic, lamentable career as an educator comes to a close, I damn myself for never having exhibited a fraction of his cruel flair — If there were a God, he told Cathy Catholic, our religious student, we would have long ago discovered him with a telescope.

Perhaps God finds the idea of your puny telescopes laughable, replied Cathy Catholic, a brilliant, drab girl whose work he unfailingly graded with swollen Ds.

You and your *God*, he would moan. Where was he when Keats was being murdered by a disease so vile it produced the dreadful final verses of "Ode on a Grecian Urn?"

Even if I had his savoir faire, what difference would it make?

I am not allowed to talk to my students that way. They, on the other hand, are permitted to hold millipede races in the aisle while I lecture; to scream, Run, Crazylegs! and parade the victorious insect through the room as the others throw the confetti that damages my school-issued hand-vac.

They are otherwise insolent, often hurtful.

People either love you or hate you, one of them said to me, in confidence. Like me, she said. I hate you. I totally hate you.

I loved Professor Harold, and tried to work hard. I would come home from a night at the Cameron House, or the Goof Fort, and fall asleep reading *Don Juan* or the *Lyrical Ballads*. And I would dream of Byron and me on the Bridge of Sighs; of him closing his cape around me like a crippled vampire; of Coleridge's forlorn "young ass"; about my fingers slowly opening a row of metal teeth sunk like pickets in lush, red velvet. And wake up anxious and ashamed of myself.

At exam time, he would tell us to memorize some "choice snippets." I chose "The aching of pale Fashion's vacant breast!" and worked it into my essay response to the question, "Whose lyrical puling about animals is the least objectionable, and why?"

In the Coleridge poem, the little creature is tied up and isolated from its mother.

He returned our work with comments dashed across the front pages in shocking pink ink.

Wretched work, he blazed on a fellow student's paper. You should be direly ashamed, he added. On mine he wrote: While Sammy's affection for the repugnant creature, stimulated, doubt-lessly, by an evening of controversial lovemaking with Kim Novak, is beyond one's comprehension, one enjoys your use of the word "breast." A great deal.

I got an A+!

Imperious in class, he seemed vulnerable, defiantly so, at his poetry reading. He prefaced each poem with a long, horrible story that was, invariably, far superior to the poem itself.

"Goat Stink," a series of rhyming couplets about his bête noir, Dorothy Wordsworth, and her personal hygiene, was introduced as follows: On the farm where I live, there are goats. I raise them and care for them. They eat diminutive tin cans from my hand when they are mere kids.

When the time has come, I load my rifle and shoot them. I skin and eat them in stews and casseroles.

They have the most extraordinary look in their eyes when you place the gun barrel against their skulls.

They know they are going to die.

Then: A stink in the pink, do you think / William wore her pelt like a mink?

I was starting to write poems of my own then, and invited him to a small, ill-attended reading.

When I had finished "Ann Romonologue," a poem from the per-spective of the mother, played by Bonnie Franklin, in *One Day at a Time*, there was a nice wave of applause.

As Professor Harold was leaving, he said to me: That was not bad. But you read far too quickly. And, "I feel this," "I remember that." No one gives a damn what you feel or remember!

A couple of years after the class, I heard that when Harold 's grades were read aloud for transcription, the room would go wild at the high grades, when assigned to girls.

I remember feeling embarrassed that my grades were so high compared to Cathy Catholic's and the two boys in the class.

Now I feel differently.

I remember a man who believed in me, who could see past something inside me that has set me apart my whole life.

That he set me apart.

I was always frightened then. I was sick and glorious; I wallowed in dirt and vomited stars.

I have the most extraordinary look in my eyes.

I know that I am going to die.

IT IS A MATTRESS IN THE RAIN

Darling, I cannot stop them, they are on their way.

This is Nora, telling me that when she asked if I wanted a mattress yesterday, she meant business.

I have been lying in bed, listening to Frank sawing wood, to the rain on the windows. And I jump up and start throwing pillows and sheets, baring the mattress I have had for fifteen years.

I cut a thread from its centre, its skinny white umbilicus, and am sick when two guys come in, wrench it downstairs, and replace it with a clean white slab.

The mattress, pocked and yellow-mooned, rests against my fence until they haul it into the truck and head for the dump.

Christ, I'm sorry, I say.

It has been so long, Francis.

Lafitte and I inherited that mattress, our first.

Our hamster Honey would tear around a pillow obstacle course on the bed, where Marvin slowly died, leaving a faint hemorrhage the day I brought him in to be euthanized. Jerome, wasted away to four pounds, his eyes bulging, bled out there too, as I read him stories, and before we made the same, terrible trip.

Mary and Lucy and Veronica and Nora and Lil slept there. Two little kids crashed over, their mom in the middle.

My mom, crying in her sleep.

Man after man, spreading out and making horrendous sleep-noises while I chewed my nails until dawn; the occasional press of gold, gypsy skin, some sweet *sexual chocolate*, a hand, beautiful in its deformity. The rare time I was able to sleep, my arm flung loosely over a damp, sweaty mass.

Steve stayed up with me and read me comic books, Frank took all of his puppy steps.

My father wandered off and took a nap —

I remember how many times I cried! I think. And fell in love.

I fell like rain, rolling myself up like a falafel and sighing as Frank and I spun ourselves forward, toward this day, other abject days to come.

I SHOULD HAVE KILLED MYSELF WHEN HE PUT IT IN ME

I wanted to like Brian so badly, I started buying bourbon by the gallon.

The last time he came over, I played him my iPod, and he said, I keep waiting for the song that will make me love you.

And when a CCR song came on he shouted, I love you, I love you!

This was our third date. I was being solicitous because I had been unkind. And because he'd brought me a present: a ceramic angel in a white billowing dress, leaning in for a kiss. She looked impudent and aggressive; her hands were loose white mittens.

It was a beautiful, cool summer night.

I want to ask people sometimes, Have you ever seen the rain? he says.

By this he meant turbulent depression, or shocking misery.

In the calm before the storm, we held hands and drank the bourbon. Later, I lay on the grass, watching him. He took off all of his clothes and was standing in the moonlight, lightly raking his pear-shaped belly with his long nails, revealing small, perfect breasts.

He barely had a penis: he was the only girlfriend I had ever had, and he wasn't even pretty.

137

You looking at my tits? he asked.

I shuddered. I still do.

I had showed my class *Carrie* that day, and laughed a lot at Carrie's mother's outrageous regret about carnal sin. I should have killed myself when he put it in me! she says of her husband. But I was weak! she moans.

With the right woman, Brian once said, I could go places.

Go by yourself! I wanted to say, but I was too weak. Instead, I started composing the message I would send him the next day, about how good he was, and how much better he deserved.

How, I would write, he deserved an angel, closing her white eyes and pressing her body forward, because she is filled with grace and believes in him.

Because she has seen everything, and wishes simply to come in from the rain. To shake it off.

I WOULD PREFER YOU DIDN'T CALL ME THAT

Jess, I mean Jesse, says this.

He knows me through someone, has looked up my poems in the college library. I run into him now and then, strolling around the food court in flip-flops and a towel, about to grab some soup and hit the gym.

He does not go to school, so it is a little odd.

Jesse aggressively promotes his career as a spoken word artist by challenging older, fatter writers to bare-knuckle boxing matches, by promising to scare children and eat insects.

He wrote me and said he liked food. Correction: I like *cooking for people*. I do not like beer, he said, but I will drink.

We met and I got drunk and stupid; asked him to come over and make food. Need a small nap, I slurred, and left him with the brief entries in my wet, sticky fridge.

I heard the hissing of margarine and some tentative chopping. Jess! I mean, Jesse! I called. Come visit!

He came upstairs where I was rolling around my bed, cursing the sheet corners for always popping off.

He sat at the end of the bed, looking seasick.

Do you have a girlfriend? I asked. And then I threw up all over him. It's okay, he kept saying as I cried, Things have been so bad!

So bad!

He left the pot of noodles, broccoli heads, and muffin mix on the stove, bubbling, and left, pulling his shirt away from himself.

It's not like I was coming on to him! I think, spooning up the green mush.

I am in the food court looking at his sweet face with the scar that cuts from his forehead and through his eye, his small smile that seems infinitely forgiving.

I tell him I have been undergoing medical trials to make money for my cat, who needs robotic legs. The side effects, I add, are *terrible*.

That's all right, he says.

The cat is like a pancake! I say, and he nods solemnly.

Later he will write and say, Thank you very much for the delicious beverages!

This guy came over and basically raided all my food, I told people. The noodle-thief! I don't wish to call him that anymore.

How does someone get a scar like that? How much has he seen; how much does he see, in his near-blindness? How much does he forget? is what I wish I could ask him.

And tell him, too, that what I threw up was all the bad things in my life, and those did not include him.

BEFORE YOU WERE BORN

My mother said, perched on the edge of my bed like a humming-bird, drinking milk and rye,

There was a man.

Your father was always away; I was a young mother and very confused. I had wanted to be an acrobat, she said, deftly twisting her leg into a pretzel, then falling over.

She resumed her story, lying on her back with the drink balanced on her ribcage.

At the very least, a stewardess.

I don't want to hear this, I said. I was thirteen and worried enough about what I could wear to school and not get beaten for wearing; about my father walking by, in his pyjamas, yelling, What's all the noise!? My retired father worked hard. At what, I never could say.

He is not your father! she said, loudly, of the man.

She told me he was made of snow and petroleum; he taught her to love, and say, What a beautiful fat baby! in Mandarin.

Chow Pang-Tzee! she said, speaking Mandarin, I guess.

He lived in filigreed cage, and had the most delicate wings of green and silver. You could point anywhere on a globe and he had been there. Illinois. Russia. Hullabaloo.

That's not a place, I said, kicking at her to get off.

He was graceful but more manly than most simians, she told me. But I've said enough, she added.

She rolled off the bed and sat in the lotus position for a while, letting her glass catch the moonlight.

I was joking, she said finally.

I pretended to be asleep and I heard her close the door, and then say to my father, Burglars!

It was burglars in masks and I had to take off my top.

My mother calls me every night to tell me she is about to take a bath and go to bed. All right then, I say.

I never wonder what she has done with the crazy imagination that hulked after her like Godzilla for so long.

She seems smaller now; she may use her pockets and purses.

She may howl at the moon for all I know.

Her mysteries were too difficult to solve and too painful, ending always with her in that same house, like a wildcat in a trap; a hamster in a ball, rolling like thunder.

FRANKENTREE

Eddie called me out of the blue not too long ago and told me he wanted to take photographs of old men's tattoos.

He thought I may know someone and I do.

We went to see my friend Raspail, a wiry ex-con who, for reasons too complicated to explain, believes that we are husband and wife.

Raspail has jail tattoos: pale green, smudgy letters misspelling his son's and mother's names; an eagle that looks like Karl Malden; a thin, watery heart.

Eddie shot these and the whole apartment, things I had never noticed: Raspail's abstract paintings; his tin pineapple-shaped Jell-o Mold; a mesh bag of onions growing wild green shoots.

Eddie asked me out and we went to High Park and walked around: he was unusually quiet and gentle. We sat on a bench and four frat boys came tearing by. I caught the tail end of what they were saying. "Grease her up —"

He heard them too.

We walked back to the car and saw this crazy tree on the way. Its foliage was sheared off, and growing from the cut base was another, upside-down tree.

He explained how this worked and I told him how sad I thought it was.

And blamed him for that, somehow, too.

He is compact and muscular. I once called him my tiny tawny superhero.

You are nice, aren't you? he said.

He said my eyes were like a hawk's, cruel and vulnerable.

To what? I said.

Oh, flying into Hydro wires and stuff, he said.

In his pictures, I am myself on the best day of my life and passing through it, passing through the sun.

He never even flinched when those guys called me a pig.

I took a picture of his key in the ignition; the steering wheel looks like a black happy face.

You use people, I said.

He sighed.

His voice is sandpapered sugar and Wild Turkey.

Mine is flat and dry as dirt, coughed up by the wheels as some woman stands in her seat and howls through a hole in the car, then falls back as he drops the clutch.

Stars making snowflake holes in construction paper and the moon waxing into a knife: some of the things he set into motion, when I was almost young and made out of pieces.

AND THEN HE KISSED ME

Perhaps you are a misunderstood genius, like the author of *Right On, Rhoda!* my agent said in a long message on my machine.

At one time, I did not understand such poetry, he said. Listen! "Sometimes Valerie and Rhoda are hard to tell apart. Clue? Valerie cannot abide wearing head scarves!"

Nevertheless, he said. Your book is hideous. I ascertained this by feeling its nauseating heft and I cannot represent you any longer.

He then told me about a story he had read in *Scientific American*, "oh, years ago," about a teenaged boy who was discovered to have no brain, just a stem and cerebral fluid.

This chap was a B student! he enthused. Something to think about.

DO love you! he added. Do not think we shan't meet for a lovely glass of champers again and soon!

He has never sold a single thing I have written. He likes to send me long letters about my "bewitching wordcraft" and then, after sitting on a manuscript for months, dash off comments like My, aren't we moody? or Well! This will never play with the book ladies.

I have met the book ladies. When I was publishing, many years ago, I would go to festivals and be picked up at the airport by the same baggy-faced woman, driving a van filled with stones, and who, after asking me hopefully if I was, possibly, Aritha van Herk? would fall into a morose silence.

After the readings, they all stand together holding their cloth bookbags and swarm whatever handsome man or complicated, frowning woman they can find.

Make this one out to my daughter, D-A-U-G-H-T-E-R. And on this one, could you just sign your name?

And then draw yourself being stoned. Like in "The Lottery."

And the readings. All of them sitting upright and pitiless. Sometimes writing a small, crabbed note in a fabric-covered book and then smiling, smugly.

Occasionally crying into wet, shredded tissues.

I listen to my agent's message several times, then call him back and leave a message.

I will write you something amazing that is also a bestseller, I say. It will be a mystery, told by a Cambodian car salesman and set in the disputed border territory around the eleventh-century Preah Vihear Temple. There will be terrible deaths, and terrible irony (machine guns in a holy pagoda!). The salesman will be named after you, Keith, and he will speak lyrically and urgently.

He will have an assistant he has forged from vegetables and voodoo. It dresses in a coarse opera cape, and has a single blue eye and a slash of tiny, pointed teeth.

This assistant's name is Hun Sen, and will guide the hero on his quest to find an American car filled with cash and girls in bikinis entombed inside one of the temple's stone Nagas.

Keith will, of course, have flashbacks about growing up in Point Douglas, about how conflicted his identity was; how drinking Brador-lychee cocktails and killing deer with ninja stars confused and excited him.

I will call it *Apichat*, which is the name of the Cambodian War Pigs' military captain.

Or Caps, as Keith may call him.

Champers? I add.

It is very hard to understand you, Keith once said, and his eyes floated away, like pale blue junks on the white horizon.

And then he kissed me.

THE NIGHT CRISPIN DROVE ME TO THE BAMBOO

Another of the switchboard operators, Crispin was dark and vast.

After a shift, his chair was soaked through, the board sluiced with palm-prints.

Veronica called me one night and invited me to the Bamboo Club. She was dating an older man named Ashton, a wealthy Australian publisher who had dated Kelly LeBrock.

He had showed us slides of him and Kelly LeBrock kissing on a sectional, button-tufted leather couch; of her coaxing scorpions into a small wooden horse; or reading the Odyssey and eating slices of lotus fruit. (Frightfully long story, Ashton said.)

Crispin drove me to the club in a small car; I drank Windex-coloured cocktails with Ashton's rich friend and he tried to get me into bed as we all did rails at his immaculate loft.

This new year, my good intentions perish quickly. Within days, I am consumed with bad memories, like the rich guy and his blue poison.

Or the time I threw up on myself in Old Montreal and reeled to a sidewalk where a stout older boy squatted and chatted me up.

You look like you've been a bit sick, he said.

Bleccchh, I said, pawing the mass of bile on my peasant dress.

How about you come to my place? I'll make you feel better, he said, gesturing to his lemon-yellow Camaro.

I think of male shamelessness, of so many penises opening their urethras at night and singing low-down songs of where they'd been and what they'd seen.

I think of the gay boxer, the man down the hall at the Epitome, the building where Steve and I lived. The boxer would stand in his open doorway and squeeze his cats, then squeal, Ooh, you're hurting me! Then squeeze harder. The cats would curl into fetal positions and moan.

Hero, you need to take it easy on them, I said one night as he was setting up bowling pins in the hallway and getting ready to roll a squashed-looking tom.

He lifted me up and threw me down the stairs. It took two cops to get him into a squad car; the cats didn't make a sound the whole time he was gone.

I think of the good friend I called because I was feeling bad who said, You are so overweight. I say this as a volunteer badminton instructor: all of that fat is what is hurting your bones.

The body cannot carry so much: it is not a tote bag!

I was as crushed as I was embarrassed. I had no idea I was still fat.

I hung up and took a walk.

On New Year's Eve, I recorded one of Rocky's speeches in *Rocky Balboa*, and I played it back.

I lost my job at the college when I kept getting sick. You are your own worst enemy, my boss told me.

The driving examiner who failed me, on my second try, told me the same thing, after having spent the road test yelling in angry disbelief.

I go to see my hairdresser, Lesley G. She is the last in a harrowing line of coiffeuses including a woman at Supercuts who looked me up and down and asked me, bluntly, What's the point?

I tell Lesley some of the bad things I am feeling.

A mermaid, she sits on her rock and twitches her tail before speaking in beads of coral.

You look nice, she says.

I play her the tape. Rocky is talking to his son, telling him that he has changed. That he is no longer himself. You stopped being you!, Rocky says. You let people stick a finger in your face and tell you you're no good.

That's rad, she says.

I will listen to what he says from now on, I tell Lesley, whose sea-green eyes widen, admitting light, and in that light see slender, shimmying plants and fast little fish.

I will change back, I say, as she lowers my head underwater.

The night I drove with Crispin, I was flattened against the window.

He never let on how much it may have hurt him, all of it.

It did not occur to me to ask him along.

You're a doll! I am sure I said before springing out, leaving him there, and saying hello to the very beautiful people who made me so sick.

The intangible things matter the most, I tell my enormous old friend, in my heart, and hope he hears me.

By the time I am home, he and I are on our way to Niagara Falls, honeymoon capital of Canada, and ready for anything.

THE BEST THAT YOU CAN DO

It is raining today and I pass a woman, on my way to the Price Chopper, who looks sharply at me, and I think of Lorelei.

I am under the overpass that says FUCK SOUP and is hazed with blue and red tags.

A train quakes past; on the sidewalk, I see what appears to be a bag of blood.

Inside the store, I select one pre-made pot roast for the dog, which is far too salty. I cannot bring myself to cook: it is enough to get up and run a lint brush over the filthy sheets.

I cannot ask for help, either. I place Bounce sheets, bottled water, and processed cheese into my cart and pause by the discounted cakes. By one in particular, shaped like a teardrop, that says, in pink icing, *See, see where Christ's blood streams in the firmament!*

I am consulting the back of a love letter from Eddie that says, You're not fat. You're PHAT.

And whispering into a digital recorder. I have to write a lecture on *The Arcades Project*, and I think about this as "Arthur's Theme," performed on what could be a Pianosaurus, plinks through the speakers.

I remember the stores in the strip mall I pass every day, and decide I will revise them into the Paris arcades.

I record the names of the low, dirty shops — QD COMPUTER INC., COMESS NEW AND USED RESTAURANT EQUIPMENT, TYLER'S PLACE, JANE'S HAIR, PARKDALE INTERCULTURAL, GOSPEL LIGHT TABERNACLE, and SUPER COIN LAUNDRY — as a woman with a black wooden hand reaches past me for a tub of Miracle Whip.

I add to my cart one bag of BBQ rice crackers, a comb, and a pineapple, and stop beside a pile of bagged marshmallows and say into the recorder's mouth, As one approaches the arcades, the light becomes faint, then collapses above the strip: the light is a woman taking off her clothes at knife-point.

I continue to move from row to row, characterizing the shops in note form, and moving toward the biggest, brightest objects.

The super coins are casual friends who never keep in touch; at Tyler's place, rat-tails construct the art of the Ara Pacis. The snakes and tongues; the small, contagious boxes of Tide.

Everything diffuse becomes unified, I say out loud to a man squeezing a cantaloupe.

Like Lorelei, who enters me like a splinter as I walk back and see the bag of blood that is the husk of a fruit I cannot identify and remember the book she wrote for me.

I see her in one of the shops, sweeping up shocks of hair.

She wrote about living in a city filled with deformed vegetables and fruits she was desperate to taste.

I pushed her out of my life as though my life were a cliff.

I try to feel remorse, and then wonder why they still make twist ties. Who uses *twist ties*? my arrogant letter to Glad will begin.

Speak plainly during the lecture, I say into the recorder.

Later I will note that it has picked up the sound of a man whimpering, Please.

I will say that Walter Benjamin looked up and saw a sky of iron and glass.

I look back and see her, curled at my feet, listening, and feel the iron that has always been there. She still disgusts me.

Why are you still mad? I want to ask.

I know what I did, but look at me. *Look at me look at me.*

SCÈNES D'UN RÊVE CASANIER

They are dioramas, filled with light and sound.

In one, a woman stands on a bridge, throwing stones. Beyond her is a lighthouse, the ocean.

She is me, praying.

In another, Lorelei is sitting at a sewing machine, stitching together a white bed-skirt that will flow like a tide over the entirety of her bedroom.

A window is open behind her. Gauzy curtains flutter over the mouth of hell.

Miklós Rózsa orchestrates the sound of a knife entering a cataract of pale skin. A woman crying, a cat drinking milk from a china saucer.

When you look at it a certain way, Lorelei's projected image disappears.

The room is then merely menacing; its curio shelf — filled with monkeys' paws and birds' nests — seems to attract the music, and the flames.

But Lorelei's bent shoulders, her pleated neck!

The dream she is making, of extravagant, pure love — it is hard to watch.

I seize Margaux's hand and whisper that I am afraid.

Me too, she says. We leave, stopping at the last glass pane: *Lorelei's Absence*. A shuttered stall barn, shaking as a train rattles past, hauling boxcars.

At the crossing is a silver ventilated truck; a scratchy old record plays.

The song is just screaming; lights search the dried grass and low, bald hills.

Outside, Margaux and I talk about the show, and how happy we are to have come out to see it.

We stop to buy books, and sift through a box of old photographs. I find one of a man with short, shiny hair modelling a leopard coat and spectator pumps for an elderly man who has his hands on his hips and is squinting through thick glasses.

Who takes a picture like this? Margaux asks.

We have reached the park outside the mental health centre. A few heavily medicated patients shuffle through the leaves. One wanders up to a woman wearing a sequined wristband and says, You always had it, Neely — we both did.

The legendary white squirrel declines, as always, to appear.

I need to tell you something, I say to Margaux.

Her face crumples a bit because she is concentrating.

Lorelei was my best friend, I say, a long time ago —

I tell her about Lorelei, about the stories she wrote for me. In one, a darkly handsome criminal and I hold hands under a table; in another, a little comb sings joyously of my long, red hair. In another, I stand in the centre of the 7-Eleven, in a coat that makes me look like Dracula, imperiously asking for the precise location of the Cheez Whiz.

The stories are true, but lovesick and slanted.

Lorelei had no family, and her other close friend was a born-again Christian who sent her drawings of Jesus yelling at her.

She eventually met a nice, younger man who happened to be staggeringly good-looking, I tell Margaux.

Tony? Neely exclaims. Tony Polar? Is that you? They break into "Come Live with Me" and Margaux says, They can really sing. We clap when they finish and the man bows and slides into the shadows.

Then, The younger boyfriend, was he nice to her?

No, I say.

He cheated on her, I say. He and this girl both lied to Lorelei; they made out in her bedroom and he slept in long-sleeved shirts to cover the girl's claw and bite marks.

Oh no, Margaux says and looks sad.

Yeah, she even bad-mouthed Lorelei all over town.

We walk deeper into the park, past the stone walls, and I start a different story about something that happened at work that week.

They want me to have a DNA test, to prove I am a human primate! I say as I think of the last time I saw Lorelei, at a terrible literary party. I was leaving, saying, Worse than Screamers.

You haven't changed, Lorelei said. And cried.

She is right.

I would steal her boyfriend again if I could.

If I were young and strong enough to see the moon break through the bars of a park ladder, where I stood, as if invincible, and sort of in love.

With him, with myself.

But not you, Lorelei.

In another of the exhibits, she is setting out a plate of runny cheese and wineglasses on a long table.

She is squeezed into a black dress. Her eyes and lips look like injuries in her pale, drawn face.

I am standing on the porch smoking a cigarette. One of my hands reaches for the door; the other holds it back.

The street behind me is the future. The young boyfriend is walking with his daughter; both carry lashed ice skates on their shoulders. Far behind them, a mean-looking woman in bug-eyed sunglasses is walking a dog, and for her tears, the artist has used red jewels.

Look, Margaux had said. If you move, all you can see is the smoke!

That poor girl, I said, moving closer.

You can tell right away what will happen.

NERO

When I got my first arts grant, I spent it all on a pair of $500 Peter Fox shoes, model number 7700, size 9B. I still have their deep blue box.

Billy was furious. He had just started his first job in two years, washing dishes at an Italian restaurant. You are the kind of person who makes me sick, he said.

The shoes are black leather, with an inverted three-inch heel. Ventilated across the narrow front with slashes and punch-holes, with a silver vamp and two thin straps with apse-shaped buckles.

I will never outgrow them, I argued.

They are art, I ventured. Art about Nero, their namesake.

They are sitting beside me now, sweetly. Asking me to step into them, ignoring a body and a will I no longer possess. Love me, they say, a little indifferently, as if afraid of being hurt.

The other day, I read an interview with Billy.

He is a famous TV actor now, the lead of a passionate drama about aristocratic assassins and the hemophilia that besieges them.

He talked about his lean years as an addict, and said how grateful he was that one person was there for him.

That person was the barber I brought him to the day of his first audition.

I feel like Santino put my *whole life* in Barbicide, Billy is quoted as saying.

Love me? The little shoes squeak.

I remembered Billy screaming at me, unusual for him, outside a drugstore: You just want a man to drive you around, taking you shopping!

The year he spent in rehab was hard: I was working for a manic-depressive professor, Wilson, at a university two hours away. He'd decided we should teach our first-year students *Remembrance of Things Past* in one week, augmented by critical essays and cookie baking.

He explained this to me in his office, while twitching and lovingly watching his yellow dog lick her distended genitals.

I would go to class, and tutorial, then visit Billy at the hospital, then go home, as the winter telescoped my life into a black, narrow tunnel filled with ice.

Wilson would explain away my ragged weeping in lecture: She is moved by the plight of Humphry Clinker's travails at the seaside, by the jellyfish I have asked to you dissect and discuss in no less than nine million words!

Or: She laments Clarissa as her rapist would, and let this — an assignment in which you will duel with a man of low character and then summarize, using only punctuation — expiate!

I continued to expand on the meaning of the shoes to Billy while listening to some other maniac on the rec-room piano stabbing out Sinatra songs.

Nero, ultimately, may be characterized as a great, if terrible, aesthete, a man oblivious to others' small-minded morality.

A violinist, really.

I told him this as he nodded off — because as it turned out, he was smuggling heroin into the hospital and passing it off as dough-nut sugar.

I can still smell the soup and puke and ammonia, and I realize that I now pay men to drive me around shopping. For cat litter or vegetables, for bulk rolls of paper towels.

Is this what you had in mind? I wonder, contemplating yet another man who has left me behind like a distasteful habit.

Dishabelle, Billy called me.

Lynn! He wrote on the title page of his first script, which he would star in, so many years later. *My pure sweet angel. I love you always.*

In the first scene, he is Nero, gazing dreamily as everything between us catches fire and burns.

Later, he and Santino find a violin at a flea market in Aberfoyle, and he plays it so beautifully, Santino catches the notes in warm towels and attends to them as angels.

WHAT I MEANT TO SAY

I didn't recognize you, I said to Melanie, outside of the hospital.

She flushed and asked, Why would you?

She was twenty-five years old and dying of cancer; she was holding a yoga mat and her long, red hair looked as sleek as satin.

That wasn't what I meant, I meant she had surprised me, and for a second, I'd been trying to place her. She had not cut my hair in more than a year.

That was ten years ago, and the last time that I saw her.

I switched to her colleague Julie's salon: Julie was a nervous, solemn woman who would listen to me talk as my hair processed in a Jiffy Pop bubble, a cigarette burning between her clenched beige lips.

I started missing appointments when I got sick.

I'm not *mad*, Julie said, about the missed appointments.

I managed to make it in one day, and she hugged me and said, We've been so worried!

I have never been good about my hair, I told her.

When I was six years old, I used to see a barber in Brome Lake. I would squirm so much as he was crewcutting my hair that one day, he cut open his face with the scissors.

He never worked again.

Isn't that weird? I said to Julie.

She looked over my head in the mirror and frowned.

You are going to need to give us a credit card, she said. There will be a fine if you cancel again.

Julie had never spoken coldly to me. On her birthday, I had given her a pink studded harness for the Siamese hairless she liked to dress in evening gowns and carry in her purse.

Melanie, what has happened? I thought.

Melanie, whose boyfriend had the same name as mine, and who mapped out my hair as if it were the world, in curved sections of blue and green.

Who laughed like a snap on a cymbal, and told me it was our turn now.

Before the cancer exploded inside of her and ate everything but her teeth.

As Julie silently sprayed my hair into a helmet, I imagined she was Melanie.

That it was still our time, more hers: in this daydream, the very good and the very brave have all the time in the world.

I CRY

It is almost Christmas, and I am watching advertisements for needy children. In these ads, people are stuffing boxes into bigger boxes, and strange little kids are opening them and freaking out.

I wonder: What kinds of gifts are these people giving?

A teddy bear, blocks, a doll that screams and urinates?

I think of my son — Mick, let's say. Who is getting pizza for dinner, the pizza my husband likes: no cheese, triple pineapple.

And a sweet beating, for dragging in a dead plant and stringing it with mice he found stuck to the glue trap.

One has no feet; it wrenched them all off and rolled away to die.

Mick's list: a cellphone and a buck knife.

What he gets: a checkers set and a warm rayon sweater.

I tell him to be fucking grateful as my husband grabs his own gifts and sells them at the Happy Time.

Depression ferries you to an underworld of unimaginable cruelty that operates every minute of every day.

I decide to give nothing, and watch the Santa Claus Parade instead, waving idly as Santa finally goes by.

My friend once took a class about child abuse, in Montreal.

This one baby, he told me then. Its mother took a cigarette and burned I CRY into its chest.

Santa waves some more and I wave back in earnest, There he is! I say to no one, filled with the warm belief, as John Berryman once sighed, that *we are unregenerate*.

The hammer in the head, the anguish unheard.

Where I live, indigent people wear Santa hats through January for the warmth. Ears covered in white mush — whatever blocks out the screaming of hateful children and everything that is being murdered.

What I thought it would be like, covering you in flannel blankets, and rocking you to sleep with my black hoof.

THE WOLVES

The day Raspail's wife died he parked himself on the street, shirt-less, in Grumpy-the-dwarf slippers and denim shorts. And howled.

I had just started speaking to him and Larue, his wife, who tended to hover around the birdfeeder on their lawn, filling it with raisins and saltines.

She would open and close her toothless mouth, making bird calls.

He told me about a time he and she racked up a two-hundred-dollar bill at the Dufferin Gate ordering sambuca shots all night.

So I bought him a bottle and extended my sympathies.

This was three years ago, and when he is piss-drunk, which is all the time, he tells me the same story about how some redhead came out of the blue and gave him a 40-ouncer.

His memory comes and goes. Occasionally, his eyes are black lasers, when he is That Way, as he puts it.

He tells me that one night, he almost choked his wife to death. I blacked out, he says. The last thing I remember is saying, Call an ambulance, Larue.

We are both afraid, he said to me recently. Afraid to love each other, he meant.

I look at my hands. They shudder to hold memories of everything vile they have ever touched, including Raspail's pig-bristle back, by accident.

Raspail lives by the church and park where I like to walk Francis when there is snow covering the trash, or in the summer when a crew mows the lawn and indifferent lifeguards patrol the kiddie pool.

There are three other options for these walks, all loud and distressing.

A drag of King Street where zombies slouch between enraged crack whores and, sometimes, men or women crawl on their hands and knees, pawing at change or bits of cheese and meat stuck to squares of paper.

The part of Queen where Caterpillars park and men in orange vests keep drilling the same patch of asphalt, every day.

The parkette in the middle. The trees there are stripped bare of their bark. Someone knifed them all one night and the next day there were handwritten signs taped to them that said I HOPE YOUR HAPPY THEIR DEAD.

Raspail started running outside every time he saw me with Frank. Calling my dog a bitch, or asking me if I needed a massage.

I have put up with all of this because he seems to mean well, because he is small and shattered.

The day after Christmas I went over with gifts after he called me, many times, enumerating, in his morphine and vodka stupor, each gift he had bought for me and my pets.

I got Whosit some tuna and a catnip stocking for the other one. And a ball and a three-piece suit for Flimflam —

The list was interminable and soon disintegrated into some racy gibberish about chimneys and silk stockings.

I brought over more sambuca and a toy parrot that repeats what you say and more gifts for his friend Kim, whose dentures look like tombstones and who is so loaded on meds she just sits, smiles, and drools puddles into her lap.

Raspail and Kim were wasted and so was their friend Bob, who immediately taught the parrot a string of obscenities.

Bad scene, I thought, absent-mindedly feeling my scalp for head lice.

I went to the bathroom, paused to look at the squeezed-out tube of Poligrip on the sink, the orange slime on the walls, the filth-larded wooden toilet-paper holder shaped like a tabby cat's tail.

The slivers of Irish Spring and the contusions of hair and scum.

Raspail offered me a shot in a glass covered in brown streaks, and I declined. He sidled over and kissed me wetly on the lips, crowing, I love you!

He pulled me to my feet and grabbed my ass with two hands and squeezed.

Before I left I told him something in words cut from ice about the terrible familiarity of what he had done.

I'm fuckin' sorry, he yelled after me.

How's I supposed to know you were done that before! he screamed, then started to break things.

He had given me a nylon blanket with a wolf on it and a pullover with the same wolf.

I brought everything to Anna and she took it and said, I'm sorry.

She was drunk too, weaving back and forth.

"Appetite, a universal wolf," Shakespeare said, of the way my anger stands on hills in forests, waiting for the call, to strike.

Raspail phoned the next day to ask if I liked his presents.

I went to his house and mauled him.

It took four men to pull me off, and a shotgun.

This will never happen again.

I am sick to death of men and starving for blood.

BLUE THUNDER

Is what Elmore called that nasty blue car, and I could hear him, burning down my street.

I was trying to learn how to drive again, and Elmore offered to help.

Just drive, he said. I'm not scared of much.

The car, filled with trash, books about sound and science, and lingering cigarette smoke: I accelerated and drove like a bat out of hell, three times a week, with Elmore.

Blue Thunder had no radio, so we would sing together or at passers-by.

"Instead a makin' love you play head games!" I serenaded a man who blushed, prettily.

Elmore's jam was "Carry On Wayward Son," which he sang in a surprisingly sweet voice.

"Don't you cry no more!" he once warbled to a hysterical child in another car's back seat.

Hey, screw you! the child called back. You and your fat wife!

This New Year's Eve, he partied with some friends and his heart stopped. They stuck him in an ambulance and took off. His heart started again, in a coma.

He is the loneliest man I have ever met. He came over two months ago and held my cat Blaze so tightly that she bit his head.

He also has two cats, a brother and a sister, that he carries around at home. They just lie limply over his shoulder. At night, they slither around his neck, his feet.

I do not know their names.

I hate stupid people, he would say. This jagoff I work with said he was setting the computer code to Pi. And then set it to 3.15!

The woman he married left him as soon as she got off the plane from Poland. He had been saving teddy bears and dolls for her daughter for a year, saving for a place.

He liked coke and strippers; he played guitar in Veronica's band, when he showed up.

He showed me a thick album of the time he spent in Poland, when he met Ludmilla and was happy.

Who is that? I ask of the handsome, dapper groom.

That's me! he says. Me! His eyes red, his skin sallow. But he still has a great, wry smile.

Shooting up insulin as we drove, I'm good, I'm good.

His car died and I stopped hearing from him.

Then, a little while ago, Elmore showed up in a crazy white car, looking clean. He drank water, and I drank beer, and we talked about going driving again, other things we wanted to do.

You're looking good, I said. I was happy to see him.

This morning, they took him off life support and he died.

I heard the news as if hearing blue thunder in a dark sky, warning me of other jolts of lightning to come.

I close my eyes.

And hear him roaring toward me in a streak of pain that starts with losing something, then everything.

I CLOSE MY EYES

You should listen to Kansas or this story will not make sense. Even then —

Veronica called and said, I guess it will start happening more and more. Our friends are dying.

She had put me on speaker-phone and I could hear her doing deep squats and lunges, the odd angry Oof!

Not you, I thought. Death would not dare to interfere with your busy work and physical fitness regime.

Death has me on a fear and attrition plan, at the moment.

I found Elmore's obituary today. It is a few lines long: Beloved son, beloved brother, "suddenly." Not listed: felt mice, stacks of black sweaters, a poster of ELO.

His mother had Animal Control remove and destroy the cats, and banned everyone from his funeral.

Elmore, I didn't know.

I am talking to my mother and looking at a hinged wooden box she has just sent me. I will fill it with contraband, I tell her. Pills, battery-operated items, Polaroids, including several of Billy, risqué and poignant — in one, he is slumped on the edge of the bed, naked except for black socks.

There is worse, I warn her, thinking of the soiled hand-towels, bags of hair, and stack of perverse diaries, mutated with taped- or clipped-in evidence.

You can throw it all out, I tell her.

And remember I was once a woman!

I did not say this: I was thinking of Anna Nicole Smith saying something similar when she was obese and no one wanted her.

Instead I asked my mother to tell the few people who show up at my funeral that they are filled with mendacity and say it like Big Daddy in *Cat on a Hot Tin Roof.*

And then I want you to play "U Can't Touch This."

My little mother gets very tired listening to these plans, which always change, and always involve her assaulting someone and hiring professional mourners.

If Frankie eats my arm or leg, he is still a very good boy!

Where do all of your ideas go? I wonder of my friend. Your lists and half-finished projects: where does their meaning go?

I was a strange and quiet child, who read David Niven books at eleven.

I would, preposterously, try to tell his stories to people.

When Clark Gable was filming *Gone with the Wind*, I would say, he got roaring drunk and said, of simulating the burning of Atlanta, Let's torch the whole fucking set! And they did.

Do that, I tell my mother. Torch the parlour! Get in the mood by playing "Disco Inferno" on the way over.

How was the memorial? she asks.

It was nice, I tell her. Veronica said some really nice things about Elmore, and someone bought a big plate of nachos for everyone.

I'M PRETTY LIKE DRUGS

This is how I described myself on Craigslist, using a Photoshopped picture of a pink bevelled pill nestled in cotton.

I said I liked shopping for munitions online and that I did not like men who thought I should wake up or use the oven I keep my bats and crowbars in.

That I am a borderline sociopath who likes puppies and rain.

Don't assault me unless it is a game, I wrote. Think of me with love and anger.

Men obviously do not read these things or care about much except your age (I said I was twenty-one going on twelve!). I got a hundred replies.

I live at home, Peter wrote, because my mom is sick but not so sick she can't make me a seven-egg omelette for breakfast every day! I am a "shut-in," I guess, but there is a lot of me to love, including my tasty uncut wiener!

Gary wrote: I have a yacht and a villa in Spain and I drink champagne with caviar chasers. Are you my lucky princess? My phone is cut off right now because I cannot be bothered with such trifles. Write me and I will tell you more about the good times we will have eating rare steak and living *Miami Vice* style.

Johnny said, I type with my stump. Fuck you if that's a problem, bitch.

Dal said, I have always settled in my life for girls not pretty or smart enough. Could you be the flippy-haired debutante who actually understands *The Da Vinci Code*?

I wrote back to Johnny, obviously.

Stumpy, I wrote. I am considering our sexual options with a great deal of excitement!

I agreed to meet him at Yonge and Dundas, where he panhandles with a sign that says HOW WOULD <u>YOU</u> LIKE TO LOSE AN ARM TO A THRESHER?

His stump was bright pink from the cold. I could see it a block away, and I ran to him, calling, Johnny, Johnny!

You're a fat girl, he said, looking me over. I have some standards.

I have some heroin, I said and heaved him into a cab.

We watched TV as he randomly ran his stump over my poussecafé of a belly, and finally, he thumbed himself inside of me and I yelped with pleasure.

Every day, he cuts another piece of my skin off.

I'm going to be a skeleton soon, I marvel.

We hold each other in the pool of blood and gore and I say, No one has ever understood me. No one has ever loved me, baby, not once, not ever.

THE DJ

Jinkum came to my last book launch, at the Cadillac, which was advertised in tiny chalk letters under the bold, big news that a PORK SANDWICH LUNCH SPECIAL was going, W/FRIES, for $7.95.

The book, a biography of my colitis, featuring interviews with doctors and repulsed commentators, was called *This Too Shall Pass*.

Jinkum showed up with Nora, who told me that he liked me.

Another friend told me he had dated a nice fat friend of hers named Donna and was a total asshole to her!

He came to my place that night, and folded his body into a grasshopper's. I mentioned Donna, and he said, She wouldn't even be friends with me after, the dumb bitch, and we both laughed.

I am a DJ, he said suddenly. My style is fresh and funky. I will sample Clara Peller saying, "Where's the beef?" and scratch Billy Ocean over the Culture Club.

Here he demonstrated, *War war is stupid — get outta my dreams!* Then made his move.

I really like him, I thought for a few days.

I like how he seems so distracted when I call, and talks about hunting squirrels and deer with his dad; I like his adenoidal voice, his long, plasticized limbs.

But he stopped calling, except to ask that we still be friends.

We never were, I said coldly.

I used to think anything was better than nothing, as my friend Farrah always says.

A while ago, she met a guy on a dating site. After their first date, he told her he was not interested in a steady relationship.

Can you believe that!? she asked, popping carrot circles into her tiny pink mouth. The guy's dick is so small, I asked him if he was in yet. *In my ass!*

Later, though, she won him over, and I feel embarrassed every time I see him.

Anything is not better.

Jinkum sleeping on his back, sighing: a sugar cookie baking on a sheet.

Then waking up and shaking off the sweet starlets and looking back to blow a kiss, his eyes filling with me, how I look.

How I look on my knees, already furious, already miserable.

Just a snatch of a song he frees from his head when he shakes his lightly browned hair.

GUZZLES

Lafitte and I went to a New Year's Eve party, in 1999.

He had not had a drink in six years. When he drank, he would start yelling things like, I can't believe you kissed that *drunken Indian!* Or start sucker-punching people.

We had been invited at the last minute by casual friends who worked in fashion and journalism.

Dress as though you are going to the Oscars! read the breathless note.

So I wore a black sack dress and the skull of a baby fox that ties around the neck with a Chanel ribbon.

I would get in trouble for this. From Jill, the hostess, a nineteen-year-old journalist who wrote a Hot or Not column that routinely suggested poorly dressed, unhealthy fat people should live in a well on a diet of tissue paper and warm water.

Jill had been talking about her pneumatic breasts for a while when I decided to shut her down, and then I noticed Lafitte burning them with his eyes.

I call them My Girls, she said, as he crossed his legs into a knot. I saw he was drinking fast from a glass of what he called water. Give me some, I asked, and he said, "Ssss dirty, lemme get you new waters!"

Let's go, I said.

You ruining it! he yelled before breaking away and declaring, Naked Twister!

I held his ear and screamed at him for twenty blocks in the blizzard.

This is how I entered the new millennium.

Jill would go on to say I ruined her party by "wearing a garbage bag and a dead squirrel!"

Lafitte would sail the seas of his own devising.

I would come to like Jill because she was what she professed to be, a serious girl. And because I had liked her sexy show as much as Lafitte but was too mean to say so.

In eight months I would meet Francis and he would cry when I picked him up and chose him.

In the meantime, I would call Lafitte Guzzles, and we would laugh, as if it were funny how we ruined everything.

THIS GIRL IN MY CLASS

In grade seven Mrs. Ross asked us to do presentations on something unusual.

Several of us went to the front of the class and talked about pterodactyls or Tunisia or whatever we had found in an encyclopedia the night before.

I talked about igloos, how round they are, how is it possible? I used several sugar cubes to demonstrate the obvious alien powers of Eskimos.

My friend Tony talked for a very long time about Barbara Astman's gelatin silver and fabric photograph, *Carol Performing Lilac Tricks*, fretting throughout about the probably purple cloth border.

Then Anguish came up. She was a malnourished girl we never noticed. She turned her back to us and then whirled around. She was wearing vampire fangs.

And she stood there and stood there.

We waited fifteen minutes until Mrs. Ross gently led her out of the room.

Anguish has epilepsy, she informed us when she returned.

We all nodded, well of course — epilepsy.

Anguish never came back.

Why would she? She is likely still flying into houses at night as a bat or a shadow, as a shining, fast thing whose bite is this sharp memory of her stillness, and guts.

ALCOHOL, ADDICTION, MANIA

I am looking for a book about how I feel at the Mount Sinai Indigo/ Chapters. I stand in Health, beside an ancient woman poring over a book called *Skinny Bitch*.

Every book is about cancer or dieting. I am surprised there is no book called *The Cancer Diet*.

Look how thin I am now, my aunt said as the disease went through her like drain cleaner.

...*drunkards like Poe, Faulkner, London, Chandler* —

I am reading a book, my mother says, where the daughter hides her mother's "sad bottles." Isn't that beautiful?

In this story, my mother is a writer of fiction who writes mysteries about wolves in the Deep South and cannot stop eating chitlins with fried chicken even though the chicken hearts beat so horribly beneath the floor.

Her narratives are "hallucinations" produced by alcohol's adherence to necessity, to the functional labour of forgetting.

My mother, alone in a chair with the lights out. I love this time in my life, she says, when we try to get her to go to bed.

And my father, changing at the melting point; and those I love, unable to understand the ends of this beauty.

Walking around like a sick animal, ignoring anyone who says, I am worried, or, You are getting worse.

Would you like to donate your thirty-four cents' change to children's literacy? the young man at the counter asks.

I think about how much I read when I was a child; I see myself holding an Ann Fairbairn novel, the dark circles below my eyes.

I read late into the night; *Five Smooth Stones* fell to the ground.

Buy them a drink, I said, throwing down a twenty. A double.

I want to have a baby and I want to give this baby a credit card and a gun.

I GET A LITTLE BIT CLOSER

She has covered the Plexiglas of her cubicle with snow-in-a-can and textured angels. She has a glass angel, a chia angel, a rattan angel, and a wood angel.

She has a knitted white cozy on her telephone and a mug with her name on it, which is Glo.

She offers me soft, quilted tissues: I am often crying.

We sell aluminum siding over the phone to strangers.

I sit there talking about "retro-chic" and "a shiny outfit for your home!" with my head pressed flat against a desk that is covered in peanut shells and lists about other lists or ones I have lost or lists I would like to make.

I cry for a variety of reasons. A woman who asks me to come over and play "Smelly Hands" with her. A man who roars, The chains in the dungeon shall remain silent!

I think of the procedure I had during my lunch hour, when the technician showed me urine shooting into my bladder in red jets, then probed my fat, jelly-covered stomach.

On the monitor: the sky at night in my yard, spiny black branches hooked to the grey sky, its seizures of white. The moon, higher still, hard and swollen.

A haze of light on the wall I thought was the breath of God.

I got to see my empty uterus, the small indentation or crater.

I had told Glo I was going to an extreme-sports match. When I returned, she had left everyone their own jewel case with a DVD inside, labelled *Zack!* That is what she is calling her baby. She has also drawn loopy hearts and written *I AM SO HAPPY* in bright, blimpy letters.

She is so pregnant.

She can only work a few hours a day, and when she's there it is Ooof, I am so bloated! or This one's going to be a soccer player! or, disgustingly, My nipples are so tender!

Worse, she is always talking about her sex life. Robbie is way turned on by me now, she tells us all. Everyone smiles or says, Good for him! Or, Good for you!

I write *He likes to cum on your fetus's face* on the back of a call sheet, then draw her and her ugly cop-husband doing it doggie-style.

I watch *Zack!* when I get home. I take a glass of bourbon and a tray of cookies with me and sit in front of the TV. And by a tray of cookies I mean a foil-wrapped square of cardboard covered with plump, immaculate OxyContins.

A logo appears: 3-D Baby Vision.

I put on the powder-blue glasses Glo has folded into the case.

A clay-coloured baby comes into focus against a sepia background. It has one visible eye and it is dark and piercing. Rubbery lips and a nose like a fingerling potato.

The timing is appalling.

But I am stoned and I just roll on my side and watch.

The baby moves in the fluid, waving its leafy hands and feet to a song about the vicissitudes of life.

Every day is a winding road, this song goes. That was Shirley-Flo! the DJ announces, and I write her name down.

When I was at the hospital, a very old woman was sleeping on a stretcher, her hands pressed to her face.

I wondered how they had hurt her.

Before I left, I wiped the cold medical-splooge off and looked at the white robo-cock. I considered referring to the entire event, with some modifications, as a nooner with a well-hung scientist.

I am considering it again as I whisper *help me* to Zack, who suddenly starts kicking like a horse in a burning barn, then looks right at me with his shrewd, sad eye.

DID YOU THINK WE WOULDN'T NOTICE?

Ponyboy and I put the car in reverse, accelerated, and drove into the ditch.

My friends were inside with the Otterburn Park boys I had invited over. Silver, my best friend, was trying to lose her virginity with Darry, a JD I had set her up with, in my bed.

I need Vaseline! she called up to me when we came back inside. I'm dry. I'm frigid!

Darry put on Silver's jeans and came upstairs. We all tried to move the car and ended up stripping its transmission.

We hid in the basement until my parents came home. At one point, Ponyboy put his head in my lap and I ran my fingers through his long, white hair. He was thirteen, two years younger than us, and to this day, he is still the prettiest boy I have ever seen.

He called my friends for months, asking them to convince me to go out with him.

Oh my God, gross, I would say. I feel like a child molester, I wrote in my diary. The truth was that I could not stand the thought of anyone liking me, and this remains the same.

But Stephen —

All of this mayhem — my parents' outraged return; the mechanic's bill; the news hitting the school—would set the stage for my one and only date with my true love, and so I say to the silver Impala, the husk of which is growing wildflowers in a field, Thank you.

Stephen walked over to the bench by the school entrance where I was sitting and asked me what happened.

I am grounded for a month, I said morosely.

My family was moving the month after that, to the West Island, where I would attend Disco High—in homeroom, the teacher would shimmy down the aisle as the glitter ball flashed, handing out discussion questions like Gino Soccio vs. K.C.: Discuss!

The date—like the time we held each other on the bridge—ended badly, and then I saw him one last time and he touched my hair, or I touched his hair and we were speechless.

I had become brave and beautiful; he had decided to stay where he was.

I would think this until I saw his picture so many years later; until I called his mother and she cried and asked what had been going on in his mind; what was he thinking?

I have spent twenty-eight years, on and off, spinning myself back into the clutch: his black windbreaker and brass ring; his messy blond hair and hands fastening me to him, still representing something about virility and love that shakes, then eludes me.

Then, the red and black squares of his flannel coat and the kiss that branded me; then, my hand or his hand, a warm imposture of the river that snaked behind us, from my house to his, ferrying great, spangled fish with gaudy red scales.

My father called downstairs, What's with the car, Lynn?

Did you think we wouldn't notice?

A silver car, jammed into dark space and dirt—this could be the image of his blessed body, being buried.

This is the image of the first crash: the one that hit me so hard that my mind began, that very day, to produce his image like a printing press.

Image after image — Stephen reposing in the grass; Stephen reaching for me; Stephen waiting to hear my key turn in the lock — there is sound also — then saying, How was your day? And I say, Hold on, hold on, laughing, because I am not even inside and I already have to push my way past all the flowers to find him.

IF YOU PLAY THE RECORD BACKWARDS IT SAYS, I LOVE SATAN.

The rain presses hard for days.

A cigarette gutters by my door, pooling orange.

Marlowe has left the cherry blossoms behind, the way squirrels do. My street is one explosion after another, pink, white, yellow. I notice these fireworks as I think: I hate you.

His letters are light and thoughtful; they tremble with fear.

I send him money for a photograph; he sends me a blurry crowd shot with his thumb squarely in the middle. "I hope you like it!"

Don't get weird with me, you promised, you promised, he says.

I know, I know. And I am helpless against all of it. All that I want.

If my safety is threatened, I will go out and get a gun, he warns me.

I am trying to find a safe place to remember you well, and not feel bad, but I am so sick. He writes me this and I am curled up on a stretcher puking into a cardboard bowl, thinking about my mother, calling for my mother.

I am worried the pilot won't shut up. Tell your dog to shut up, he writes.

A roll of messages, unspooling. I still miss you and love you. Or, The way your eyes look.

I am sorry I left you there.

The clinch in the doorway: his beard is a nest and when he says goodbye, all these little black birds are singing; they are opening their throats to be fed.

He is folded over like a knife on my bed. Don't go yet, he says.

I tell him about the Trail of Tears, the Chickasaw migrants dying of smallpox and starvation there as they were forced to push west. And the Cherokee fugitives who lived off roots and berries, circling the mountains of Unega. Refusing to move.

I am reading to him from *Quest of a Hemisphere*. About the muscle shoals in the great bend of the Tennessee River, the food the settlers ate. I tell him the names of each treacherous spot, each meal. Boiling Point, the Suck, Frying Pan, the Narrows, and Tumbling Shoals. Broiled venison, hoe cake, boiled greens, and parched corn.

That sounds so good, Marlowe says.

He brings a bottle of bourbon and an ashtray upstairs.

Prior to that, he was lying on the floor. I lay down beside him, and got a sense of us, how we looked, dead.

If you sit on my lap again, he warns me. Then, Get off, I hate you.

My dog won't stop barking. Shut up, shut up!

Bourbon and Perc chasers; the room starts to smudge.

We walk to the store, and I hold his cold, thin hand.

He sits on a green wooden chair, like an elegant, reticulated insect.

He looks like something from a monster movie, something barely alive and shuddering.

He is leaning against my door when I get home, smoking. Are you still married? I ask. He stomps the cigarette and nods.

I have been out driving in the Beer Store parking lot, doing 360s.

The wind lashes the car, and I am on a flatboat, heading downriver, trying to cross the rapids, where he waits for me.

THE CRACK BABIES

The last time I got bronchitis, I quit smoking.

Then I read about my lungs, which are upside-down trees. Their branches and leaves capture dirt and debris.

The leaves become paralyzed after too many stormy days.

My lungs start to fret and whimper things to my brain, things that this nefarious organ interprets as follows: Go to the store. Buy a package of cigarettes.

Do it now.

Put the package in your mouth and eat it.

A little while later, my lungs start to falter, their whisperings becoming mostly unintelligible: red match-head, sulphur, nice. That hit, the first one, oh that's so good.

Then they start screaming.

They have turned into furious, neglected, filthy infants. Crack babies, desperate for something they need or all it is they know.

Babies in black singlets, howling.

I lace my hands below my ribs and squeeze, cradling them.

I fall asleep and dream of a woman and her strange little daughter who wears thick glasses and a beehive.

The girl is drawing a picture where everything is upside down.

A speck-sized white bird walks carefully across the grass, and the green sky is filled with even smaller, paler mice.

Nice, the babies say, and it is their first word.

RAY OF LIGHT

When can I see you? Nora asked, and I said, Not now, meaning not ever.

I am a bad friend at the best of times, and it has been hard to let her go.

She is never angry with me, and understands that I am largely unavailable to others because I am building a Fortress of Solitude out of space debris.

Our lives are always falling apart, but she is better at this, and more stylish.

She is smart, and fast — she is too fast for me.

I think of things I would say at her funeral. She read some of these stories a while ago, and she read them out loud.

Write about me, she said. Don't be afraid to go deep.

But what if I did?

Could I pretend to find her glamorous, still?

She used to be. I think of how she would get dressed in her filthy room, the room where she once found a dead mouse in her lingerie drawer; where she got into bed and felt, with her feet, a half-eaten chicken wing.

And emerge, in her little gowns cut at the top of her sky-high legs; her heels with tight ankle straps; her big, expensive hair and eyes like pale blue saucers.

Drawling about a writer she loved, absolutely adored; about her fascination with the Treaty of Versailles; an amazing person she had just met who I had to meet, who I would love, love!

We would cut lines and go out and sprawl around bars, causing small scandals, or sit at each other's tables until our mouths were dry and clicking, our bodies twitching, and the fear, for me, took over.

But that is going too deep.

What if I explained that her beauty was modified, embellished even, by her cruelty, laziness, and monstrous appetite?

That I became afraid of her as well, in the end?

Or could I just mention how I loved her? How she was, at times, a white comet. A long, clean line.

THIEF

I heard someone banging at the door last night. It was very late, and I was working with pompoms, confetti, and glitter.

The project was called "Marlowe Disguised as a Version of *Ten Oxherding Pictures*"—sixteenth-century koans about ox-taming and enlightenment.

I would make ten dynamic variations of the same image: the pack of matches he left here last spring that say Thank You, Come Back Again.

And write, beneath the images, things like, The yoke slips from his neck: he writes his wife's name in the sand, or, The beast follows a crab along the shore, breathing hard.

The banging got louder. Who is it? I called out. I was apprehensive: this is a bad neighbourhood.

I heard a man yell, Mablicilus! Blabbaloosa! He sounded happy.

Get out of here, I called back. I don't know you.

I went downstairs a little while later and no one was there. The seven garbage bags I had filled with clothes for the Children's Wish Foundation were still there, tagged "CW" on slips of white paper.

When I was going through my clothes, I could not believe how small and pretty they were.

I had to keep some things — the gingham bikini I was wearing when Lafitte carried me through the Caribbean Sea; the first vintage shirt I ever bought, a black-and-white lace blouse with pearl buttons; a silk, cream-coloured tea dress with black ribbons.

I was so careful, so nonplussed, that it felt like I was going through a dead woman's belongings.

That is what I was doing.

I called my mother and told her I thought a burglar had just been at the door. She was mildly interested.

I thought about Marlowe, and how I missed him.

In the morning, I was thinking, nervously, about how I would go out that night and see one of my exes read; that two others would also be there. And feeling a bit angry that they all had children. (Those children should be mine! I sometimes seethe, if I am wearing a mink stole and drinking vermouth.)

Who's my baby? I ask Francis.

I read a story the other night about a woman who, after her husband and daughter died in a car accident, raised a chimpanzee and became very attached to him. They ate and bathed and slept together. The chimp dressed himself, combed his own hair, and liked to look at pictures of animals online.

He got Lyme disease and started to become moody, often taking the house keys and disappearing; dressing carelessly and sleeping more.

The woman's friend came over and the chimp ran out and tore out her eyes, jaw, and nose, then started to eat her.

The woman stabbed him, then the police came and shot him and he crawled to his bedroom and died.

I have never had a bath with Frank, but still.

I was thinking about going to the reading, and Marlowe wrote me. He wrote that it had been him, banging on my door.

He said he was going back home shortly and that it was a shame I had been busy or had "company."

I called his mother's house and begged him to come and see me and he said that he had to teach his aunt how to play Scrabble, so, no.

We can't speak to each other anymore, I said.

I'm afraid to see you! he sobbed. Because I love you. He kept crying for the rest of the call.

The first letter he ever wrote me began, Dear Ms. Crosbie.

There, there, I said. It's okay. And then I gently clicked the phone off.

It was like a breakup even though I saw him so infrequently and knew we would never be together.

His wife seems like a nice woman. She designs cakes that look like different cities, and cities that look like cakes.

The chimp's owner said, When I stabbed him, he looked at me like, Mom, what did you do?

I never did go out that night. I stayed in and petted my dog, and told him he could eat any one of my friends and I still wouldn't stab him.

I was going to say, of the married man, that he was a thief: that I had so little, and he stole it.

But that is not true: I took all that he could give me and I fenced it.

A TORN LIGAMENT

This is the name of a story by my old friend Daniel Jones, who killed himself on Valentine's Day, more than fifteen years ago.

His stories are laborious and exceedingly precise. They are invasive, neurotic, and unseemly: I admire these stories very much. They were published after he died, and the launch was held in the same bar as his wake.

After he committed suicide, using instructions he procured from the Hemlock Society, I helped his wife identify his body at the morgue.

The woman in charge was a scowling, sponge-shaped loudmouth. She was yelling at people to "Wait ya turn!" and "Fill out tha form!"

When it was our turn, she flicked a switch, her mouth still making an upright staple, and there he was.

I was young, and I took it hard.

When I tore a ligament in my knee recently, I thought of the story again.

In the story, he wakes up with a bandaged ankle and a pair of crutches. He does not know what happened.

He resumes his affair with a woman with deformed limbs and

long feelers of hair growing from intimate and unusual parts of her body.

He describes her, naked on top of him: the story is repulsive and beautiful.

I smashed my knee by falling on an icy sidewalk. I went down hard, got up, and wiped out again. I lay there as people walked by, saying nothing.

Before I fell, I had been very ill with bronchitis, and when I started to get better, I would walk. At first, I could only go a couple of blocks before getting winded and dizzy.

Then one day, I walked for hours, making stops for dog cookies, red scalloped knee-high socks, a tin robot in a pink checked dress.

I talked to everyone I met, and the more I walked, the happier I felt.

I knew, somehow, I was going to walk all the way to Steve's grave.

When I got there, I was tired and I could not find it. I kept walking back and forth, above the dog-run, where a chihuahua was riding bareback on a basset hound.

I realized the tree that had been planted for him would have grown, but I could not see it, and I left.

The next day, or the day after that, I tore the ligament.

Daniel was a pragmatist, and an atheist. In his story, the protagonist (who is him, in a manner of speaking) finds himself under his lover's window after she has broken up with him, staring up and crying.

It is raining in the story, so he cannot tell the tears from the rain and vice versa.

I felt like something flesh and bone, he says, something almost human. Or this is how I remember it: I am always misplacing the book because it upsets me and is, of course, unsigned.

This passage is derivative and desperate. He loved art; he was compelled to rifle through it, and his past, for meaning and hope.

When I couldn't find Steve's grave, I thought that it was because I was not meant to keep looking for him there.

If all the trees in the park had started singing, they would have sung, It's too late to say you're sorry.

To him, to others I have loved, and have made almost human by missing them, entirely.

AND THE WHIRLWIND IS IN THE THORN TREE

Written on a chalkboard in front of Koma Designs: CHANGE IS IMMINENT.

Kanye, folding falafels, two doors over, inside a nest of bright pink turnip; the stuffed pheasants at Salvador Darling staring dolorously.

Grocery list on the sidewalk: Skippy. Bred like GOST. Mayo. Salty Munkees.

A red seed pod whipping down so fast it seems sad to leave it where it lands, but not today: the signs are all in place.

There is the miracle of the pennies, everywhere I look, and the branch sheared off my tree by lightning, and then truly, there is the pigeon laying eggs on the spikes on my windowsill.

Two large, white eggs that she has tried, with her mate, to make a nest for with some twigs and a piece of yellow fabric. The spikes hold the eggs as if they are marquise-set into the sill. It is sweet and frightening, like a candy cat-o'-nine-tails.

She laid the first one the morning I told the married man that we would not speak again.

And when I saw the egg, I saw it as a covenant.

That same day, I heard from a woman who was my best friend

when I was seventeen. Until I caught her in bed with my boyfriend, a man I have all but erased from my life.

She asked me to be friends, on Facebook.

I sent her a poem, instead, that I had written a long time ago, about what she did. The poem cites the Hexhammer, and casts her as a sorceress I drowned in a Turtle Pool.

She did not write back, and then the second egg emerged.

Two covenants, then. Involving all of these lonely years, and the good that will surely come if I keep my loose morals and cruelty in check.

Two eggs that may hatch into tiny nightmares.

I know that something is happening. I hold it close yet I also shudder, that it may be, that it is filthy still.

Amen.

I NEED YOU

This is the last line of Jacqueline Susann's *The Love Machine*. It is a telegram that Robin sends to Maggie, causing her to walk off her movie set and fly to him.

It is also what the vibrator said, the other night, before I stuffed it into a pillowcase that I duct-taped and dropped into the garbage can in the park.

I can still hear a little zzz of despair.

This is what happened. I bought a nice, small-ish vibrator. Purple and curved, with a black wrist loop and an oscillation dial.

Its imperviousness to water reminded me of an old jingle that went, Why just take a shower? When the Shower Massage is around?

That was awesome, I said out loud one night, putting my hair into a turban.

Are you sure? I heard a nervous voice say. Because I felt that you weren't all there —

The vibrator was lying on its side in a puddle on the counter, *talking to me.*

When I held it, it said, That feels nice. You never seem to want to touch me . . . after. Do you like me, even a little?

I said Yes, really fast, and slammed it into the lockbox I'd bought at the same porn store.

It started making noise and bumping around, and I opened the box.

Why does THAT have to be in here? it yelled, gesturing to the gigantic mechanism beside it. I know you two have a history, but why do I have to be reminded all the time? I feel inadequate —

I locked it in again and thought about this, my life.

Then I took it out and said that everything was good. That I definitely liked it a lot, actually, and yes I did think of it — Marco, it said, shyly — I did think of Marco when I was at work sometimes.

What kinds of things do you think? Marco asked.

Well, you know. Dirty things. And, ah, how much I like seeing you?

I was trying to fill the malevolent silence.

I sometimes want, I want to call you!

I wonder if you are okay!

Do you need me? Marco asked in a tight voice. Because I need you, he said. And hopped back into the box, rolling as far as possible from the pink Rabbit.

I *dig* you! I protested, and thought of taking it out with me the next day, maybe sunning it in the grass, or treating it to some shiny new batteries.

I turfed it instead, and I heard it crying — I definitely heard it say, This is how you always solve problems! — as I slammed down the lid of the trash can.

And then, of course: Walk away like you always do!

FRANCIS IS A DOG

I once knew a writer who suffered from OCD, who was very afraid of leaving his apartment because of what could happen. When I would visit him in New York, I would never reassure him, but instead teach him new strategies.

Have you considered unplugging everything electrical? I would say. Or, Put your hand flat on the stove, four or five times.

He got a new psychiatrist who encouraged him to stick up Post-it notes around the place to remind him of their sessions. Shelley is a dog, one of them said.

One summer, Frank and I went on a road trip. When we stayed at the Motel 6 in Van Nuys, the couple in the adjoining room had us over for dinner.

They made me a nice plate of mashed potatoes and carrots and turnips, and put out a bowl of dark, oily red scraps for Francis.

He's a dog! the husband yelled, noting that I looked uneasy.

They were loners, like me, they said. Vagabonds! the wife trilled, nudging, with her shoe, a large, moving bag under the bed.

Is that...an animal? I asked, and she cleared my plate and smiled.

No. No it isn't, she said. Now get your nosy cunt-face out of here.

Calvin, the famous writer, was obsessed with angry women. He watched Joan Crawford films all the time, and would call me and speak so earnestly about them, I would feel restless and roll a Pepsi bottle beneath my foot to strengthen my arches, as Joan advises in *My Way of Life*.

You know that when Joan was in London filming *Trog*, he might say, she had Mamacita wrap all of her blouses, skirts, and dresses, and her good day and evening suits in crisp white tissue. The lingerie was placed into sachets, as were her shoes, and Joan always travelled with wide, round barrels for her hats, each of which was lined to match a different ensemble.

Her jackets were also lined to match! Such exquisite attention to detail. I am currently shopping a novel, he confided, called *The Red Moiré Silk Snood Goes with the Red Moiré Silk-Lined Capelet*.

It is a thrilling tale of a masquerade ball in Capri, told by Joan as she receives a sexually charged surgical procedure!

Calvin and I had been very close, but he went off me one day, just like that. This happens to me a lot, and I blame, in part, my charm, which is both fraudulent and short-lived.

My charm is a trompe l'oeil of a mayfly!

He went off me the last time I stayed with him. We were collaborating on an essay about the trope of nefarious women and powder rooms in American cinema, and he told me, suddenly and tearfully, that he felt I was not at all passionate about the work.

You thought we should call it "Pee Girls"! he cried, then, Oh God, NO! — I had just chucked a ball at Shelley that knocked over his framed rendering of Joan murdering her husband, Alfred Steele, with a lead pipe, in the drawing room.

I need to decompress, he said. I need you out, he said.

I get thrown out or stormed out on a lot.

People have very intense feelings toward me, I say into the mirror, circling my mouth with thick, red lipstick.

Lynn is a <u>friend</u>, I wrote on a Post-it note. Before leaving, I slapped it onto his ashen forehead.

A couple of years later, not too long ago, Calvin started sending me chunks of a new novel, signed with kisses, and his name.

He had called first, suggesting I call him right back — Because, he said, I do not have a good long distance plan. I said no, and there was such a long pause, I knew he was counting to a hundred.

The novel, *The Backstabbers*, uses an epigraph from the O'Jays song.

Unfortunately, I am a barely disguised Backstabber, and I rate a whole chapter. To be polite, he changes my appearance a bit: "Linda is a small African-American woman, with thin hair and a musty odor."

In the chapter called "Leave Shelley Alone!" I stay at his place and smoke huge cigars all day and night. I eat handfuls of warm, runny cheese and vomit into the pillowcases, and whenever I go to the bathroom I "act funny after."

I am not mad. He and I are peas in a pod.

This year, Shelley died and I called him and we cried.

I walked around the yard holding Francis like a sack of potatoes.

Calvin collects Tintin paraphernalia. He spends a lot of time arranging Tintin and Snowy on his mantel until they look perfect, and then he is so nervous someone will wreck it, he is mad already.

He is writing that book.

THE OLD FIRE

At night, I have been taking — I want to say *eating* — pills and writing notes about stories I would like to write.

The notes rarely make sense, including this one: That it is all GAUZY!

There is another one that is two pages long about an episode of *Happy Days* I pretty much remember seeing on the Christian Network.

The one where Al's burns down because of Chachi's carelessness, and Fonzie stops Al from moving to Kenosha by offering him his life savings and a partnership.

Marion sweeps helplessly in the middle of the ashes and debris; Joanie says, Parties make me wild!

Fonzie is very hard on Chachi, saying to him, You don't *burn down a man's life!* And say sorry!

It is hard to watch these old shows because they almost always carry with them a measure of uneasy nostalgia, and shame.

Ralph Malph looks all right with longer hair, and is anxious to go to a tavern before the fire. I've still got it!, he used to say.

He doesn't say it anymore.

I have been taking taxis almost every day for seven years or so.

With Saah, Varney, Wleh, Mamadee, Solo, Kwesi, Jim, Przemek, Vlad, Abdul, Dharma, Goma, Faaris, Mohammed, Lalit, Teddy, Farzaneh, Afareen, Klaus, Jenghis, Taj, Ezra, Dominick, Alijah, Jerome, Adonis, Henry, Hansel, Kennedy, and Diskobolus, to name a few.

These names used to come with numbers, on the receipts. They have offered to take me out for dinner and dancing, or invited me to come over and watch a movie.

They have stopped the meter and the car and talked to me, for a very long time, about how they feel, and where they come from.

I have seen a man's tribal scars shine like rivers of silver in the light of the moon.

I have cried, and one man cried also and said, I feel like it is happening to me!

We have prayed for each other, and laughed so much I have had three accidents.

When I went into seclusion a few years ago and gained all the weight and all the age — age like a disfiguring disease — they stopped talking so much.

Or they would admire my pregnancy, to my embarrassment, saying, Be careful, nice lady, as I leveraged myself out of the little door.

Fonzie, long after his debut as an almost credible hoodlum, has not aged well. His leather jacket is puffy, and banded with elastic; his jeans are quite tight, revealing a mushrooming ass.

His hair is ridiculous.

I remember an even later episode where he has a fight with Richie, who has returned from his army training. They meet in a bar and Richie beats up some guys and gloats about it, then derides Fonzie by saying, I'm sorry, is that not *cool a mundo*?

Fonzie answers, with considerable dignity, that he has not said "*a mundo* in a very long time."

I watch him and feel some of the old fire, spreading.

And I flirt my head off with the next drivers I meet. And they say dirty things and ask for my number, and I say, Give me yours, and I add them to my collection.

The fire raged through Al's, scorching every song in the jukebox, igniting bottles of ketchup and mayo, turning forks into tridents, divesting the place of everything.

I have always thought of people on TV as my friends.

I have a hundred men's phone numbers: *I've still got it!*

OVERDETERMINATION

Since I quit smoking, I talk all the time and largely to myself. I have so much to say!

Or I will corner someone, a student, and start yelling about one of my new theories (technology is furthered only by perversity) or recipes (macaroni, chick peas, and Corn Curls).

I pretend I am someone else, looking at me living my life, and I keep up a lively commentary. —She is wearing Stendhal couture: red sweater, black coat and scarf, black dress, black boots, red tights, black gloves with red stitching.

— In her human-head clutch is a warm, beating heart.

— She is walking to the corner and she walks catlike!

Alternatively, I pretend I am John Crowe Ransom and construct insular, close New Critical readings of my life in an accent I feel closely approximates his.

If he were loaded on bath-house gin.

— In her bedroom, on the sward of the dresser: five jewelled bird rings, feather earrings, a black metal birdcage. The Blue Girl sleeps with her "head in the crook of her elbow," an image that, with the preponderance of avian flourishes, suggests both her desire to be free and to fly, unbroken (no longer "crook[ed]") from the cage she has built for herself.

Or I dance, the way an old man danced with me once when I was very young, with elaborate hip rolls and hand waves, a big loose smile.

I stand in the corner when I am very worried and think that life is too much and not enough.

A scene from the 1971 movie *The Zodiac Killer*: Grover, the truck driver, is sitting at his vanity table. A Taste of Honey is on the record player. He is wearing a pressed suit, a shirt and tie, and is carefully placing a wig on his bald head.

He then sprays its bangs into place with a huge aerosol can. Too much action, he says, checking himself out.

He slips a gun into his waistband and admires himself again. He calls himself one good-looking son of a bitch.

I see this scene so many times. As directed by Martin Scorsese, Girish Karnad, Zhang Yimou.

As a series of drawings or in Morse code.

The world is bursting open and it is too much action, I say, smoothly or with terror, when I open my eyes and the sun strikes.

CRASH

This morning, April 7, 2009, 11:43 a.m.

Is when I fall apart in front of Cantaloupe, the taxi driver.

What just happened? he asks in his low, nebulous voice.

I have not been sleeping; I have run out of the painkillers I have been taking. I received a performance review that translates to an F or D–. Part of it reads, "Lynne has some problems with organization and responsibility."

The superfluous *e* is struck out with blue ink.

It is raining: cold, terminal rain.

I am soaked, holding a box of my students' final projects. Several of them made me presents; others wrote me notes.

The girl with the small, frowning face declined to sign the evaluation card I bought and sent around that read "In Sympathy."

You need a man to love you, Cantaloupe says.

I have my dog, I say.

You need a man to make love to you, he says. Not to make babies, he adds. No babies.

I am looking out the window at a man in a silk dress chasing a wet red lobster.

You need him to touch you all over, and taste you.

The I LOVE YOU graf on Harbord.

And make you feel like a woman.

A chalk drawing of a rainbow.

Take his big, hard —

You cut that out, I tell Cantaloupe.

I feel very calm, as if my failure is a warm cloth bag of beans.

I think of my three taxi crashes. The last time, the guy hit an old Chinese man and tried to take off. I got out and found a speaker of Mandarin.

The old man said to the paramedics, when they showed up, I. Love. Canada!

I am just telling you, Cantaloupe says.

Later, Cantaloupe bangs on my door and Frank barks so loudly that he takes off running.

I have some problems, I tell Frank.

But you aren't one of them, I say as he happily pumps his short tail.

BENDER

Babe, I had the most morbid scary intense bizarre dream with you in it last night.

My gay students have started to have confusing thoughts about me.

They are all very tall and strong, with shocks of dark hair and long, black lashes, lurid nail polish.

You were pretending to be a serial murderer because you were doing research for a book, he writes. And you had me in this small room in a basement. And you were repeatedly breaking character to ask if I was okay with it, and I said yes! And so you started cutting my upper arm with a straight razor, and I was really scared. And the whole dream was black and white and grainy.

Oh no! I text back. I am in Kensington Market, listening to Nicki Minaj sing "Shingaling" and drinking mango tea. An aggressive couple has crowded me to the end of the bench. They are eating plates of quiche and trying to sell — it sounds like *sustainable vampires* — to a polite, incredulous couple.

Outside, a woman throws up her hands and spins.

You must be afraid of me!

No, he writes. You were really nice, and worried.

What was I wearing? I ask.

You also looked extremely intense, he writes. Very dark and mysterious: wet black eye makeup and a black tank top.

It was like watching evidence, he adds.

You were like Karla Homolka.

My parents knew the Mahaffys, he writes. When I was three years old they would come over for dinner.

When this student was three I was living with Lafitte and writing a book about Paul Bernardo based on the romance novels of Barbara Cartland.

Send me a picture? I ask.

He sends me one of him and a little girl building a snow fort.

He was in my writing class this summer. It was rough going at first, but pretty soon we were having parties and making balloon animals.

He tattooed my name on a banana for one of the HOW TO seminars. Others performed the Thriller dance, joined the Peace Corps, and had lunch with a Hells Angel.

Several Christmases ago, Raspail gave me a tiny pair of diamond earrings. He told me to open them at my parents' house and call him right away.

I had brought him a bottle of Glenfiddich, which he splashed into his mug of Diet 7 Up.

I opened them when I got home and felt bad: he could not afford them, but I knew what the gift meant to him.

I called him on Christmas Day and tried to say You shouldn't have as meaningfully as possible. He was bombed and kept cackling, How'd ya like me now!?

He would say that every time I saw him until the end. It had become a confusing story, in which my patrician parents dropped their mimosa flutes in shock as I defiantly screwed the sparklers into my ears and rushed to the phone, nearly knocking over my brother playing Handel's *Messiah* on the violin.

He crapped his pants! Raspail would say of my brother. Whatta they thinka me now!?

Have you ever seen *The Breakfast Club?* I asked the class, as they, as a group, performed one of the complicated licking and grooming sequences from *Cats.*

I love the scene at the end where Claire, the Princess, takes off one of her big diamond-stud earrings and places it in Bender, the Criminal's, palm and kisses him and he staggers; he actually swoons.

It is like watching evidence, that love can be pure and true.

Open your hand, I said, and I placed Raspail's diamond there, and he slid the bar from his lip and replaced it with the brilliant little stone.

This was the cut and after, that was us, Bender and me, picking up handfuls of snow and patting them into new shapes. Changing them; love changes you and everything.

THE WAY SWANS SLEEP

Jelly's stories were always the same. He was dating or living with a "world-class" beauty, or acrobat or scientist. And had to leave her because of her wanton bigotry, meanness, or aggression.

I perceive you to have a beautiful soul! he said in a letter written a week after we met, on Facebook.

Like Brian, he had been a friend of Steve's.

You showed such dignity at his funeral! he wrote.

He begged me to let him call me. He spoke in a little voice, with an affected Yiddish accent.

When we had a small quarrel, he told me he went and held AIDS babies to feel better.

I decided then that he was a kind man, and, in spite of my reservations, I agreed to meet him. Oh, I am so excited, he said.

I knew everything about him, it seemed, except what he looked like. He was fifty-five and lived in a basement apartment with a pot dealer, and was waiting for the next big idea. There is crazy money in reality TV, he told me.

He was a recovering coke addict who wrote ten-page letters at four in the morning, claiming excitability. He was in recovery, he said.

He drove a beat-up beige Ford Escort and used to be a performance artist called Misterio.

I got the name from a very nice, and surprisingly affordable, Cabernet, he told me. When I asked about his shows, he said they were hard to describe: Oh, I would pee on flags and stuff, he offered. Once I was a dinosaur coming out of a steel egg.

Jelly was planning to go back to school and study. Not what I should know but what I should feel, he said. For example, I want SOC101 to teach me how communist people act in breadlines. With sadness? Or élan!

He confided that his thirty-year-old daughter kept having molar pregnancies. They look like bunches of grapes or falling snow in the ultrasound, he told me. She named the last one, which looked like a snowman, after Jelly, before evacuating it.

It was a world-class child, he texted. COL, he added, his acronym for "Crying Out Loud."

Jelly called and wrote me all day long for the week leading up to our date. The night before, he sent me a disquieting rhyming poem he had written about wanting to hold me. It's called, "I Want to Hold You," he told me, when we spoke the next day.

I came close to backing out. I phoned him, but he had to take another call. He answered it, then came back on the line. One of the AIDS babies just died, he said. She was my special friend and she died alone. I have to go, he squeaked.

He called ten minutes later, and said, Hey! How are you!?

What about the little girl? I asked.

Yes, Oh my God! Life is so crushing, but you have to go on! I cannot *wait* to meet you and simply stare into your topaz-coloured eyes, he said.

My eyes are blue, but when I had corrected him in the past — the time, for example, he had called them blazing, hot coals — he snapped, For a free-spirited receptionist at a thriving new hair salon, you are so literal-minded!

I was unable to correct him on the matter of my job either, and from then on, I remained silent when he referred to Your gallant prosthesis! or Your death-defying storm-chasing adventures!

We finally set a night, and that day I had my hair and nails done and a dress dry cleaned. He had told me he was not tall. He had not told me that he was a midget. He reached my knee, which he embraced and, fleetingly, humped.

He leaped in the air to take my hand.

We went into the living room and he clambered onto a stool. Class, he said. You've got it, all right. He was staring at a painting an insane woman had given me, of a white cat with large red lips playing a harmonica.

He took me to a restaurant on the Lakeshore called Jaks. No C, no apostrophe. The waitress brought over a couple of phone books for him to sit on and I had a grilled-cheese sandwich and fries that smelled like the fish he was shovelling into his Tic Tac–sized mouth.

We drove down to the lake, and at first he did not feel like getting out of the car. I'm wearing a light jacket! he fretted. But he followed me anyway as I walked over to look at the swans, sleeping, their long necks curved onto their backs. They made me feel tired.

As he leaned against me, I thought of how much I have had to change to let anyone touch me.

Jelly drove me home and we sat on the couch, drinking tap water. I had been clean for thirty-seven days.

I have not dared to dream in so long, he said. I keep thinking, I don't want to blow this.

Me too, I said, my eyes passing over the crotch of his tiny, pleated slacks. I thought about my days as a drunk and that I may have slept with him then.

He missed the joke, kissed me, and left. When he kissed me, he clamped his lips together tightly, while folding and unfolding his legs and making them chirp like an insect.

After a week I called him.

You're so angry, he said. I am not about anger and cynical Ponzi schemes! I smoke cigarettes and dream of art and performing with power and fire!

I apologized, I was so shocked.

My father is dying! he yelled. And my huge fat diabetic brother has to have his legs cut off. He will be at the funeral in a wagon!

He then held the phone to the radio (I heard a DJ speaking mellow Hindi), and said, That's them, they need me.

And just like that, Misterio was gone.

Never to return, but I think of him, once in a while, shivering by the lake and looking mournfully at the dark, churning water. That is one world-class swan, he must have thought. But cruel. Cruel!

SWAN LAKE

It is a bright spring day, before the weeks of rain, and Lil and I walk toward the lake. We stop at the Skyline, which we now call the Place.

We sit in the booth by the end of the counter, where the plants are. And, surrounding them, little dolls and animals, toadstools and palm trees that are always being moved around.

We are working on our soap opera, *Don't Walk Away*, in which Lil plays herself, a replicant, a rigid Scottish matron, and a pharmacist named Gordy. I play myself, another replicant, an angry Scottish matron, and a dude named Brick.

There are roles for our pets, and there is a great deal of confusion about the replicants who are trying to kill us and assume our lives, and whose master is named Dragon Revival.

They do something called the Dazzle to stun and immobilize us, but we are not sure why they want our lives, and what they will do with them.

When Lil makes a joke about her milkshake, the young waitress laughs and Lil blushes strawberry.

We take pictures as we walk: a phone booth with a Mountain Dew can and Advil blister-pack on its ledge; the word *grace* scribbled behind an elderly couple smoking in a doorway; a tiny *hi* on the sidewalk.

I have been feeling good, being clean. In the morning I found a fat picture, and in it, I am wearing a huge black coat, with a big, baggy black skirt and blouse. I am using my dog as a shield in the picture, to cover my face.

I want to wear things that fit, no matter what.

Lil and I go into a vintage store and she knows the owner, a thin, sinewy woman with a mane of dry grey hair.

I find a coat and like its soft fabric, but when I try it on, it is enormous, and I remember the picture and start to take it off.

Hey! the owner calls over. We have lots of Big Gal stuff!

I walk out, and Lil follows after a bit. She says the owner is worried she hurt my feelings.

I hold up my hand for a taxi and when we get to my house, I go right in and lie on the floor for a long time.

I call my mother from the floor.

What a stupid thing to say! she says, when I tell her what happened. I say that the owner is an evil sorceress, and that she turned me into that woman in the black baggy clothes.

What will I do? I ask, and after a while I get up because my mother keeps making me laugh. Did you ask her how the Dried-out Crone Couture was moving? she asks as I glance at my convex body in the belly of the tea kettle.

I look out the window and Lil has left me three tubs of hyacinths, pink and yellow and blue. I put them near my bed.

Later, I see a woman on my street I have not seen for a while and have been worried about. She is very big, breathless, and has to use crutches.

She is smaller now, and has a cane: her hair is cut into a short, feathered cap.

You look pretty, I tell her.

Is my hair flowing in the breeze? she asks, and poses dramatically.

She is on a diet of bananas, oranges, and food she likes that is good for her.

A blind girl walks by and tells her mother she knows a dog is near her. The red-tailed hawks charge the sky, heavy with pale blue light, and an army of ants hoist a pecan on their shoulders.

I mean that kindness rushes in like white cells, hauling pails of clear, cold water to the injury.

TRAIN I RIDE

Going back to Montreal, sitting beside a young guy with earrings and a crewcut who immediately jams in his earphones and torques his body away from mine.

I think of all the old ladies who used to talk to me on this train. About their grandchildren (She is marrying a coloured boy! one fretted) or the filthy stories in *True Confessions* magazine: "My Husband Was a She-Male's Plaything!"

Life's a pain in the ass, one cotton-top drawled at me. She went on and on until I changed seats. Then she kept talking over the seats until I gave up and went back.

Not so long ago, I asked a girl if she wanted a peanut, and she said, very slowly, Look. I do not like to talk on trains. I like to read my novel, and think. I hope that is all right.

It's just a peanut, I said.

I used to think the old women were lonely and poignant, but they were just tough.

The livid hulls of passing trains, the rusted-out swamp-car. The pitch pines and scrub brush. The snakes of water and neon-green new grass, the lazy cows — rushing past all this, I have a memory of my past that is not a thought but a feeling, like choking.

Coming home and moving forward, is the idea.

I see my grandparents' grave in the Mount Royal Cemetery. They are buried together, snugly.

The rectangle of dirt in front of the grave is bare. Plant a flower, would you? I say to my father. Some grass, anything.

He always irritates me. He walks around like a bear at a camp-site, shaking trees and yelling when his snout gets caught in a beehive.

You look like a giant oyster, I tell him when I happen upon him, half-asleep and making noises.

Those paintings you bought are junk, I tell him and laugh.

I stay in my room and read most of the time. When I leave, he takes me to the train. He tries to help me get my suitcase on, and they won't let him.

He starts yelling.

What's wrong with us? he asked me once, when we had stormed out of two restaurants in a row.

When I got home, I called him and we had a fight.

Today, I walk Frank to the west side of the park, straight into the wind. An old lady is doubled over on a bench and I call out, Are you okay?

She looks like she has been crying.

Are you okay? she yells. Leave me alone!

I am sorry, I say, and feel embarrassed.

I am not thinking about old ladies as I turn back, or of how I might talk better to people, but of one time my father met me at a bar I like.

When I arrived, he was wearing a jean jacket I had given him and strolling around holding a martini.

I wouldn't let him order another one and hurried him out.

In front of the church, there is a mother blowing soap bubbles for her baby and she says to Frank and me, Look!

The bubbles rise to the cross as I look up, stumbling on my bad leg, and I remember my father, rushing to me the day I twisted my knee and carefully lacing my leg into a splint.

I'm sorry it hurts so much, he said.

He looked fantastic, walking around with his drink.

Look, the mother says again, and I stand still. I want to listen; I want to listen to everything, then say, No, Dad, I love you. I love you more.

TOO DIRTY FOR A RAT

Farrah and I meet on Mother's Day at a restaurant near her studio called JOE.

She wears a little slash of pink lipstick and a scrim of mascara; her long, blond hair is spilled champagne.

Do what you want to do, she says. Marlowe is coming over in two days and Farrah and I have met, between rainstorms, to talk.

Marlowe is coming by "just for a short visit," he has warned me. There are other caveats, about him being clean, "super-exhausted," and probably in pain as he has booked four hours for a tattoo just before he comes.

What do I wear and how do I act and feel? I ask Farrah.

Something that looks good, she says.

She wears troll-sized tops and skirts and looks sexy as an unmade bed. She likes to read a book called *Men Love Bitches*.

I ask her what the book would say, and she says, That bitches do what they please, and too bad if men don't like it.

I mention seeing a man we used to know twenty years ago who was so good-looking it gave us heart attacks.

He was riding a little kid's bike, I tell her, and his face looked like a raisin. Or a brain.

He comes by my place every day! she tells me. When she impersonates him talking, she looks like a crazy parrot.

Farrah has as many enemies as I do. I love her little purple-blue eyes, and the sad stories she wears like a perfume that suggests a woman lying in a pool of cold, cloudy water.

In the kitchen, four Chinese women in hairnets peel carrots and turnips into tubs. And in the bathroom, someone has written TOO DIRTY FOR A RAT on the wall by the mirror.

My father died on Mother's Day, Farrah tells me. It was so many years ago, and it never gets better.

I think I keep him alive by hating this day so much, she says.

She looks beautiful, hating this day, and I kiss her goodbye and her skin is like new bark.

The sky turns pitch-black as soon as she leaves. Why come at all, I write Marlowe enticingly.

I'll be there, he writes.

I see myself cleaning and cleaning; see the black half-moons under my nails, my eyes; him leaving after getting a call he drags out by saying, repeatedly, "No, you hang up!"

I see myself slamming the usual doors.

But before the call, I'm no bitch.

I am a baby rat opening my pink mouth and quivering: love feels so good!

STILL LATER, IN THE TORRID SPRING: MARLOWE

This is what I wear: gold and black, Farrah's screen of Axl Rose with my name sliced into his face; and this is how I feel: cool and composed.

Marlowe drinks a tumbler of bourbon and we go to the Cadillac, where he positions his long, aristocratic body into the chair and orders a plate of poutine that arrives as big as a flying saucer.

He eats three fries and pushes it away.

A table of tattooed men wave at him and follow him to the patio for a cigarette. He did blow with them the night he showed up at my door, as it turns out.

They jump up and down like small dogs and laugh when he calls one of their friends' parents "Wop socialites."

We tumble around in my bed, and Marlowe keeps saying no, like a schoolgirl, then suddenly takes off all of his clothes and says, I feel so vulnerable.

He is one of the birds in the window, pink and helpless, almost hideous with need. His eyes, also — those great, green lilies — they are a drawing of portholes made by a child with only one crayon, a child who has broken and eaten the rest: I call this damaged child Reverend Mayhem.

Reverend Mayhem writes this, in blocky letters: "The old lady and old man were kissing and other gross things I LIKE DINOSAURS AND GUNS RULE!"

And he draws me two days later, walking across Queen's Park to see Al Purdy's statue. Tears as big as pears on my face, the sun a guided missile. "She sat up high and held the statue's hand and went AHHH! The statue was hot and black."

Marlowe had called to say he was leaving, and that he was never coming back.

I feel it in my solar plexus, Reverend, I say. All the days and nights of loneliness, then him holding me like a rope ladder, those ladders that fall out of helicopters during emergency evacs.

Yeah, those.

Stop kicking me.

He wrote that I was a panther, I say. Your body like a tsunami, he wrote, and, Goodbye.

My father beats me, the Reverend says. With his belt and things he finds, even lettuce once.

I hold his hand with my hand warm from Al's and we make a serious plan to go somewhere where no one can hurt us again like THE PAST! the Reverend says, and I tell him that is even worse so we start a list that begins: INSIDE THE MOON, then Chips & soda. Then, SPRING RULES!

AND DAWN

Orlando and I met in the hall at school: he was quite striking, with his feathered headdress, buckskin vest, flowered shirt, and the bright beads woven into his long, braided hair.

He handed me his card, his face impassive.

Orlando Magicality! it said over a series of numbers and addresses. The magicality on the card was a painting of a man bagging a caribou as the sun set over a purple pond.

He placed his hand on my leg — I was wearing purple tights — and hiked up my skirt. My colour, he said thickly.

We were having a pleasant-enough date, in my backyard with tea and ginger cookies. He was leaving for the B.C. interior in a few days, to spend the summer with his tribe, and then he was going to study in Paris.

He showed me his book of pictures, and I was forced to linger over each image, asking, Who is that? Or, Where is that? To exclaim, Those poppies look so real! — the kind of horrible things one has to say about other people's vacations or work.

Oh, is that the Coliseum? It looks so beige! Your music is so heavy, I just loved that long ballad about the Girl with the Sad Eyes.

I decided to pursue my feelings for Orlando, possibly because he was leaving.

When he moved, I hung up his painting, *The Whispering Wolf,* in my hallway. I spent a lot of money on it, and was promised it would look different every time I saw it.

So far, it still looks like a deranged purple dog staring down a shovel.

I wrote Orlando a bit, and we back-and-forthed and then he called me one day when he was watching the ice break on the river and felt lonely.

I am learning the guitar, he said ponderously. Let . . . me. Get my song. List.

After a lot of rustling, he produced the list and read it. — I want to learn, he began reciting, "Yellow Submarine."

"Peggy Sue."

"Chantilly Lace."

"The Boxer."

"Love Me Tender."

"Fuck the Pain Away." I had stopped listening. I was thinking of the trellis of broken capillaries on his nose.

Oh no, the door! I yelped as he continued — "At the Hop," "Scarborough Fair," "Monday, Monday," and more.

So sweet of you to call, I said, hanging up abruptly.

You should know what kind of sex I like, he wrote me, the next day. If you were wearing underpants I would cut a hole in them guess where.

I responded, coquettishly, that he was being so silly!

He wrote, I like to fuck up the ass, or stick my fingers there.

I said I did not like the conversation. You are rude, I told him.

I know you want to be my girlfriend, he said. And I am rebelling. I am a rebel. Also, my people are more earthy.

Really? I asked. Because I have dated a native man, and he didn't talk to me like I was a whore.

That ended things between us.

I got a gross card a week later, of two insipid-looking seals capering underneath a dream-catcher.

I miss you, he wrote. And Frank.

When he was here, Frank and I sat on his lap, and my cats took turns sitting on his head. I thought he was so gentle, and sweet. This excused a great deal.

Are all men gay? I asked a man performing in front of Designer Fabrics.

He played a bit of "Tie a Yellow Ribbon Round the Ole Oak Tree" by rubbing the tops of bottles. Then he did "Knock Three Times."

It sounded really good.

BLACK PEARL

She is in deepest disguise. I will add details designed to deflect superb detectives like that excellent private eye, Monsieur Clément, whose small twin grows from his side.

The twin is named Marcel and he does wear a monocle, and a partial, very fine, linen shirt, and cufflinks, topaz I believe, on his single, curved arm.

This is what I call an unfair advantage! I tell these chaps, who are familiar with the Dick Tracy villains, and, of course, The Black Pearl.

I have cast her in the role of a ferocious pig who rolls in her own ordure while boasting of her tremendous military successes and the many people she has destroyed because of her ruthless need for perfection.

Ah, but you would make short work of that pile of chops, Clément says, twirling his thick, black moustache, and Marcel exhales, windily, through his single, tear-shaped nostril.

I have loved and trusted her, I tell them.

They seize on this clue like hungry predators and shout out a number of names.

This was too easy, I say. There are so few!

Marcel thirsts and must take of drink, and Clément retrieves the eye-dropper and the ROCKST★R beverage he enjoys. Clément then advises me always to be silent about this matter.

Even if her squealing should keep me up nights, throwing my Toledo knife at her image on the wall, because I am certain to regret having said so much about one so little.

Littler than I? stammers Marcel. Or enormous; we shall not say.

I write this on a tablet: She smells like smoke and ginger; her smile is the convex shell this siren has placed over her lips and there are starfish on her dark, hollow eyes. There is also the rustling of crêpe du chine.

Clément snatches up the paper and devours it.

When Marcel starts speeding, he tells stories about his time in the Prussian army, Dragging *this one* around, he says of Marcel, and he starts to tell us a vulgarism about Field Marshal Derfflinger but cannot finish, he is laughing so hard.

These exquisite friends have often led me to consider taking down the painting that hangs in the centre of my living room and reads, GOD, I'M LONELY.

When the smell of pork roast assails me, I think of Marcel's eye, wet from laughter under the clouded monocle, and it lashes me securely to the mast.

WHERE THIS WILL LEAD

Walter has a garden in front of his house that he works on every day.

We met shortly after I moved in. He came over to tell me bur-
dock root was growing on the edge of my lawn.

You will need to take it out, he said, or its roots will spread. He
described it as a kind of fast-acting poison, or a very bad cowboy
with an itchy trigger finger, motionless in front of two quaking sal-
oon doors.

It took me over an hour to dig it up with a shovel, then a shovel
and crowbar.

Walter came to my house one day and planted something skel-
etal, and carved branches off two trees to give it light.

Not too long after, he had me over for lunch, a simple affair with
a few reserved elderly women who spoke quietly and concisely about
current events, fine wine, opera, and things I know very little about.

The food, as food by elderly bachelors so often is, was dreadful:
a fish with its eyes intact, chewy from being in the oven for hours,
on a bed of limp lettuce with a side of hard lima beans, cubed ham,
and pineapple on toothpicks.

I was quiet, and uncomfortable: soon enough, we were reduced
to nodding coolly at each other.

But Frank is crazy about Walter. When we walk by, every day, on the way to the park, he looks longingly at Walter's door or breaks away and tears up the stairs. If Walter is outside, Frank yelps with happiness and runs up to him and places his paws on his knees.

I began talking more to Walter about how he felt after he told me he'd had a painful procedure. About the sunny or rainy days; about relatives who say they may come visit, and forget, or change their plans.

It doesn't hurt my feelings, he says. I just wish I knew what the plans were!

He and I live alone, and understand certain things, implicitly, when we speak. I *am* hurt, he is telling me, and angry. I am afraid someone will drop by when I have been drinking. That they will come when things are very bad and it will be like being in a small boat in a storm.

I walked over to see my new friend, a funny man who is scared of spiders. You need to see all these spiders! he yelled. One, the Leader, climbed to the top of my fence and dropped a drag line for the rest, and they all came out from under the stones and swarmed!

I saw Walter being taken away in an ambulance as my friend tried to show me evidence of the spider-caper.

The last time I saw him, he was pale and trembling, and I asked him to please see a doctor.

He gave me five bags of cuttings that all died moments after I planted them in my barren yard.

His own garden is a lush square of vines, shrubs, and stalks in alternating bright and deep greens; of heart-shaped creepers; of showy purple orchids and bright bursts of yellow and red among ripples of glowing sapphire blue. Of scarlet tea roses that began to unfold the day I went to see him in the hospital.

He was lying on something like a medical deck chair, his feet sticking out at sharp angles.

He was gaunt; his hair and skin were leached of colour.

I talked to him as orderlies came in and out, emptying his bag of fluids, rolling him around like a sack of mulch.

Are you scared? I asked, and he managed — it was very hard for him to talk — to say, I was scared. But not now.

I told him that Frankie missed him.

I miss Frankie too, he said. I touched his hair and face, which were painfully soft.

He doesn't know where he is, his best friend Tristan told me, later, on the street by his house. He is dying of cancer, he said, and Tristan looked tough, weak also, as he drew on his cigarette. I am taking in his mail and watering the garden, he said.

The little roses are blooming, I told Walter, when I visited him.

I am happy to hear that, he said.

I told him that his garden was opening up, and that he should come home to see it, and he smiled.

I repeated this to Tristan.

He squinted through smoke. He is never coming home, he said.

THE HEDGEHOG

Pornography comes up during one of my students' presentations.

She mentions Ron Jeremy and I say, I totally kissed him.

Gross, she says.

That don't confront me! I say.

I am already letting my thoughts wander away from her, a girl I dislike because she told me, in a personal note, that she likes "to read *People* magazine at my friends' places while taking a dump."

And when I see her, all I can think of is her shitting a pile of black and tan logs and waving the smell at me.

I went to see Ron Jeremy being interviewed at the Gladstone Hotel, two years into my direst celibacy, brought on by men — incredibly — not being attracted to my big, fat body and face.

I went looking for him before the show. I slipped through the back doors and ran into him, standing on top of a small flight of stairs, composing himself.

He looked handsome in black slacks and a white linen shirt, his long black hair combed straight back.

He smiled sweetly at me.

The talk went fairly well, but the audience did not like his raunchy account of making *87 and Still Banging* with Rose Agree.

You don't want to be just, you know, giving it to her, he said, making a thrusting gesture.

Well, you don't! he said into the aghast silence.

I waited in line to get his memoir, *The Hardest (Working) Man in Showbiz*, signed.

When it was my turn he stood up and said, Come here, beautiful. And he held me in his arms and kissed me.

He smelled like sharp cologne; he smelled like the sun.

He wrote something in my book that suggested we had made an adult film together.

I wore a perfume called Lovebirds to that event and when I smell it, or feel warm and happy, I am also feeling Ron Jeremy's arms wrap around my soft, eloquent body and smoothing out my hostile diffidence in two, long strokes.

MICHAEL JACKSON WAS MY LOVER

Você encontrará este duro acreditar.

It is hard for me to believe, also. So much so that I wrote my love story in Portuguese, in the manner of Elizabeth Barrett Browning, the famous English werewolf.

Wha aconteceu entre nós estava tão sujo —

That is a dependent clause that makes my heart clutch.

Something happened in Los Angeles, when he stood with his arms extended like Kali (I meditate on him *raimented with space*), and the sails of ancient ships opened, reaching forward.

I looked good; someone told his friend that I was holding, and the rest is a love sonnet about wild animals.

During our time together, I took rhyming note of what hot, huge muscle pressed where; how did he seize me, what sounds did he make. On occasion, I used these indiscreet metaphors: an anaconda, a panther, a dove.

But I never could explain all of him, standing on his toes, his hips like claw hammers in my ribcage, starlings there also; that he smelled like something growing in the warm, wet ground; that he was liquid and motion and wildfire.

This happened in a broom closet. I knocked over pails, and

barrels of industrial cleaning solvent.

You are like the white butterfly that alights, in early summer, on the flowers and vines, I said.

You move like a frightened account of wild mustangs.

Your tongue —

He untaped his fingers and closed my mouth with the bands. He ripped open his white shirt and unbuckled his black bondage pants, which fell to the floor in a crash.

He made me promise never to tell what happened next, which is why I keep naming the animals, and then I feel each of my teeth being extracted with a clam-knife.

I got to see him dance, what was that like?

It was like watching the last living creature on earth collide with a spaceship.

He sent me a card from Bangladesh that read, Thinking of you. On the card was a picture of his brothers performing; of him, some distance behind them, quietly on fire.

He would send me things for years. Popcorn shaped like people, including J. Edgar Hoover and Minnie Riperton. A drawing of a dead cat in a sombrero. Tiger-striped Sally Hansen nails; a porcelain baby in a white velvet wetsuit. A string of wooden beads, tortoiseshell reading glasses.

I read that he had been ill, and someone asked him who to call. There is no one, he said.

There is someone, I always wrote, on my packages of pink makeup sponges, paper cranes, or Robo-Fan, a robot-shaped fan.

But I have said the same thing, and I understand.

The last time he wrote, he sent me a list of names he liked, including Prince Michael Infinity and Small Pillow. His signature crawled toward the card's end and collapsed like a victim of violent crime.

I do not know if he read my letters about choosing a lighter lipstick shade, maybe plum? About eating better, and purdah, and every spring, the robins singing go bird go.

The day he died, I was at a bar called Sin and Redemption with my students, after our last class. One of them got a text and said, Michael Jackson is dead. I think he is, she said.

What will I do? I asked them.

On the way home, I checked the news and they said he was in the hospital. He will be okay, I thought.

I looked at my emails and they all said MJ Dead, or *Jacko*!

I wrote about him, an article that someone would call the "maudlin ravings of a nightmare spinster."

And Frank and I watched CNN all night. I saw so many images of him dancing beside the words MICHAEL JACKSON DEAD.

I took a shaky photograph of my television as if I had seen a monster in the forest.

He burst out of his skin and became a ravenous wolf: there are scars.

He kissed me like a child, later, and thanked me.

Not too long ago, a man yelled, Move it, Fatso, as I laboured across the street.

Hold your head up high, Michael said. Say, I know I am some-one! It is hard to do. I just walked home slowly, and sat quietly, my head in my hands.

I believe in you, he wrote, on thick, creamy Shangri-La Hotel stationery. He drew us holding hands and hanging off the top off the Burj Dubai, our mouths wide red Os.

I watched his body in a bag, hitting the road.

I was holding the walnut he sent me, with a diorama inside — of him, on one knee, extending red roses.

My hand pressed flat on the screen, only electrical fuzz be-tween us.

No one can hurt you now, I said.

I felt that this was true. I felt it with such passion it was like making a pearl.

I cultivated a pure memory of him, of me, moving in a circle, saying *Eu te amo* like we were saying grace as his legs snaked around mine and I fell down where heaven is, surprisingly.

It is down there.

AT THE ORIENTAL HOTEL IN BANGKOK

The week before he died, the last of Walter's summer flowers bloomed, showy and pink.

By then, he had been moved into palliative care, a few blocks south of here. And that is the direction these stargazer lilies have started leaning: they have listed nearly to the ground, tracking him down.

Their petals look like the soft flesh on a dog's belly; they look like pricked dogs' ears, like sleepy dogs' paws.

Frank continues to charge the stairs; I continue to pull him back.

The last time I saw Walter, his face was marbled with pink, and he opened his eyes and said, Yes. Yes, yes, yes, yes.

You always say yes, his nurse admonished him.

I held Walter's hand, and he squeezed mine hard.

A few days earlier, he'd been receiving guests in the hospital, a group of stunning old men with pomaded white hair and important jewellery who'd smuggled in a few bottles of wine.

I remembered our strained lunch with the old women and thought, Now this is more like it.

Walter's roommate, a small stick of a man with a racking cough, came over and sat on the bed, smiling; laughing too.

Walter had asked a friend to bring a camera, "Because my hair looks fantastic."

The day we held hands, I did not say goodbye. I had been trying not to breathe and was light-headed. I would smell Lysol, shit, and milky vomit for days.

The day after that, I was at the Oriental Hotel in Bangkok, isolated by my increasing dependence on painkillers and tranqs, and terrified of my new enemies, accusing me of lies and filth. The lies, however, bore some relationship to the truth: at the Oriental Hotel, I read Derrida for the first time. It was slow going, but not unlike pink champagne. I underlined this passage:

When activated, the scrubbing bubbles release a fragrant series of signifiers that are constantly deferring grime toward an unattainably shiny home.

I thought of the ways in which the lies could be so easily spread because of my weakened condition and my desire, always, to dress my dolls in sexy little numbers and talk to them, really talk to them about quantum mechanics.

When the cat is *dying*, I ask, is its super-positional state still more super?

When I asked Walter if he was all right, he said Yes, and yes, yes, then Super a bunch of times and his friend was incredulous. I have never heard him say that word in his life, he said.

In the hotel suite, I started throwing up on the plush carpet and I cried so hard that I broke a rib. I whispered orders to room service for marshmallow puree and skinned, purple catkins. I started writing letters that said I love you, and sealing them and smiling as I slipped the envelopes into a bowl. I said: It's true, you know. I do love you. You're all my children.

I flew home holding a bouquet of lotus flowers, in full makeup and a long, shiny wig.

The lotus rises from the mud in sublime filth that is why it is perfect. This is the note I passed to the stewardess, who liked it so much she let me comb out her hair and tease it. I used a hot tomato juice can to give her volume and panache.

They will do what they have to do, I said bravely that night as I walked through my wild garden, my eyes on the stars.

So much death invites magical thinking, and the pink stars lurch and fall. Finding me: someone in trouble, but still dangerous.

DEVIL TIMES

Homicide Detective Kang Oh Soo is perplexed when he finds me in my office with a tarot card thumbtacked to my forehead.

The Eight of Swords: Sickness, calumny...treachery, he murmurs and pockets the card as the paramedics roll me onto the stretcher.

The detective stays behind as I am ferried off and asks quiet, concerned questions about who did this to me.

Office is a converted bathroom, he writes. Smell of urinal / puck like dragon fruit mothballs / smell of ukime.

He is writing in a Blue Octavo notebook, the kind Kafka used for observing things like "Evil is the starry sky of the Good" or "Bed, constipation, pain in back, irritable evening, cat in the room, dissension."

The detective and his colleague Oh Seung Ha write haiku because they are always being mistaken for Japanese men, or Chinese men. They also make ostentatious reference to, say, Bruce Lee's Shadowless Kick or the daring fundoshi he once wore while eating a bowl of Ants Climbing a Hill.

The masked Tarot Card Killer was unsuccessful: after kicking in the door, he used a ligature until I passed out, and was pulling out a serrated knife as he pressed the tack into my head.

At that moment, my boss, Dr. Bale, peered in, her hands clawing a formal reprimand from a student who testified that she "didn't appreciate it" when I said I would burn her essay proposal with my eyes.

The killer bolted, knocking Bale over, and everyone rushed to her side. It was ten minutes before Creation, the AV guy, punched in 911 on his cell. The numbers made a sound like a snare drum and everyone went Ohh.

Assailant is probably a man, Oh Soo writes, Three of Wands, Five of Swords, The Tower: will the assailant complete the reading?

The others were dead, sliced to ribbons, stamped on, set on fire. The connection is obvious: we all work in colleges and teach writing or are tutors. We spend a great deal of time reading up on strategies regarding the use of articles in English, or how to best explain a dangling modifier.

We are often impatient and wish to snatch the paper away from the perspiring, scrunched-up student in our office, swiftly correct the mistakes, and hustle him out the door.

That may just be me. My colleagues speak slowly, and hold long meetings about outlines and mapping symposia while eating rank, damp food from waxed paper envelopes.

They wear shapeless clothes and let their eyebrows grow wild. They photocopy articles about the ways in which other colleges teach and they pass them around, leaving oleaginous fingerprints on the paper.

They sit aggressively in their chairs, straddling them as if on the verge of heroic bowel movements.

These people make me sick. I look at them and all I can think of is striking them with a two-by-four.

Of course I staged the attack.

But I was able to get Sally Peppertree's smelly fingers all over the card by passing it under a collated article about a conference in Las Vegas, or, "Syntax City!"

Sally, a butterball with square little eyes, likes to sidle up to Bale and tell her stories about me.

I saw her talking to herself in the hallway, she will hiss. It is abnormal!

Bale will then say to me, Someone told me you have gone crazy, I mean is everything fucking okay, goddammit!?

You're creepy, Sally once said in a tiny voice as she passed me in the cafeteria, picking raisins from a dry muffin.

I killed a classmate in high school, Oh Soo tells me as we slowly turn the Lazy Susan to pick at the Hanjeongsik. It was an accident but —

He spears a red chili from a small blue bowl.

He was needy and cruel, and he had wide, womanly hips and a perm.

How unseemly, I commiserate. Devil times! I say, and he nods. Seung Ha announces that he will perform an act of psychometry on a single grain of rice.

The rice was planted on a patio bar in Da Nang, he begins.

Tell me everything, I say.

Oh Soo makes his voice high and sexy.

Every-ting you want! he says.

THE DRUGS ARE MORE IMPORTANT THAN YOU

Last week I told my psychiatrist of sixteen years, Fuck this!

Fuck you too! I yelled at a woman waddling down the hall who had interrupted our session.

And when she interrupted, my psychiatrist had not reached into her chest and torn out her bloody, beating heart.

He is thin, frail, and afraid of anger. Stop yelling at me! he once cried when I raised my voice. He put his fingers in his ears.

He is, at the same time, fascinated by details about my life as a writer. Or he used to be, when I had stories to tell. Oh, you are joking, he would say, leaning forward. She let him *do that* in Banff!?

When the woman came to the door, he and she whispered back and forth as my brain jammed on the story I had been telling that began, I don't know how he could do this to me.

That story.

After I stormed off, I visited the Rexall and bought sexy rubbers — as I do every time I shop. I buy Vibrating Ring Trojans or K-Y Touch Massage, or these black ribbed numbers called Let Me Do the Work in Bed. Yet the last date I had was with a married reiki practitioner who said he would prefer that I not hug or otherwise touch him hello or goodbye.

We can still have a good time! he said.

I buy tiny fitted jackets and skirts that I cannot pull past my knees, then write "Dreamy" on strips of masking tape and label them. Just today, I was getting ready to leave for my first spin-class with a new friend when she wrote me to cancel: I have a friend in town + electrolysis, sorry!

I hope your bush looks wicked! I wrote back disingenuously. And your stache.

Instead, I make an event of my day off, of walking to the 7-Eleven and carefully selecting processed cheeses, then walking back, my face turning tomato-red by the end of the short, hilly jaunt.

I then take a handful of Ativan and watch Michael Jackson videos on YouTube. I watch one where he is in a car with his friend, in Miami, listening to R. Kelly's "Ignition." When Kelly sings "Bounce, bounce, bounce, bounce," Jackson pantomimes dribbling a ball.

A woman wrote, in the comment box, I can't stop watching this!

And someone else wrote, You think that's bad, I can't stop and I was supposed to meet my husband two hours ago!

Steve and I were obsessed with a number of movies, including one about a sadistic Los Angeles serial killer who would pace his empty living room, bellowing obscure, racialized insults: Mistah BIG TIME PIMP! From Van Nuys Boogalard!

In the same film, a social worker eases her client into a breakthrough. The client, sobbing, addresses her family as if they are in the room: Mom. Dad. The drugs are more important than you!

The film is about absence and authenticity. It is a Zen koan called *Tosui's Vinegar In Your Wounds!*

When I re-enact it, I play the patient and the killer. I often speak when no one is around, quite viciously. I threaten to ruin people, or hurt them. I stagger around, crying and shaking my pill bottles like castanets.

I shot a film of my dog the other night where I am slurring,

Where's the snowman, baby? The TV is on in the background, and I have no memory of watching the show.

Where's Frosty?

I went to the Goodwill the other day and picked through clothes until my fingers felt gummy. I bought a paisley suit with a stiff white kerchief sewn into the pocket and picked up several pamphlets. One says, It's A Honey of a Deal! and features a bear sitting on a tree branch and raiding a beehive. One says, How To Be Saved and Know It, over a drawing of an ocean liner dragging a man in a life preserver.

Another says, God Loves You.

I wanted to read that one because it made me feel good. I opened it and it said, Please do not resent us for giving you this tract. We love your soul, and we want to tell you that if you have never been born again, you are on a journey to a place where you will burn forever and ever.

That is harsh, I thought. I wondered how it was we both believed in the same God.

My God roars, I HATE YOUR SINS, then sings "All Right Now" to me while playing an electric dulcimer.

It occurs to me that it is a matter of reconciling disparate information: that same day, for example, my friend Lil had sent me a card she'd made from pictures of things I like, a squirrel water-skiing, Michael Jackson, and her parrot playing with the present I gave him, a tiny, knitted monkey.

Inside, she wrote, You mean a lot to me, Linda.

I need to write the words *Joy* and *Grace* on the pills, I realize.

As I labour at this task, the phone rings and I jump. It is always a carpet-cleaning place, and they are very nice so I finally book them to come by.

To clean the stairs that have vitiligo.

And make them as smooth as sand, sand in my feet in that piercing vision of me driving toward water, then accelerating at the shore.

I WANTED TO WIN

Bobby Clarke is now an "award-winning investigative journalist," I discover. I watch a video of him talking about infiltrating a Mexican drug cartel — "I wore a sombrero, chaps, and distressed leather boots. Code name: Tito. When the narcos started searching my donkey's saddle-bags, I thought I was a goner."

Bobby writes for distinguished men's magazines also, about finding "a sturdy, mischievous shoe" or the taste of several rum beverages, marked on a scale of one to five "iries." About the woman he almost married, a paralegal named Sharona, and this is where I come in.

When I knew him, he did not dye his hair with what appears to be black shoe polish, and his face was less wide and pleated. He was not yet a writer either, although he was working on an outline for a book, a racy legal thriller called *Permission to Treat the Witness as SEXY?*

He was the host of a literary game show, loosely based on *The Price Is Right*, where writers were asked to appear and guess, as frantic yodelling played, the correct price of Canadian novels positioned below an Alpine climber.

He asked to meet me to work on a screenplay about two kids,

named Ron and Cherry, who discover the enraged ghost of a Spanish conquistador down at the old Johnson Manor!

It was a pick-up and it wasn't. The day we called off our young love affair, he asked me if I had only agreed to work on the film to spend time with him.

The film we had roughed out on a cocktail napkin was called *Hockey Fright in Canada!*

No, but it is not my best work, I admitted, letting my hand wander up his leg.

He was the first and last smooth, polished man I ever dated: he had an MBA and a loft filled with state-of-the-art tech and a sectional sofa so large it appeared to be forming a conga line.

His show was popular and he was inundated with sad, racy fan mail.

He wrote a lot of his own material, he told me. Life is like a box of books, he once observed, as a show-closer. You never know what you're going to get!

What did that mean? I asked him on our first date, having watched the show the night before. Are some books filled with coconut and others contain nougat?

I was on that show. He invited me himself, after meeting me at a writers' event at a karaoke bar. We chose songs and read our work over the melodies. I read about a thrill-killer in Reno called The Toupeed Menace over "Run Joey Run" and "Copacabana."

I was wearing a black leather dress that fit like a firm hand on my ass. And Bobby thought I would be perfect for the following panel discussion: "Should Canadian artists make a stately, twenty-five-metre-high nude statue of Margaret Laurence, then, using steel ropes, oxygen cylinders, and metal-cutting blowpipes, knock it down and replace it with a flag embroidered with the face of avant-garde feminist Nicole Brossard?" The winner would drive off in a new car!

It is important to know that the statue is wearing high-heeled pumps and carrying a boxy purse, Bobby told me, to give me an edge over my grim competition.

I arrived in a sexy T-shirt I had made at a head shop, with a quotation from *The Diviners* in puffy letters across the chest: "Ride my stallion, Morag!"

The makeup artist, after applying hand-tan to Bobby and writing her phone number on his palm with glitter, made me up with black raccoon eyes and smeary orange lipstick. You look like Bette Davis! she said. After her stroke! she muttered. She was seething with jealousy, because Bobby's beige handprints were visible on my face where he had grasped it and said to me, Look at you!

On the show, I said, laconically, No, that statue idea is absurd, and was free to spend the rest of the panel staring into Bobby's Gumby-green eyes and watching how, when he shook his head, his chestnut-coloured hair, dashingly, stood on end.

He called me the next day and the dates began. We dated for about three weeks, but I had two serious boyfriends at the time so it was complicated.

One was Lafitte, who would invite me over and start yelling, Don't see him! then stalk around his small apartment in a blind rage.

The other was the farmer, a good-natured man who gave me some sensible advice like Don't let on how interested you are and Be a good listener. And, rotate the crops or you'll be sorry.

Bobby and I would meet at disgusting bars and wander around, winding up at his place. Once I lay on top of him and he made an *oof* noise.

Another time, a friend called him and he wept openly. You mustn't talk that way, Checkers! he cried. Checkers, no!

Checkers is an old friend, he told me. He has just threatened to masturbate while suspending himself with a pair of nylons by the neck because he has just seen an image of a chambermaid refilling a mini-bar that he finds unbearably erotic.

I held up a framed photograph of Bobby and an attractive woman that I had plucked from his coffee table.

Who is this? I asked.

My sister, he told me. I adore her, he said and stood up and asked me to leave. I am worried sick about Checkers, he explained. One time, we had to revive him with smelling salts after an extended stay in a five-star hotel. It was weeks before I felt clean, he said.

The light just then caught the picture —

Later, I would move in with Lafitte, and he would finish this story.

In his story, this is the ending, more or less: And when the light hit the glass, she saw that it was smeared with thousands of oily fingerprints!

And that was true — but Bobby and I did not quite end there, or when he told me the truth about his love for Sharona, or even when I finally gave in to Lafitte, a mistake that was my Alamo.

I went out drinking with a girlfriend, and Bobby showed up at the bar. He was with a famous filmmaker and we all did shots of tequila, and Lafitte, I would discover, was walking back and forth outside in the rain.

Bobby and I split a cab. I am not allowed to talk to you anymore, I told him. He pulled me deep into the red velveteen seat and kissed my face off.

Let me know when *that* changes, he said, and pulled me back into the car when I got up to go; another rain of lavish kisses.

When Lafitte left I wrote Bobby right away, anxious at that time to connect with all the men I had pushed away, out of love, or fear.

He wrote me a note so short and terse I felt like it was a communiqué intended for one of Tito's dangerous enemies.

A Panamanian drug lord, maybe, who likes to get high, stroke his belly, and shout at his minions, Oye! Gimme tha number of that chica, you remember, muchacha attractiva!

I was trying to let him know I was available, and may as well have shown him short, devastating films of myself trying on expensive clothes in well-lit changing rooms.

But you told me to let you know! I wanted to write. My understanding of the past is different than everyone else's now, because it is all that I have and the newer parts are like a horror comic I read once, but that is another story.

He was called Bobby Clarke because he played hockey in his youth, violently and well.

YOU EXPECT MORE FROM THEM

My cousin Yoko, a soignée intellectual living on Park Avenue in Montreal, between Crémazie and Chabanel, handed me a spliff and said this.

Finding the boyfriend cheating, well that is hard, kiddo. But with your best friend? I mean, she said, stroking her tabby-streaked hair with her sharp, shapely nails. One expects so much more from one's girlfriends.

Yoko is twenty years older than me. When I was seventeen, she was so lucid and strong, I tended to shrink in her presence.

She would pick me up in her Jag, and we would flash through the city as she assailed me with questions.

Are you hungry? For what? Tapas? Dim sum? A hearty Polish sausage? She would drum her fingers on the wheel as I watched a gale of wind tenderly lift her long silk scarf.

Um, I would stall, thinking of the few steak dinners my family had gone out for at the Ponderosa, on special occasions.

I like sandwiches, I finally told Yoko, which led to a barrage of new questions, and, finally, a grilled Red Leicester cheese on sourdough bread that I still remember, and miss.

Yoko would curl up on her red velvet club chair and, as I got more and more stoned, tell me about art and poetry and politics, occasionally getting up to pull a book or object from a shelf.

The showy curve of a painted apple, a doll from Moscow, a shoebox filled with her dead lover's ashes.

I told her about the cruel cinephile I was seeing. He hits me, I said. Oh, never let him do that! she said. Never let a man touch you!

Yoko was like the older sister I never had, and I lived for her advice and kindness. My home life was difficult, and she blasted that all away with her extravagant compliments — You are like a young tigress! — and gestures: Here's a stack of fifties. Have fun!

My mother was less compassionate, it seemed.

I never confided in her, and she treated all my boyfriends with the same cool indifference.

When I confessed that one had left me, she threw his only novel, unread, into the trash and said, You have made my day.

I feel terrible! I protested.

Sorry, she said. I just can't stand the fact that he gave your father a Speedo for Christmas.

I would come to venerate my mother for her remoteness, her cool.

When older friends would take a maternal interest in me, I would think, Yes, you are mother-ish. But can you scream, I'm on the warpath! and scatter a crowd?

And be genuinely stylish, in just an oversized T-shirt and head rag, holding an industrial-sized can of bug spray?

I recently saw Yoko in Montreal, very briefly, and she was tense with me, speaking mostly to Frank.

O what if it gets colder and you are stuck outside with nothing on, not even a beanie? A beanie! she purred at him.

Everything is great, I told her, when she asked. She was pawing the hotel coffee table for her "critical documents," whatever they were.

I took in the violently coloured kimono on the hook, the shabby copy of *The Wretched of the Earth*, each succulent item in her toilette laid out like a small city of chrome and glass on the counter.

Thank you for saving me, I wanted to tell her, and did not.

Not too long after I told Yoko my secret, I went over to the cruel cinephile's place and knocked him down.

I broke my hand.

In the middle of the night, my mother changed the bandage and we sat at the kitchen table together, her tiny hand lost in mine.

He deserved this, she said.

He did, after all, quote Rex Reed at the dinner table.

I smiled at her as the snow hit the window and the night darkened into the nights I will miss her, all my life.

WITH LEGS INCOMPARABLE

This was long before she fell down, which took forever because of her height and good, shapely gams that go on for miles.

There is the middle and it is comparable to a many-storied building before the wiring — held together with silver duct tape and bald splices — blows. Comparable to all the people living inside the units, and their families and pets and flatware and shoes and mittens and photographs, and all the people in the photographs standing in crowds or below huge monuments, waving at people taking photographs in a group, or on a grassy hill swelling from the Earth as it pulsates in the Universe among fierce stars and speedy meteors.

And before that, Nora walked down my street, in an abbreviated silver dress, stockings, and high black boots, causing a small commotion because she is that beautiful — ladybugs are moved, for example, to assemble in patterns on the spangles of the dress. They cluster in poppies, a bolus of pink opium, and the lips of a tenor singing "O Sole Mio." Her eyes are not visible beneath her large, black glasses, but I know they are great, tensile coneflowers called the Green Envy. She is smiling lazily as she bangs on the door, and I freeze, then let her in.

THE FOREST

On a rainy fall night, Margaux and I went to an art show about the end of the world.

The exhibits were spread over a number of vacant lots: there were boxes filled with tin cans that damp, angry children were throwing at each other.

Is that art? we kept asking.

An old man passed out, twitching, about ten feet from the installation. Art?

He was cradling a bottle of Listerine; his lips were ocean blue. The exhibit beside him was called *Hobo Utopia,* in which there were sausages and hot chocolate, and a lot of kindling.

He dreamed until I slapped him awake and made him walk until he could do a passable Mashed Potato. Shake that moneymaker! he and I yelled.

A white beam of light pulsed WE ARE SORRY in Morse code, and a few, enormous construction cranes were dancing, moving their articulated parts slowly across the steel girders and full white moon.

People in giant paper bags crowded around us and apologized also.

We had wanted to see *The Forest*, which was billed as a spectacle of recycled metal parts and a galaxy of lights. We were talking about steel trees glittering with frost and blackly banded together, carving the light into ghosts.

It was by the train tracks, in a field, on a scorched part of the grass.

It was an aluminum trailer, with some trees cut in its interior. Overhead, there was the sound of hammers. The plaque suggested we would "emerge back into another part of the city."

It took less than a minute to walk through the trailer and out, to nowhere new: the same officious volunteers with clipboards milling around, the same lonesome train bearing down, then away.

I started to wonder what other things I had missed while seeking out truth and beauty.

Margaux writes me letters from the Yukon.

She went to a museum and saw a stuffed fox. The night before, she'd seen a red fox's tail twitch, then dart like a flare. This happens a lot, she writes, seeing the same things, dead and living.

Hegel imagines beauty and truth as a compound, beginning when a caveman carved a little bison out of wood and did not pop it in his mouth.

She tells me that she is painting animals: a dog called the Miracle, and a basket of baby animals she is holding, fiercely, to her chest.

She has painted me without a shirt on, holding Frankie on a chair in the middle of a lake. I call the first study *Heaven*, and move it around my house, from nail to nail, restless to live inside of it.

Most days, I realize I have used up all of my love and feel resigned.

Or warm and contented — this fall, in the gold light and leaves, slowly detaching — with the love I have already had, and so much of it.

There would have been owls in The Forest, diving for scurrying creatures. Their eyes would have been made out of segments of egg carton; their feathers, scraps of owl-coloured paper.

A man walked by me today and I caught a bit of what he was yelling: It is a bakery now, Lord Antonio, what was once a verdant 7-Eleven! A bakery where the social workers may procure their precious pastries and muffins!

There are cloth cobwebs on many of the porches. Dolls, beheaded and suspended upside down. Small and huge pumpkins, some of them with wide mouths barfing seeds and guts.

The girl across the street is moving. The Two Guys And A Van are parked outside. Last night, I watched her take pictures of the fat little shrub on her lawn that bursts into a bright red fire each fall.

I bring her a bottle of tequila, and she shows me around and gives me her fiddle-leaf fig tree.

I wave awkwardly as I cross the street. I did not know her well, but it was nice thinking that she was there, writing or bouncing on the tiny trampoline I saw in her study, by the circle in the carpet where the tree was — Rachel, I named it after her, and the minute I put it down it began crying its leaves off.

The Forest intimates everything I have wasted as I stood, watching rabbits and moles dart past, plastic shopping bags on tripwires.

Other allusions: a galaxy of plastic diapers that have been rinsed in grey water, a field of plastic water bottles painted emerald-black.

A hole you might fall into, beyond the eggshells and rancid vegetables and green bread, then emerge again, in an inverted world of steel.

It was The Forest we could not see that told us about truth and beauty, and many of us missed it.

When Margaux is away, I miss her. My friend who stands like a Crimson King Maple in The Forest we imagined, where she would explain photosynthesis so earnestly she would catch fire and cool in the dark rain and then be golden.

She is the light that lowers sweetly in the fall to break the blow of sad endings.

STILL THE DAINTIEST

Your book is too small, the Grindhouse's publisher tells me.

We publish books that are fleet, muscular Olympians. Books that leap from the shelves at the sound of a firing pistol and race to the finish line, where they collect substantial monies and golden medals set in lush velvet bands.

A book like this, he says, pushing it across the table at me. Well, it simply won't hear the gun, let alone give its hamstrings a damn stretch!

Ha ha! he laughs. Ha!

My book is small, he is right.

I keep it in a little house I made, long ago when I was a visual artist, taking a course in furniture making.

It is a replica of Ed Gein's house in Plainfield, Wisconsin.

A pair of miniature lips opens and closes the blinds in the living room; on the table, made with pieces of my own skin, lies a shoebox containing nine radish vulvas.

The book is on the shelf — a finger bone, mounted with knotted hair — beside a glass bowl filled with smoking liquid and a filleting knife.

It was Ed Gein's idea to call my book *Blood on the Gizmo*. I mean the figure I made of him — in a hunting cap, gumboots, and peach-coloured caftan.

Which gets to walking the floors and shouting advice I can rarely make out.

Life is a bowl of cherries!, he might snap. It starts out sweet and then it's the pits!

No one says "the pits" anymore, Ed Gein doll, I tell him.

I am putting you in the cellar, I say. His lips tremble and then he flat out wails when I toss him inside, and he bumpity-bumps down the stairs.

Later I hear him bang at the door, pleading, and I throw a blanket over the whole mess and shelve it.

No one wants to know what happens to people long deprived of touch and love.

It is far too disgusting — this morning, I looked deeply into the publisher's eyes as he laughed, and I laughed too.

I let my bandaged hand crawl across the table onto his sleeve and light there as my soul clawed helplessly at its restraints.

I'LL KEEP HOLDING ON

Tyler came over one night, just before Valentine's Day. I met him at the door.

I was holding his present in a little Chanel bag.

Blanketed in white tissue and ribbon: a tube of deep-red "Vamp" lipstick and a palette of the Coco-revival gold eyeshadow. He was my Michael Jackson friend and I liked to draw him wearing these colours, floating in an emerald sea on a silver inner tube.

When he arrived he was holding mannequin legs and arms and crying.

I can't do this anymore! he sobbed.

Are you joking? I asked as he began stacking the body parts in my foyer.

Take these back... please! he shrieked. I had given him the vintage baby girl and mature woman mannequins some time ago. He dressed them as Cher and Chastity, and offered them cocktails in the evening, and made light party chatter with them.

I need to call my mother! I can't... I can't do this! he said again, before bolting away.

That was awful, I told the man I was dating, who came by out of the blue to give me a box of Ferrero Rochers on which he had written TO: *Delicious Lady! FROM: Guess Who?* in leaky ballpoint.

That is fucked up! he agreed as I stood there, the black bag dangling from my fingers, my mouth an O of shock.

You want me to go beat him with them doll legs? he asked, distracting me with his good heart.

For two years, I avoided even passing Tyler and his husband's street, and when I thought of him, I would flinch. He had seen me at my very lowest and worst.

For example, one night, I went out in my pyjamas and scored crack and made him smoke it with me, then pull my belly-button ring out with pliers: I was getting so fat, the whole thing must have looked like an outlandish carnival game.

Years ago, I was his English professor. He used to call and ask, Dr. Crosbie, may I have an extension?

I had long since been demoted to the writing workshop, where I would arrive in the morning smelling, more often than not, like sweet smoke and dressed in rubber boots, a variety of large black jackets and a skirt so stretchy my refrigerator could wear it as a tube top.

Grammar, I would tell my students, cannot be taught. You need to absorb it, through reading. Read this, I would say, handing them *Penthouse Letters* or *Guns & Ammo*. Circle the most striking punctuation in remarks like this: "Her milk kegs were huge; however, they were not the biggest chebs I had ever seen!"

The semicolon before the conjunctive adverb is perfection; the exclamation point a daring gesture. "Cunjunktiv" and "Darring," I noticed my Persian student write in her sketch pad filled with drawings of rainbows and dolphins.

I have anal cancer, I would whisper sometimes, to make them leave so I could cry and wonder when, exactly, I had stopped being able to cross my legs or put on socks while standing up.

Tyler was the last friend I had other than the man I'd been

dating (who was killed by a speeding bus), a couple of junkies, and the dealer I was falling in love with.

I'd often wanted to write Tyler and ask him what had happened, but I couldn't. His husband, who manages several busy Red Lobsters, called me, instead, not too long ago.

Tyler is sorry, he said.

Tyler would like to be friends again.

I said okay. I am sober now, and I feel I look better. Mannish, with hair that looks, as my two pretty students said, Like you got gum in it? But better.

And he started writing me again, about his new job as a porn film fluffer and stylist (I'm living in the "Thong Song!"); about his workouts and continued devotion to MJ, to projecting "You Are Not Alone" on his wall and freeze-framing Michael's cock when it peeks out from the towel.

So I thought of him when I got press tickets to *This Is It* from the *Homeless News*, a paper I write poems for, using the name Sister Freefire & L.O.V.E!

We went together and sat in the first row.

The critics for the big papers were in the back and did not make a sound for the whole film.

I was worried about how bad I felt, and scared.

When MJ sang "I'll Be There," tears started rolling down my face and Tyler took my hand and held it tight.

I want to fuck him so badly, he whispered.

Me too, I said. Our hands sent messages back and forth about regret and forgiveness before letting go.

On the screen, Michael Jackson had wandered onto a riser and was singing like a diffident angel: *I like living this way.*

THE GLORY OF LOVE

ONE.

I pushed Lucy down and she landed hard, on the gravel, on her knees. I baptized her with the sludge water of the Mississippi.

Her short red hair swallowed the sun. The way it looked burned into me: it is an apostrophe after "the pretty girl with the luminous skin" and "the collar of diamonds on the neck of the slender doe."

I met her when I first came to Toronto from Montreal. She was living with my only friend, Misha, in an old candy factory: they bathed in a laundry sink and roller skated around to the songs we all liked, *When you're all alone and lonely* —

She agreed to meet me for a drink, and I stood and waited not too far from where I live now, except I was filled with joy then, and hope, and there she was, loping west toward me, and my heart jumped.

She was born with crazy legs: she showed me a picture of her as a little girl, underneath the Christmas tree in a full body cast, presents piled up around her.

She was slender and stylish, with big violet eyes and freckles making a starry night of her pale skin. We would walk and talk; eventually, a bunch of us formed a club we named after a sign we saw for a huge bingo excursion, The Super Nevada.

In my favourite picture of us, we are so young our cheeks are fat and our hair is as glossy as the pelts of strange, beautiful animals. We were posing outside the Grand Ole Opry: later, we would go to the bar next door — where Hank Williams used to knock back shots, waiting on his set — and sing a song with the entertainment, a one-man band called Sherman Tank.

I think of the letter I would write her mother, if I could. Dear Mrs. ____. Do you remember visiting Lucy one summer and drinking with us at the Black Bull? You smoked Buckingham Flats and called gin "panty remover." Lucy was so easy with the unusual, the awkward: the clay figures she made for her animation were, to me, ugly and deformed, and I was so irritated with her the last time she showed up, *uninvited*, that I tossed the little painting she'd made me, a dull orange, banana-headed male nude. Who knows where!

What am I saying?

Dear Mrs. ____. Lucy and I always managed to get into trouble. I mean this in a good way! Over the last three years, when we managed to write, we always said, I miss those wild times! And that's about it because I didn't know her anymore, and she didn't know me.

I can't write that either.

The next-to-last time Lucy visited me, I was thin and smashing. She and I stayed up all night with two men I knew, doing rails, and much later, three of us went to my bed. I clung to the side of the mattress as they fooled around, and that is some of what I meant when those Got Junk? guys came and took my mattress away and I patted it and said, bleakly, A lot of memories.

But the last time, I had crashed. I was wide and angry and dressed in alternating black feedbags.

She was visiting indefinitely. Didn't she know I had things going on? Every day it was something else. I need paper! Where is a good copy place? I'm hungry!

Mind if I make some tea?

She offered to cook me dinner; that is, take all of my food and mash it together, then serve it as huge plates of what smelled like warm garbage while watching her demo reel of clay people living in clay castles cleverly making smaller clay people out of clay, who in turn were making clay elephants with clay howdahs and spraying the clay village with tiny clay peanuts.

Lend me your alarm clock!

I'm cold!

I ended up asking her to leave. I have to write my column, it is a matter of some urgency! Kirstie Alley has just been photographed eating gorditas from a *trough*!

I had just been hired by an up-and-coming website to write "Kirstie!", a regularly updated profile of the voluptuous *Cheers* star.

As soon as she left, I called Veronica and complained bitterly. I am a writer! Just because I don't work *in an office*, people think they can call me at all hours asking me for things. Lynn, I need money; Lynn, I hit an artery!

People are assholes, Veronica said, like she always does, and I glowed: our mean streaks were completely in synch.

When I look back, I see that I was ashamed that Lucy had found me this way: fat, alone, and going down fast. But that is an excuse, and does not excuse the way I acted.

The night I did try to rally, we went to my local, and one of my sister's friends was hosting a karaoke night.

I heckled him a bit, and he called me a cow. I lowered my head; I may have lowed. Cows have feelings, is what I was thinking at the time.

I felt like a cow tearing up the pasture because the grass tastes cold.

When Lucy left town again, she forgot to drop off my alarm clock. She said her friend, where she'd been staying down the street, couldn't. He had better, I said, or I'll go over and get it myself.

I waited two days and went over. His girlfriend answered, holding several expensive clocks. Take them all, she said.

I didn't speak to Lucy for years because of this.

Years!

The alarm was a chubby little digital Lafitte had given me. I was unreasonably attached to it.

Lucy and I loved a story in a *True Romance* comic we kept tacked to the wall of our apartment, called "THE SKAG!"

This story is about a girl with bad skin and greasy hair who is unpopular in high school. One day, she is daydreaming about a handsome boy riding toward her in a convertible, wearing cool shades and a billowing printed scarf.

Pardon me! the teacher snaps, unable to get the girl's attention.

The Skag's in a world of her own! the handsome quarterback says and the whole class laughs.

The girl moves to another city and lives with her older sister, and learns to manage her weight and take better care of her skin and hair; eventually, she is going to drive-ins and soda shops with this guy and that guy.

I am now The Skag, living in a different time-space continuum, where it will surely be possible to regard my luscious skin as the skin of the peach, to see myself in the arms or the crook of the elbow of one of the many men I have loved and lost. Any day now!

Dear Mrs. ____. Your son told me you are asking questions he has no answer for and I do not know if he is suggesting that you have memory loss or that you are philosophical by nature. That your little girl is gone and why should that be?

TWO.

Veronica wrote a simple letter to Mrs. ____. Lucy was so nice and filled with girlish mischief, she wrote above the gilt letters spelling In Deepest Sympathy.

Mrs.____ thanked her profusely, and Veronica called me. Well that just breaks my heart! she said cheerfully.

I wanted to start over. I would buy a proper card and write, in lavender script: Lucy changed me with her sunny smile.

This time, I would win.

THREE.

I have to go back and look for her last letter. It says: "hey girlfriend... miss you. trying to get to you soon. maybe before xmas we'll get up to no good and then you can write about it. love you and I know we've been shit keeping in touch. always in my thoughts darlin' kisses n smooch."

It was never complicated with Lucy, if she loved you.

I want this to be true, I want to be in her thoughts, always, like a bird on a silver branch, its eyes gilded with sleep.

FOUR.

We are making plans all the time, and we do not know we are making these plans.

I am heavy with the thought of your plans, Lucy, to be loved, to have children, all the creatures you wanted to make, and where you wanted to make them.

I keep trying to write your mother.

I wrote your brother, who sent me a picture of you smiling, your red hair clashing so well with a pile of red pillows.

And I asked out Veronica, Lil and Susan Chesterfield, who I have not talked to in years. The Super Nevada, more or less.

We are not friends anymore, not really, but we wanted to meet, for your sake, and we did, on a cold, bright Saturday morning. We went to Fresh and had lunch and Lil ordered the way that she does. Lucy, I wrote a little story for you about Lil ordering food at the Skyline:

I will have — do you, oh, do you have? I need. Some. A boiled, something boiled, a potato? I am frightened if they have black spots or sometimes big, green shoots like ha ha a thick potato beard, no, I am kidding. I know that they grow that way but *I don't want realism. I want magic!* What soda do you have I do not mean Pepsi no, Oh! A float that is what I want, I think I want to have that, could you use half the chocolate though, and warm the chocolate...could you put the chocolate in a separate, warm glass, and heat the spoon and I am not sure what malted milk is, is it a skim milk? If one is chilly and the other is warm, it can be very nice. I am...I think I would like you to come back and then I will probably ask for a saucer of coleslaw, with no mayonnaise if that is possible, and a spoonful of chocolate powder, and a thimble of some game meat like venison or bear —

When she and Veronica sat down, I saw that they were both very thin, and wore bifocals. Lil's were pink diamanté cat's-eyes; Veronica's were a no-nonsense black, rooted in a horseshoe of grey hair.

Side by side, they could have been sisters. Veronica looked like the mean one, the tax accountant who did Lil's return every year, snorting, I told you to get a file folder!

They looked at the menu, and then they talked for a long time about the weather while peering down their noses and murmuring,

Isn't that something, fresh arugula in the autumn!

Susan Chesterfield came late, in a silver jacket and tight jeans, looking the same, but not, like she was a badly fabricated version of herself.

We used to go to Niagara Falls every summer, when we were young, and raise hell. Lucy had moved by then, but the rest of us would walk the strip, always cresting at the Criminals Hall of Fame. Inside there are a variety of criminals with bloated faces and coarse horsehair, staring balefully from behind bars.

That is what I mean: Susan looked trapped. We all did, like we'd eaten our young selves and were having difficulty digesting.

When we were teenagers, Susan Chesterfield used to walk over to my house in her pyjamas almost every night, and we would draw how we would look when we were old.

We drew our faces, then added horizontal and vertical wrinkles. I like wrinkles, she or I would say: they are like ritualized scars, signifying maturity and wisdom. Pretty young girls with some heart say these kinds of stupid things all the time.

We could afford to be generous because we had no idea that such lines are a mere flourish: that age is like the boy that vigilant Italian fathers are terrified of, the one who will ruin their daughters, who will disfigure them and take away their honour.

Lucy aged better than us all: she filled out and grew her hair past her shoulders; her eyes deepened into aquamarine.

I was ordering a salad called "Jerusalem" when I realized that I had not sat in a room with these women since — while holed up in the back room of Veronica's summer cottage — I wrote a poem about drowning them. I would have liked to elbow you, Lucy, and roll my eyes.

I listened politely to Susan Chesterfield tell stories about her expensive dental work, hassles with her renovator, and a fantastic play she saw. I was moved to tears, she says. I was so surprised!

We had all gone to that cottage together eight years ago. In the car on the way up, the three of them talked about *Confessions of a Shopaholic*: I know it's not *Shakespeare*, Susan Chesterfield said, but it's so funny! In one part, she explained, the Shopaholic tries to buy a low-cal lunch after purchasing these amazing emerald-green suede Christian Louboutin pumps and a rich brown wool Prada suit, and her card is declined by a former Nicaraguan guerilla whose ear was damaged by a bayonet. She orders samosas!

She'd laughed and talked until we all had a fight: she told Veronica that her husband had probably left her because he didn't love her, and Veronica countered that she was a lazy, imperious pain in the ass arrayed on her tiger towel all day ordering drinks and snacks with snaps of her fingers.

Lil stayed out of it and sat quietly painting rocks to look like kittens, adding rolling eyes and pipe-cleaner whiskers with a glue stick she kept in her arts and crafts satchel.

I never said a thing, just seethed as we all drove home from Crystal Lake in malevolent silence. When I developed the pictures I had taken, I exhibited them at a papusa restaurant as the *Sexxifulicious Bitches*.

At Fresh, we asked a stranger to take our picture, and recoiled from the image.

I'm ugly, Susan Chesterfield said. None of us disagreed.

And when I said I did not want to walk through the park, that I wanted to leave, she said, Well, that was *shit*. Veronica and Lil just said goodbye, offering small, brisk hugs.

Lucy, you used to hug me so hard I stopped breathing; I cried every time we said goodbye.

Goodbye!

I walked and met a blind, angry dog named Watson and a shy dog named Felix. I bought Japanese paper, red gel pens, and irises.

Veronica had acted like your death clarified everything.

I was never going to speak to you again, she'd said. But what does any of this—she gestured vaguely—matter?

We were intent on doing the right thing, I realize. But when we met, no one mentioned your name. We are so guarded with one another that it would have hurt to disarm ourselves.

Even to say something when Susan said out loud that she was ugly. Like, Me too.

You, Lucy, would have said, Get the fuck out of here! You're beautiful! And then we would have taken off on them.

You were always up for anything. You came with me to see the Village People in a raunchy gay bar long before they crossed over as camp; we went to a lecture by René Lévesque, who was quite stirringly insolent.

We would walk slowly around the city at night and get high and watch U of T students play the cello from the lawn, or sneak into the grounds of Casa Loma and lie by the castle and talk so quietly: we talked like the rustle of grass.

I miss you, Lucy, and I miss having a friend. I am so sorry.

Ten years ago, I bought a leather jacket from you. It had belonged to your friend who killed himself. You were reluctant to give it up, but you needed the money. It was hanging by my hamster Honey's cage and she methodically shredded its red silk lining. I gave it back to you the last time I saw you because I never felt right for having taken it away.

Do you see, do you see that I am not completely horrible?

I know that your brother cleaned out your apartment and tossed that jacket, and I wonder if someone is wearing it, if they feel the zipper as my cold hands, and smell, faintly, turpentine and lavender and see the glorious red mess my little girl made.

Almost everything worth living for is gone: gone to where we were before we were born, I tell Frank, and his Asiatic eyes drink this news in, like a miracle about a god taking milk from a bowl.

I do love you, I do.

FIVE.

Dear Mrs. ____. I emptied every box in the basement, and there it was, her painting. The orange man in profile, pensive against a bright purple background. Painted in her unique style — think Modigliani if he had made cartoons — by my dear friend, who spent all her dreamy days bent over a sketchbook or cel or computer, as all the colours of the spectrum flowed through her and left such lustrous impressions.

When I heard the news I thought of a big, goofy dog I loved, who was always knocking things over with his happy, wagging tail. One day he ran in front of a car and I watched all the joy bleed from his eyes.

And then his ears pricked up, one last time. Maybe he would be okay, is what he thought.

SIX.

Your brother told me he held your hand and you squeezed back, hard.

This was before the machines took over.

The machines taking over is what we were afraid of, as children.

Not what has happened, which is being alone.

This is what happened today and I want to tell you it, Lucy, and then I want to stop telling you things this way.

I got up early and it was the first snow, just little, loose flakes.

I put on ugly thermal boots and a gigantic parka and went out and got on a streetcar. I was listening to music on shuffle and one of Steve's songs came on, a Ministry of Love song that they entered into a radio contest in the 1980s.

It has a New Wave vibe, and a number of vocal intensifiers like "Hey!" and "Whoa-ho-ho."

Still, it is a good song, and I remembered, suddenly, being with him and calling the station all night, voting for them.

They lost.

I started singing along on the streetcar, which made the handsome Egyptian man beside me start shifting miserably.

And I walked quickly to Steve's plaque, beneath the little tree that is a bit bigger now, and it was very cold. Even the old man who sits on the bench behind the tree, singing swanky songs of love during wartime, was gone.

I thought of the man singing to me, the previous summer, about a girl he called Barb the Kraut. "She is all I thought of, even as we crawled through the mud / she was realer to me than guts or blood."

When Steve was in Trans Love Airways, he sang a song called "I Think the World Is Coming True," about him and me.

I played that: his vocals are butter-soft, his phrasing slow and patient. Content with the idea that he is right.

That he will not fall on the floor ten years later, clutching his heart, and never get up again.

I think of him smiling in his sleep, and reaching for me. Oh no, I moan, and run. I get into a taxi and tell the driver, For some of us there is only the past and that is hard to live with.

As I am saying this he interrupts and says, Left here? Or right?

I saw so many attractive men and women today: no one saw me.

I did not see you either, Lucy, in the park, on the street we walked so many times, in the trail of my tears that turned the land into a wild, snaking river.

It may be because I am barely alive, and when I go, I won't leave a single thing behind.

You leave the clay people and animals and dragons, masses of electric love: I got to feel that, surging through you.

We will start our crooked walk through the darkness, and you will start everything from the beginning by striking a star.

LIFE WITH BILLY JOEL

We are always at cross-purposes, talking at each other, listening, in our own way.

On a typical night, he will tell me, again, about writing his songs, and I will recall the mordant details of my day.

Today, he is baking when I come in, cold and very tired. I've just taught my Sentence Fragments in Popular Culture class, which went fairly well, discounting the many times I approached the screen to touch the images.

Billy Joel is taking trays of gingerbread out of the oven, nodding and humming. He is wearing bifocals and his tufted silver hair is matted; his little concert T-shirt rides his hard, round belly.

Come here, Scribbles, he says, opening his arms. He has a number of sweet nicknames for me: Pink Lady, Word Worm, Four Eyes, Goofball, and the Vast, Fathomless Tenderness.

He writes the latter on the little cards that accompany the flowers he sends me when he is touring; he uses it in conversations, as in, Don Henley! Please get the Vast, Fathomless Tenderness a drink, and step on it!

I let him hug me, then break away.

It is hard to write about Billy Joel and me. Because it is private, because no one needs to know how it is when Anthony says, go ahead with your own life, leave me alone.

Anthony is a metaphor, he will say.

People are afraid, mostly. They want to escape their pasts and start over.

Who needs a house up in Hackensack? Billy Joel sings, absent-mindedly, as he draws bricks on the gingerbread. He is making a replica of his childhood house in Hicksville. Yesterday he cooked and shaped his family, and me.

But I wasn't there, I protested.

Really, Lynn, you surprise me sometimes, he said.

He is chronically disappointed in my lack of imagination.

During the slide show I gave my class today I closed my eyes: This is me, I thought, and my friends at a club on St. Laurent and we are hearing "London Calling" for the first time; that is my hand in Carol's — there are snakes on our wrists, griffins; this is us, later, lying together on a long table at the stripper's place and the stripper says, Oh such exotic beauty!

That is the way one young man smelled, like cedar and salt; this is how his silky black hair fell like a wave in the middle of the ocean where I got shipwrecked —

What did you really show them? asks Billy Joel, who is now sitting with the cats on his lap, our two cats and three I have never seen before.

Michael's injuries, I say. Michael in a heaving white shirt, raising his arms; Michael making devil horns with his fingers and climbing out onto the roof of a car, Michael —

You still miss him, he says.

It's not that, I say.

I just think of him and dream of him sometimes, I say.

Tell me about it, he says.

I do:

The night I fell in love with Michael, he said: I will never leave you.

He wrote this on every box he packed: *I am never coming back.*

And I have been alone ever since.

Like this? he asks, mauling my neck with his rough beard.

I turn around.

Voilà! says Billy Joel, and I shake away the clouds. He is holding out a tray and smiling.

The house — now spackled with jellybeans and gumdrops — is done!

THE DEMON

There were strange noises, in the wall, by the old bassinet.

The number 7, written on the mirror with soap.

Someone yelling but no one was there.

I dreamed of a man firing up a chainsaw, then a voice said *Fucking bitch* right in my ear.

I feel that someone killed himself in this house, I said. I always have.

The corners of my mouth split open, lesions formed.

I coughed and spit blood into the sink.

It was a sleeping sickness, punctuated by shrieks and slams.

I listened to loud music to drown out the television, the persistent buzzing underneath all the episodes of *Two and a Half Men*.

There was a cello playing as a woman kept saying, Charlie, why didn't you call me?

Then the dryer alarm started going off every ten minutes.

White spots appeared on my tongue. The thrush laid a clutch of speckled eggs.

Someone is always at the door. No one is ever there.

It is ice cold, then blazing hot.

There are strange and hurtful admonishments, outright insults:

Shut up. You're an asshole, a total asshole. Spoken through my loved ones!

All the underwear has disappeared by the shameful looks of it, bras also.

The liquor is also vanishing, by fingers, then inches.

Every day I chip another piece of the frozen red soup away and boil it.

The door to the utility room opens and closes; someone says, Who is that? Hello?

My white dog in the snow, cringing. The crows follow us from tree to tree.

My father arrives in a black overcoat and fedora, holding a bag of tangerines.

I am sleeping and my mother walks in and yells, Why are you so unhappy?

The Demon says, in red, dripping paint, I want you gone.

I take a taxi with Francis, downtown. The driver, Anubis Frechette, watches me thoughtfully, his sleepy eyes outlined in black.

We check into the Chateau Versailles and spend the next three days walking along Sherbrooke Street.

The trees are laced with white light.

I leave a cookie for the ant I see in the bathroom. In ten minutes, the cookie is black with ants.

Outside, the snow presses down, glazing a map onto the windows. Below the equator are ghosts, roasting animals in the surf. Above, exactly across the street, are the windows of my first apartment, where I lived with the cruel cinephile.

The white blinds are drawn.

I consider my seventeen-year-old self living there, hanging my clothes up, and putting my shoes away.

If I threw a stone, I could hit her.

Maybe I could kill the fucking bitch.

THE ART OF DYING

I flew to London on my birthday, years ago, when Billy and I lived in a basement apartment in Little Italy with our two cats.

The house was beautiful: Donovan's family had passed it down to him, so he could sit around all day, painting wooden chairs. He would paint the slats purple and green, then upholster the seats in fur.

Some nights he would go off with a guitar case, and on those nights his wife, Heifer, would stampede in wooden clogs.

I cannot think of these people without wanting to see them again, after drinking drugged milk, and commit ultraviolence against them with a knife and chain.

I was worried about Billy and left him a Japanese notebook to fill. I began it for him, writing, Be nice to the cats. Feed yourself, beware of fires and evil. Start your novel. Be careful. Lock up. Chin up. Be v. careful!!!

Now I say similar things to Francis and the cats when I go out — with much less anxiety, as I have never seen them tying off and jacking heroin from a blackened spoon while pretending to be taking a bubble bath. They have not disappeared for two days with their boss at Value Village, a vile-tempered transvestite named Myrna Loy.

They do not crash at my girlfriends' houses after emptying their liquor cabinets and asking to try on their bras and panties.

Like that.

He continued the journal. I would get intimations of what was in it when I called, and he whispered about taping plastic sheets on the stairs, then howled in pain.

I saw Westminster Abbey and Cleopatra's Needle; I stood outside a pub in Dublin and calculated the space between me and Billy, across the ocean, maybe listening to Heifer squealing; maybe starting his novel about Godzilla's inner life, based on the writings of André Breton; maybe dead.

Don't be dead.

Everything was fine when I came home. He met me at the airport and gave me the journal. We played with our cats, and I gave them squeaky Oscar Wildes.

I am sitting with the journal now. The heavy construction continues on my street; another house is being gutted, a townhouse is going up. The property owner wrote me a letter about his vision: "Privacy is very important, and we will also be installing trees, and other landscape materials throughout the property." The letter came with a box of chocolates in cellophane and a gigantic pine cone.

It is bitterly cold and the Napkin Man was at the variety store today, buying a stack of pornography and ten packages of serviettes. He licked his lips and moved his change around the counter interminably.

I said to him, You make me sick with your dirty . . . napkins! and he scuttled around, protesting.

In the journal, Billy is reading Kenneth Patchen's love poems and cutting up old encyclopedias for images: a hooded executioner; a fallen man at the foot of a flight of stairs, papers all around him; a page from *The Art of Dying*.

Later, he will find a cache of gay pornography behind the furnace and glue in some images of men with long hair and Afros licking and kissing each other.

At the same time the entries will have become tiny, and crabbed. There are references to "a frightening, bizarre occurrence," and "what I found in the air ducts!"

When I left for my trip, my tabby cats did not take it well, apparently, and started scratching Billy when he petted them. "They are acting really weird," reads an entry from the first day. "Hostile. Marv claws and bites me when I try to pet him, Jerome just pulls away."

The days pass, and he begins to address his entries directly to me, always sweetly fluid on the topic of "your pretty face, and odd questions and long legs," of missing me.

These effusions are cramped between a story about his father excluding him from a family photograph; the news that his grandfather is dying ('Shit"); and an account of his ex-fiancée, who he calls "Patti Pigtits," showing up where he works as a dishwasher to mock him.

He brought my bike in for company and translated Ovid: "My bed hopeless and hard, coverlet and blanket fallen to the floor . . . Am I attacked by Love?"

He writes that he is worried the cats are suffering from "separation anxiety" and buys them Pounce, and changes their litter every day. He admires "courageous women" and wonders if I am flirting with "some handsome sea bass."

Almost a week in, the cats attacked. Then, Billy "caught both fuckheads pissing jauntily at the top of the stairs. The piss is drooling into your closet for Crissakes." He used a hanger to push them away and they screamed so loudly, Donovan came down and threatened to call the police.

Billy cleaned the stairs, and the closet, then covered my clothes with the tarps. "Both my hands are deeply gouged," he writes. He goes on, about "stench" and "plotting"; that "they know!" Over this sequence is pasted a drawing of a medieval Hell Mouth.

"I can't take much more," he writes.

He would just cry when I called, and whisper, They're coming, or, Don't tell them —

The entries become happier; Billy changes tack. The cats broke several lamps and busts and Billy says, of the aftermath, that he refused to be angered and instead sat them down for a real talk.

"I was quite surprised," he observes, "to discover how un-fulfilled they feel without careers. Marv wanted to be a carpenter at first, but Jerome and I broke out laughing at him. Jerome wants to be a sailor. We'll find out when he has to scrub his first deck! He says, Nothing to it. Tomorrow I'm going to let him scrub up his own piss. He's eager enough. I think he's splashing the deck right now! A trooper!"

They worked out an agreement. The cats would use my bike to get groceries and Billy would cook: "It's gonna take some time," he muses. "But it's something we all want."

Then the writing falters: he is sleeping a lot, hungry. A friend has taken him out for a salad and soup. "It feels good to eat," he writes.

But he cannot traverse the distance, he says, between him and the world; he cannot "speak well or move." "I feel isolated and dead," he says. The illustrations have stopped: "I can't see people. I feel very sick. Come home," he adds in wobbly letters.

At this point I had been gone eleven days and would be home in three. "I can't find the piss," he writes. "It's everywhere."

The cats ran away, he told me when I called. The beautiful girl I was travelling with looked up from her sewing and reminded me that every time I saw her there was a calamity at home.

I didn't see it that way. It was more that Billy was having a hard

time; that we were consumed with anxiety for each other, with love.
Love that is an egg we passed between each other, small and pale blue.

"I am paralyzed," he writes, the day I was coming home.

The cats were fine when I got back. I was concerned, though, because everything we owned was covered with garbage bags, including the flatware and lamps, and in three days Billy cut his wrists and ended up in a mental institution.

He kept on missing me, through the gap in the journal and when it resumed. Even as I sat with him, in the common room, with the old man in pyjamas performing "That's Life."

The old man made up crazy lyrics, of course — "I've been a pedo, a pyro, a pinko, a pygmy, some plonk and a prick!" — and we were strong and we were lucky, so we laughed: I loved him through all of this and then some.

A trooper!

LIFE IS ABOUT LOSING EVERYTHING

When I started to get sick, I could barely move.

I just watched Frank adjust himself beside me with Gitmo, a stuffed, buck-toothed green pepper, and read *Jacko* by Darwin Porter, which appears to be a pen name.

Darwin Porter may be an obscene raconteur, but he is an amazing fabulist, and during this time, when my life flatlined and the doctor let his mask fall like a crappy necklace and the nurse tsk tsk'd, Porter managed to offend and excite me.

I want to thank him, then kick his ass.

In an early scene, Michael is backstage with Mr. Wonderful, who raves, Outtasite, baby! and pumps his hand until Sinatra interrupts and says, Listen, faggot. You sing okay, even though it's just a bunch of goddamned noise! Then Mike Tyson says something eloquent and punches all of the Nation of Islam bodyguards until the room is filled with stars and circles of little yellow birds.

Michael then has dinner with Mae West and Liberace. Liberace keeps making reference to the vast pipe organ in his living room, and saying, Goodness, your skin-tight jeans make me horny!

Then Mae West says, in accented Arabic, You stole the moonwalk from the cakewalk.

Michael goes home and rapes his python, Muscles, and Justin Timberlake calls and says he has Burl Ives on the extension. They sing "How He Makes Me Quiver" for Michael, then start fighting about who invented leather chaps.

Michael starts to cry. It is always like this, he is a very sad and lonely man. Girls, he tells a reporter, want to get close to me and *share* my loneliness. Not change it.

Last night, I started rereading the book and highlighting large sections. By several asterisks, I write "cf., *Memoir of My Nervous Illness*."

I wonder if Darwin Porter is clinically insane, or more like Henry Darger, an outsider artist with catholic tastes.

Most of the people he talks about are dead, or ruined.

I want to pay him to tell a story of mine, in his inimitable way:

When I was a child, I spent a lot of time with my dad.

I liked being with him because he was so quiet and so nice.

He bought me a balloon one day, signed by Fess Parker and Bambi Lee Savage. It slipped out of my fingers and we watched it scaling buildings, then clouds.

My dad bought me another one from a man who was trembling, because Johnny Weissmuller had just called him a *maudit tapette!* while swinging by on a vine.

We went to see his mother, my grandmother, who has been dead for thirty years now.

I stood on her porch and watched the Rockettes for a while, and once more, the balloon slipped away.

My grandmother, who called me Pussycat and bought me illustrated histories of Canada and expensive, age-inappropriate jewellery, including an intricate tiara and gold cymbal-rings, started yelling.

She yelled at me for losing the balloon and she yelled at my father for spoiling me. I had never heard her raise her voice: her love was like a little tree-house or snow-fort.

I hid under her bed all day.

Michael Jackson had to talk me into rolling out. He held out his hand and smiled so delectably I wanted to remove all his teeth, cover them with confectioner's sugar, and carry them around in a small paper bag.

It's just a mistake, he beamed.

In the car with my dad, I looked and my hand was spotted white and black like a cow. I kissed my hand, and Zero Mostel drove by with Megan Fox and they wolf-whistled and my dad and I cracked up.

These days, I see Michael standing in the middle of a wheat field, extending his arms. Everything he has lost takes the form of ascending black crows.

He is smiling, without warmth, because he is tired and has had enough.

The stewardesses who flew with him and his children all the time wrote, in his Passenger Profile, "Very timid flyer but will get out of his seat during takeoff and landing."

They noted also that he ate huge platters of KFC for breakfast, lunch, and dinner while removing the skin from his children's chicken and refusing them sugar or the spray-butter he liked.

It goes by so fast, he said, when he turned fifty. There is a point where you can see how little you are leaving behind, and how fast what is left will catch up with you.

One time he was on a plane and a girl got on and saw him and stopped and stared as a dark circle of urine slowly appeared on her jeans.

It is Saturday again, and I am alone, and one of these days, I will be gone.

I won't leave you, I tell Frank, on one of our many moonlight walks in the slush.

The last time Frank and I went on a trip, it was hard for me to let them take him away. Take care of him, I called after the porter.

He's all that I have!

His absence would be the last piece in a pure white puzzle.

The way that loss takes shape: there is Van Gogh's *Wheat Field with Crows.*

The skies are roiling with black clouds and birds, rushing from the centre, birds I take aim at with a crossbow.

In the book Michael Jackson calls Van Gogh, who does not speak English, and he sings "You Are Not Alone," and the painter promises him that one day, he will fill a room for him with flowers.

I was so excited when I read this intimation of joy.

I pissed my pants.

MORK AND MINDY

Veronica's text message appeared while I was watching an old Julia Roberts movie, *Sleeping with the Enemy*.

In the movie, Julia plays a young bride living in a huge, immaculate house in Cape Cod: you can see the ocean from every window.

Her husband is fit and tanned: he has a big, black moustache, neatly combed, and he likes things done a certain way.

When Julia Roberts doesn't cook the lamb properly, he gives her a warning stare. And when a sailor tells him that she is always looking out the window, she gets the back of his hand!

This was the text message: *I don't know you anymore.*

I read it and folded tea towels still warm from the dryer, swept the floors, and cleaned the counters.

When I went back upstairs, the *Sleeping with the Enemy* husband had found out Julia Roberts faked her death and was living in Tiny Town, Nowheresville.

She is walking to her kitchen cabinets, trembling with fear. When she opens them, every can has been neatly stacked: they are all in tidy rows!

I forgot she used to have a big ass, I think, as he leaps out and starts wringing her neck.

Then she shoots him, steps over his corpse, and gives herself a perm in the kitchen sink.

The perm was foreshadowed in one of the earlier scenes, where she sits on the bus with a kindly old lady who offers to share her bag of apples. Julia Roberts timidly admires her short, wavy hair, and the old lady says, animated by her own sagacity: And I like your straight hair! Isn't that always the way? We want what we can't have.

Yes indeed, we want what we can't have, she says, chomping on a big Belle de Boskoop.

When she spills the perm solution all over the place she laughs, like she's thinking, I can do whatever I want! She is still smiling, revealing teeth the size of louvre doors, when her new boyfriend walks in and does a double take.

Well hello, Curly! he says.

I cried through much of the movie. My sympathies lay entirely with the husband, who is seen in flashes, howling with grief and ironing the sharp collars of his shirts.

The movie ends with a close-up of the husband's dead, staring eyes, superimposed onto a Mr. Potato Head doll. I wrote a letter of complaint addressed to Julia Roberts, c/o Julia Roberts's People, Hollywood, L.A.

Dear Sirs or Madams, I wrote.

I recently saw *Sleeping with the Enemy,* which I gather is a rather old "flick" because the star's equine features, if you will, are more pronounced and endearing, and she also has ravishing long hair regardless of her comments to the elderly razorback on the bus. And I wonder, just who is the "enemy" here? Is it your star, who seems in no way traumatized during the twenty-minute "Trying on Costume Hats" sequence, or is it the grief-stricken young Tom Selleck–type whom she leaves, none other than Patrick Bergin of *Casanova's Last Stand* fame? Please admit that you wished to slap Roberts yourself on many occasions in this film, for example when she laughed that famous WHOOP of a laugh after the young man with cerebral palsy asked her to the cotillion!

I daresay —

But this letter was never finished.

The days are long and filled with pain.

At night I dream that I have hurt myself and I wake up, again and again. I make appointments with massage therapists for the human contact, and cry there also, as someone in the next room invariably shouts, "Ahhh! That's *fantastic*, Dr. Groovy!"

Today, I went and had shiatsu. I told the girl everything that has been happening to me, and she interrupted to say, This is a place of peace and healing, then cranked up the volume on the CD of whales singing and eating plankton.

I went to the Cadillac after. I wanted to drink coffee and draw pictures in my notebook of the cops I saw this morning, forming a perimeter around a run-down old house.

Can I help? I asked the one with the assault rifle. You just look for a Flemish kid with a knife probably outta breath by now, he said gently, and I want to draw him wearing a wreath of new spring leaves.

On the way to the clinic, after I told the cab driver how well dressed he was, he told me a long story about his single mother starving so he could eat half a sandwich for lunch.

My mother gave me a square pillow with a penguin head, I tell him. Every day, I sit with it pressed against my belly so I can't get attacked.

We ride the rest of the way companionably. He opens all the windows.

I go into the bar and order a soda water. Tonight, Veronica is reading from her new book. She has invited everyone I know.

The last time I published a book, I read there too. I was very nervous and, crossing Queen Street, she and my sister took my hands.

A band called Mork and Mindy is playing: a low-key duet wearing matching grey cardigans.

The room is filled with men and women with gorgeous white hair, dressed in red and silver, who smell like wildflowers.

I try not to think of what I am missing, and how I managed to lose so much.

I breathe the smell of all the soft, rustling flowers and imagine that I am holding them, that I am being held.

HEATHER

My mother called me last Tuesday and I asked, What is the occasion?

My mother died, she said.

I started packing and making plans.

I called work, and they said, I'm sorry to hear that, Linda.

Sometimes, at the faculty meetings, a colleague will call me Linda and I will bristle. I'm sorry, they always say. I apologize, Glenda.

Less frequently, someone will ask me how my work is going: Don't you write something for the *Buy and Sell*?

Yes, I say. I write about things that people want, or things that people do not want anymore.

When I started work there, Dr. Bale took me out for a beer and confided in me. I confided in her as well, and soon I would feel a near-constant shame in her presence.

Nothing is ever good enough for you! I wanted to yell at her because I had come to think of her, in an awful way, as a mother.

I did everything I could to please her. When I returned to work, strung out and furious, I told her how hard I tried to fit in, to be a part of the department.

I tried, I said. But they spit at me and call me baby-killer!

You're the last of an elite group, she said. Don't end it like this.

No, that was Sheriff Will Teasle, in *Rambo: First Blood*.

Dr. Bale stands in front of her bathroom mirror each night, her face glazed with cold cream, and says, Yes. Lining her narrow eyes with a Magic Marker, she draws the word out, then reclines in bed, eating small slivers of wood christened with the names of her enemies.

She comes to work refreshed and radiant.

Today's eau de toilette, she will begin to say, if I pass her, is a sprightly mix of berries and cured meats.

I have learned to start yelling into a cellphone on campus, at all times. Get the blueprints to Schoolly D! I will say. He is on a goddamned leaking frigate, rapping his ass off!

Go for Delicious! is how I answer calls. If I am not barking orders I am making noises and wantonly exploring my body with my hands.

People go away and stay away.

In the months since April, I have already lost the friends I have written about in my capacity as the composer of the theme to *The Golden Girls*.

If there are still commonplace miracles — this morning, small striped snails! — I am still deep in rehearsal for the role of Aileen Wuornos, shortly before her execution.

Thanks a lot! I snap. You're killing me, thanks a lot!

The last time a man walked by and looked right through me, I stopped him and shook his hand. I am resigned to this, I told him. To living the rest of my life without love; to my deterioration.

He smiled affably, as all these newborn ducklings splashed around in a puddle beside us.

Heather — my mother's name — grows pinkish blue and wild: it forms mycorrhizae, where fungus nests, forming a symbiotic relationship.

All my life I would call my grandmother, and she would thank me for calling.

Her name was Mary, the name of my little sister, who I like to tease. Hello, did you bathe in a bottlecap today? I ask her. Did you sleep in a peapod? No! she always says shyly.

My mother is also tender-hearted but has grown a bit wary.

At the funeral, I tried to imagine how our lives would proceed now.

There was my mother, in a painted blue scarf, an apricot sweater, and ceramic bangle, her blue eyes like a blue room filled with blue bowls of asters.

There I was, creeping up to her and pressing myself to her side like a big, odious mushroom.

I'm going home, boomed Paul Robeson's voice as we filed in together.

Someone pulled me away, and I was seated far away from my mother, who wrung her hands for her mother, and when I went home I was tormented by her wild beauty, by my loss.

I keep losing things, I tell Liz, the lady beside me on the train back home. Places, people.

If I close my eyes I see myself leaning to kiss my grandmother the last time ever I saw her. Her face appeared slowly, and completely.

Liz is hard of hearing and tells me a story about a beach that was Filled with immigrants! Cooking God knows what!

I seize her hand, and say, Mother. She starts to cry because I am hurting her. We cry together and no one notices, or cares to.

We cry, Please let me go!

AND CRAVE THE LOVE YOU THREW AWAY

He is wearing a suit, and is thinner than I remember; his dark red hair falls away from his forehead in two small curtains.

What are you doing? he says angrily.

I do not recognize him — I have been feinting my way out of the chapel, where my grandmother lies in a shining coffin drenched in red roses.

He asks me to go outside with him. He calls his cigarette a "coffin nail" and still speaks in a loud bark. What do you do there in Toronto? he yells as I continue to search him for clues.

There are his eyes, still huge, still cat's eyes.

There is his height and there is the desire I feel to take his hand and walk into the blur beyond the orange and grey treeline.

I met Lovely when I was with the cruel cinephile. He drove a chopped Harley and ran with a group of vicious riders.

My chic friends, the punks he hated, were appalled by him but too scared to say so. He is an animal, my boyfriend said as he annotated Pauline Kael reviews with asterisks and other marginalia such as "visceral, vivid" or, in tiny, astonished letters, "whoa."

Even now, Lovely moves through the mourners like a blade and I soften, thinking of the time I brushed and braided his long, tabby-striped honey-and-gold hair.

I used to draw him in my diary, modelling his lean, ripped body after Laocoön, the Trojan priest of Poseidon, and we had a few very sweet dates when I was seventeen.

Seven years after that, I would go to Montreal and look him up, then write a solemn poem about him, organizing my past as though I were putting tiny, fragrant baby clothes in a pine drawer.

But when Lafitte set his schooners on fire, I became newly sentimental about all the men I had lost, for the visibility was low and the skies were dark.

I think, with a pang of grief, of the night Lovely and I kissed above the hot black water of the Sainte-Anne-de-Bellevue Canal.

I worked my fingers through the belt loops of his jeans, petted his leather belt, the huge Vampire Octopus buckle. Stay the night, he said, but I couldn't. I mustn't, I said.

I was, ultimately, more interested in the way I would describe him in the poem I called "The Hotness of the Heat" as "An incontinent volcano!" and "A plate full of Manwiches."

I continue to imagine that he is not a married father, who sold his Harley Sportster, and told me, when I called him from a strip-mall bar in the West End a few years ago and asked him to meet me for a beer, "I'm in bed by nine now! I'm an old man."

Who chopped his hair off, grew a little beard, and started wearing fierce black eyeglasses.

Here is the beginning. I met him through Ken, a high school friend who worked with him after graduation: they worked with dynamite, exploding buildings and bridges; once, they knocked down a row of townhouses like dominoes.

I used to dog-sit for Ken's mother, a trim brunette with an auburn beehive, emphatically underlined eyes, and thick, copper-coloured pancake makeup.

She had a depressive Pomeranian I could not stand who hid

under the bed shitting hard white balls. Jesus Christ, Princess, I would say. Get it together.

Ken would stay at the Spanish cathouse called Lola LaChance. And I would invite Lovely over. And watch him pull into the driveway, take off his helmet, and shake his hair free as it caught all of the sun, and his tattoos would light up and look like bright glass being passed under hot water.

I did end up sleeping with him. He bled all over me, and left, left me on the bed while Princess wept and made weak choking noises and a ferrous abstraction slowly seeped across my white camisole.

That was too bad because when we met again, I had a boyfriend I did not like to cheat on. It was too bad that Lovely was such a well-packaged specimen who whispered the sweetest endearments as he tried to manoeuvre me into the reverse cowgirl.

So gentle, he would sigh, as I stroked his hands, which were scarred from punching and covered in knife-cuts.

But we rode to the canal after we stopped at Lafleurs, where I checked myself out in the rear-view mirror — scarlet hair and mouth, distressed purple T-shirt with a yellow banana appliqué, black leather pants — and he scarfed three dogs ten feet away. And we fooled around in the grass before I made him take me back to the hotel on St. Catherine with the moose heads in the foyer and the furious proprietor who kept emphasizing his policy on male visitors.

I sat on the West End balcony and thought about Lovely, and he called and I watched the clouds leap the sun and his voice dripped like the sweet mush on Sno Cones and I could not sleep, remembering his body as a panther tearing through a drift of swine, turning over the image of his bared teeth, weeping blood.

Take me home? I ask Lovely at the funeral parlour. Be nice, I say, when he hesitates.

He and I drive around for an hour and there is nothing to say, so I let myself feel that I am beside him, moving quickly, and when he gets to my hotel I kiss his soft, luscious lips and say I always did love you and I always will.

You have a good night, he yells.

My hair is blowing into my eyes and my hands are laced behind me and the shiver starts there; it started there and never stopped.

THE FALL

The peach-coloured rose froze for thirteen days on my dresser in its
jar of water, opening only a part of itself.
Like a little thief, revealing his goods.
I brought it back from the funeral. My aunt and uncle had given
out roses to the women important to my grandmother. So many of
us loved her: our arms kept extending and retracting.
I feel so special, she said when I sent her white roses. You are
my dear girl, she said.
There is no one to say that now.
After a few drinks, a man several rows back on the train began
singing that song, "Time of Your Life."
He did all the instruments too and the crowd noise: Yesss!
This is the song that Wayne Gretzky skated to, the last time
he played in Canada, which was the night he decorated "Wayne's
Office" — the space behind Damian Rhodes's net — with a buttery
leather recliner, a kidney-shaped desk, and a jar of ballpoint pens.
I am feeling sensational, he told the press. Everything has come
together — my athletic genius, my love for my family, and my sensational appearance on *The Young and the Restless* as Victor's ambi-
tious, morbidly disabled accountant.

All of the very good things.

In the end it's right, he sang, as he moved one skate slowly in front of the other, and he and his father cried for all the dreams they'd had and would never have again.

I am every star of the game! he said to himself, although the score was tied and he spent too much ice time writing The Great One with mustard on hot dogs and chucking them into the stands.

I watched the game with Lafitte and he cried.

Adieu, 99, he whispered, sickening me.

I saw his face, swollen and miserable, the fetching eyes and comely lips of all the men I had loved, as the whistle blew and streams and pastures filled the windows.

Then, red barns and black horses; the old woman beside me sighing into sleep, her hand on her heart.

I thought of our last visit: my grandmother seemed to be doing well, and I felt good.

Her side of the hospital room was filled with roses.

After that trip home, I took a taxi from Union Station and the driver, Paladin, and I talked excitedly about his dogs, who still lived at his farm in Kashmir.

Kashmir, he explained, is so stunning, you will be stricken while looking at the mountains and then, deep inside of them, at their juicy, rich veins.

He was using his hands to show me the shape of the mountain he called Mama when the silver pig truck went by. I saw one big pink ear escape through a slot like the petal of a rose.

Sometimes it is so hot, or so cold, the pigs are dead by the time they reach the slaughterhouse, and they are lucky for it.

The next day, I adopted a pig named Stormy from a couple who had rescued seventeen of them. Stormy had fallen off a fattening truck a year before, they told me, and was picked up by a man who planned to raise him in his garage, then kill and roast him.

They rescued him on a cold and rainy night; he was very afraid. He never stopped running in circles, knowing what he knew. But when I went to visit him, I dropped juicy yellow melons into his mouth and stroked the rough hair on his head and he smiled.

The "Time of Your Life" guy finally stopped singing and the sun pierced the windows of the train like a yellow-suited armament, and I stared dully into its centre.

All I remembered of the funeral service was sitting down, then standing up. To kiss people and accept their condolences; to sing "And He walks with me and He talks with me"; to touch her face, for the last time.

It has been several weeks.

The chestnuts fall hard from the trees and the trees light up, one by one.

Frank and I walk past the same houses, a route I have plotted in order to stay clear of the alley called the Milky Way.

I am mindful of the ugliness that complements grief.

A few years ago, a woman's torso was discovered in this alley, by someone scavenging through garbage bags.

I thought it was a pig, the man said.

Her leg would later surface at a garbage dump, miles from here, still wearing a slender ankle bracelet.

The police kept searching our yards and basements.

They were looking for the head, which showed up eventually.

The woman's name was Rose.

Her boyfriend killed her, then chopped her up. He barely dragged the torso half a block from his apartment, and told friends that she and her dog were taking a little vacation.

Somewhere up north, he said, when asked. A really nice place where people go to rest and play shuffleboard and get massages.

A doctor I know told me that when he was a resident, he treated a derelict who was wearing children's underpants when he was picked up for vagrancy, that the fabric had grown into his skin.

Leave my little girl alone! the derelict cried as the doctor went about his grim work.

It is easy to see where squalor is and how it breeds, but only from a distance.

I went to the spot where her body was and left six red roses. When I walked by, a half-hour later, they had been purloined.

Your life is worth nothing, Rose, and your death is a small symptom of an illness that is referred to as being unexpected.

At least in its first blush: there you are, rolled into a pink blanket, and your face is gathered into petals and you smile, uncomprehending, at the noise of violent arguments and threats.

At the knife shaking itself loose in the jerked-open drawer and later, someone saying, My God, what is that?

It is a part of your body. There is a blossom tattooed there.

In the galaxies that reach out to heaven, my grandmother's words are converted to stars: We are roses, she said, and must be cut down, sometimes, so that we may grow more beautifully.

IN SEARCH OF THE MIRACULOUS

Lichen and I worked side by side at Semiosis for half a year before I noticed him.

He was wringing his apron and anxiously explaining to an angry customer that we could not take his green tea soufflé back because we permit "no denunciation without an appropriate method of detailed analysis."

Lichen's face was beet red; his single tuft of hair was wrenched into what looked like the horn of a unicorn.

I hate confrontations, he told me later, as we shared a piece of coconut cream pie.

People tell you who they are as soon as they meet you, but who listens? I let my fork drag toward his and when they clanged, he smiled and all the lights went on and glowed.

We were both working as waiters between teaching sessions.

I am a painter, he confided in me. We had started meeting in the break room after closing up, to drink mango tea and put off going home. My empty apartment was looking more and more like a jail cell (I had started eating off of metal trays and carrying a shank); he lived with his wife and four children — they were always taking his art supplies and overpainting his large, blank canvases with cruel comments or shopping lists.

He asked to see me on our day off, and we met at Type Books, where he suggested we pick out books for each other. He chose *In Search of the Miraculous* and I choose *Hammer of the Gods*.

I am always trying to make beautiful things happen in my life, Lichen said. We moved to a bench by the White Squirrel and drank iced coffee through bright bendy straws.

Across the street, Trinity Bellwoods Park was filled with people, lying on towels, playing ball, or sitting in a circle, solemnly passing around a clear bag filled with blue gel.

Lichen brushed sugar off my cheek, and he stammered and said my name as if it were a little animal he was keeping warm in his mouth.

I fell for him as the sun made its passionate appearance.

It was Good Friday.

Think of Jesus, dying for you! I chastised myself as everyone held out their hands, trying to gather up the hot yellow sparks.

Think of Lichen's wife, screaming, as a membranous sac, filled with squirming children, falls from her and into the hands of a midwife-flautist!

But Lichen unwrapped a packet of pink meringues and we brushed lightly against each other in the manner of fire coral. When I left, he took my arm and said, I am not very good with boundaries.

I considered myself, fleetingly, to be a beautiful thing that had happened. That night, before the pain returned like driving nails, I would see sugar burning in the sky, and feel our bodies — not touching, but yelling at each other.

When Julia Roberts just stands there with her Chagall in one of the last scenes in *Notting Hill* and asks to be loved, Hugh Grant says, Do you mind if I say no?

It's all too much, he says, and he is not up for it.

Good answer, she says, although she is very sad.

Lichen's answer, to a question I had learned never again to ask, was good enough to make me feel something new. Visible — how the sun plants its shovel in the earth and turns up, among the dark and frightening things, a new place to start.

THE RADIANT BOY

— if you don't wish to send me his picture, I understand. I will never bother you again.

I wrote this to Stephen's parents as Lafitte — unbeknownst to me — was making other plans.

As I asked him to make me triangulated sandwiches with small flags on each section, he was packing, and neatly labelling, boxes in his head. Kitchen. Bedroom. Misc.

I had become possessed by Stephen. I read and reread my high school diaries, and dreamed of him night and day.

I bought a bottle of the Head & Shoulders that he'd used to shampoo his cat I and kept it, opened, in my desk drawer.

I wondered if he meant to harm me. I went to the Spiritualist Temple on College Street and spoke with one of the ministers. At the services, they ask, May I step into your vibration? before channelling the dead. This one simply said, He is a higher power now. He wishes you well.

I wish you well, I informed his forlorn grave in the Resurrection Cemetery in Whitby, which is jammed into a small grid.

All around: new trees and hedges, violently green lawns covered in yellow cranes, pink swing sets, chubby plastic pools.

These are for you, I said, presenting him with three bouquets of white tulips.

Thank you, I whispered back in a ghost voice and jumped. So much of this was fabrication, except one thing: Stephen returned from the dead to save me.

He was there as my life imploded, beguiling me to look elsewhere for love.

I took out library books about the supernatural, like Carrie does after her first few telekinetic expositions. Like her, I looked in the card catalogue under "Miracles."

I read about "Radiant Boys," specters who appear in bright light or flames.

I just want to see his face, I wrote to J. & M. McDougall, his parents.

To peer inside the centre of the fireball that stands, holding a slingshot and dead bird, at the foot of my bed each morning.

Eventually, eight years passed and J. died, then M. sent the picture. I had called her and requested it for a high school reunion. M. had burst into tears.

I think of him every day, she said. Why did this happen?

He had been hitchhiking from Ajax to Toronto and was hit by a truck. He prevailed for three days in the hospital before letting go.

He was the sweetest boy, she said.

I have come and gone to the reunion, a brief travesty. I fled as an enormous woman in a sparkly tube dress clung to my arm, gasping, Don't you remember me?

Her hand left a peony on mine.

I have ridden in the back of a taxi on Dorchester, feeling my past shoot through me like morphine, thinking of nothing at all.

When my back exploded, he returned and stayed. Through the operations, and recovery, he has stayed, breathing on my neck, passionately, wrenching me from danger —

It is two days before Labour Day. As I waited at the intersection this morning, a drunk man threw lit firecrackers at the Hydro line until one caught and began smoking.

Then the line lit up and ran, pulsing at intervals in white stars, until breaking and falling to the street.

In the picture his mother sends, Stephen is older and has a moustache, and is tanned and fit. His soft brown eyes are shining; his teeth are warm seed pearls.

I lied to your mother, I say, walking away from the smoke and the screaming.

He keeps his hand on my back, the way he did so long ago, on the bridge over the river, on the sash of my long, belled skirt.

She knows, he says.

What are you to us? he asks, not unkindly.

I pass the drunk who is standing in the road, bowing like a toreador; I pass dogs with spiked collars, straining hard, a slam of music.

I am shaking, I notice. I can't help it, I say.

He draws me closer. He is the sweetest boy I know.

ONLY YOU AND YOU CAN'T HEAR ME

He looks out the window most of the time now, sitting on a hard, wooden chair.

What are you looking at? I ask, half listening when he says,

— The woman's octopus baby, its fleecy tentacles.

— The tiny alien crafts, beep-beeping *Radix malorum est cupiditas* and Remember to floss!

— Bottles of Grecian Formula, tinting the leaves of the trees, handsomely, naturally.

— Your shoe the shoe I drank champagne from, your white satin shoe.

Yes, yes, I say. Or, Oh. Okay.

This takes place in the world where Stephen and I met again and stayed together.

We were married in the Church of the Resurrection, and we had a honeymoon in Niagara Falls.

We pounded that heart-shaped bed into a circle, and during the days we walked under the water in yellow raincoats, hand in hand.

And all of this, up to and beyond our spotlit wedding dance to "More Than a Feeling," when he dipped me and my golden hair glanced the floor, began when I was seventeen and visiting his local bar after a fight with the cruel cinephile. It was a late summer night: just beyond us were apple orchards, livid with fruit, and the Richelieu River, running wild under the anxious stars.

The night he walked up to me and said, quietly, You look different now.

I like your hair, he said, as I stared at him imperiously.

He touched it — it was bright red and razor cut — and walked away.

He touched it — it was longer than it had been in high school, and sun-bleached — and held my face and kissed me.

The kiss is torrid and warms me from an incalculable distance, from the place where dispatches originate, arriving to me as faint sighs and shivers.

I know that we have children and only love each other.

When he is away, I sleep on his side of the bed and cry all night.

He smacks my ass every morning and says, Come here, baby.

We go to the high school reunion together and he and I don't recognize a soul.

And when he is old, I am old. We take care of each other.

A storm is coming, he says, standing up and upsetting the salt shaker.

I draw our initials in its discharge.

And hold him until we are a single breath in the dark world that shadows this one, the one where we both get to live.

AS THE SMITTEN TREE GIVES BIRTH
TO ITS FUNGUS

So it was that a very rubicund, shiny-headed man — his skin perpetually stricken with livid outbursts of acne — became, for a short time, the object of my affection.

Lichen disappeared abruptly from my life, making a line between the sea and the dirt.

Like the scar that bisects my throat, given to me by the outlaw, Dr. ____, that translates as follows: This part of my life is over.

Lichen and I grew close quickly, like a mushroom's slight elf cap pressed against the great trunk of a tree.

Beautiful things were devised and executed. We found each other, one morning, by sending cryptic pictures of our changing locations: a giant pumpkin, heart grafs, a red stone, a red forklift; finally, my red cape from a great distance, flaring.

He and I went to the CN Tower one afternoon, and he slid me, quaking, across the clear tiles at the very top. We leaned over the deck and he talked about the city below us, making a model of the water and streets and buildings or the constituency of his heart.

A little model I managed to stamp on like Godzilla, but how?

How was it that my friend became small enough to scurry in and out of the tiny structures we looked at that day? How did we become like two clouds moving in, and past, each other?

He would never say.

He would not say that he was too good for me.

THE FAT BOY

It was poisoned.

The squirrel is curled into itself, grey and pudgy. It has died with its eyes open: I see the light leaving them, like two tiny meteors.

There is not much of your world I wish to see anymore, I say to God.

The last time I went to the church, to speak more formally with You, I stepped on a filled condom snaking down the steps.

The pain is terrible. I feel like a drawing in a colouring book that a mentally ill child is crayoning in cyclones of purple, black, and green.

The body, mulish, will no longer be lashed. It is seated, half-dead, and saying, with some dignity, You may keep the carrot, thank you. I am simply not hungry.

The mind is an instance of recursion in which it is photographed holding an image of itself on impact.

It is the Saturday before Christmas.

The family down the street I usually spend Christmas with (having responded to their "Eat, Pay, Love" ad) have moved to the country and become factional Mennonites. They exiled me the last time I visited for singing "Funkite Town" while baling hay.

They were in town to shop last weekend but would not come to see me. They rode their wagon up and down my street a few times, as is common in a good, old-fashioned shunning.

I was curling my hair and hoping to hear from the adult film actor I'd met at my salon the week before.

Yes, I am aware that he is in a number of controversial gay porn movies, I tell a concerned friend. My sexuality is highly evolved, and I am sure Randy Coxwell's is the same.

He never called, however, and when I finally asked why, he said, Lynn, *my boyfriend* and I were busy.

Randy, the emphasis is a little hurtful, I said.

Whenever I go to my doctor, she asks the psych nurse — who looks like a hippo in a sari — to see me instead.

I can barely lift my arm, I say.

Families can be so cruel, she says.

It's like the whole left side of my body is disaligned.

Some people find the company of small, warm animals to be of great comfort, she says.

My Mennonite father said, I have no daughter! I say and sigh.

Tell me about that, she says.

Well, I want to be a jazz singer and he wants me to be a cantor.

In the silence that follows I ask her, Did I tell you about the man I am seeing, Randy Coxwell?

As the Mennonites raise a barn, I decorate my apartment with cotton-batting snowmen and pipe-cleaner reindeer I have made, over the year, with Lil, every time she and I visit Dr. Hop, the sweaty physician with a hand-lettered sign on a tarpaper shack.

Just give me something for the bullet holes, I say, holding my belly.

I draw myself dead of various festive suicides. Hanged, wearing shiny, black leather boots. In bed with my wrists slashed, in a Santa hat; lying in the bath with a toaster that has ejected two stigmata-riddled pieces of toast before shorting out.

I put the drawings in the windows where I have written, with snow in a can, BEWARE OF MURDERERS.

I call a distress centre and speak to a nice man named Sarge. I am not making much sense but he seems to understand.

It started with...the Class! I say.

With the terrible hunchbacked girl who put tacks on my chair and the fat boy who made me carry garbage!

And the cat—

One fall day, the Class and I walked outside to collect leaves and write poems about them.

We noticed a squashed cat in the parking lot. One of its paws was waving as yet another car backed over it.

Oh no! I said.

There was a dreadful silence and the Fat Boy said, I am thinking of translating Pablo Neruda's poems into take-out menus.

We collected handfuls of leaves and walked slowly around the campus. I'll die if I have to finish this term, I thought.

But I did finish it. And my other classes, where my students always began a conversation by saying, Listen up!

I drank fiery eggnog and flirted with solid, handsome men; I saw old friends, but still I could not feel better.

The pain is too severe...and Sarge? I say. Sarge, they don't want me there.

Yer crazy made-up maw an' paw? he asks, because he grew up in a tiny holler down south.

Yes, I say. Why?

I reckon I don't know, he says. That's hella bad, though.

Do you want ole Sarge to come by? he asks, and I hang up.

Men of the world, I declare, as I harness up Francis and fill his saddlebags with water, beef jerky, and a small harmonica.

We are done.

I am no longer interested in your cruelty or perversion. I view with contempt your assessment of where my interests reside.

As though, I say to a man on the street who is my age, more or less, As though your hard, low-slung paunch and tonsure excite me!

Just buying a few groceries, he sighs. A bag of apples and some rice.

As though *your* wide hips and ears the size of eggplant are what I long for, I tell another man, who is trying to get by.

I will devote myself to goodness, Lord, I yell in the direction of the cross where two birds are always perched as if to say, Oh, this is *on*.

The man with the big ears is walking by slowly, his hands on his belly.

Tell your friends! I call after him and steer Frank, walking narrowly between milky puddles of phlegm and flaky pieces of shit, between garbage and vomit and angry bald women and hairy, whistling men.

I always wonder if today will be the day I find the human hand.

It is waiting for us, and even though I am careful not to look at shrubs or piles of leaves, it will find me.

The cat — a little tuxedo number — seemed to be signalling for help, although it was far too late.

I understand, I say to its dear soul. I will take action next time, I swear it.

I will grasp the hand warmly and shake it. We meet at last, I will say.

It has been exhausting, the hand will concur, as it lies in the velvet-lined box and curls its fingers inward, one by one.

SAVE THE BROKEN THINGS IN MY LIFE

ONE.

I heard this song one snowy day at Urban Outfitters. The lyrics are convoluted but passionate.

The song is like Hemingway's idea that while many of us are broken, some get stronger in the broken places.

I bought a pair of black zipper-leg jeans, a notebook with a sky and a seagull and the words, in clouds, "I want to fly away," and a black-and-white bath mat that says BUST A MOVE. It will be a year until I understand the mat's dirty joke.

The people who work at the shop are young; I am not apparent to them and need to slide into their vision like a silent migraine.

This is a cool jam! I say to the clerk. Mhmm, he says, shaking his hair into his face.

I smash into a rack of sheer white dresses on my way out and apologize.

It's okay, the dresses hiss. God!

I am standing with my hand raised, thinking of the box I received this morning from Veronica, containing all the things I ever gave her. And a flat brown dog toy for Francis.

I am soaked through. I am thinking of its sad contents, of

losing my friend, when I decide to catalogue instead all the beautiful things. I want to formalize the process; to make a list, written alphabetically on index cards and cross-referenced.

This is better than trying to explain how I feel, on days like this.

A taxi stops; its back seat is filled with confetti and Kleenex flowers. The driver switches on the radio, jumps stations until he finds Orangegrass.

He says, Check this out, baby! then dials it up.

If I were making a book about broken, beautiful things, I would paste in a picture of this car. I would use stick-on stars, paint, and photographs.

Smokey Blue; The Queen of Seville; Lucy. Diaphanous loveliness. The Satyr with Glossy Braids; An Orange-and-White Cat, Cleaning Its Paws; Hercamone and Sweet Port Wine. Over this, a furious scribble of silver crayon, a chivalric angel, extending his hand.

The other day, I found the galleys for a sci-fi book called *Pioneers of Alienation*. The author has written "Interesting and Fascinating!" on the cover and, underneath, drawn a spaceship with an X on its dome indicating You Are Here!

I discovered his email address in the chapter about Miss Marjoram and a man named Disco Chic, and wrote him a fan letter.

Thank you, he said. Not that it matters, he added.

Why not? I asked him. I signed the letter *Your fan* and did not hear back. The book had been perched on a set of dinosaur stickers — most of them peeled away, a few triceratops legs and pearled frills remaining — and a macrobiotic cookbook, its pages fingered with orange crud.

I bought a nice flowered blazer that day, from Saks, and a long, hooded sweater: I found a pine cone in the pocket.

TWO.

When I was six years old, my friend André's crazy mother was taken away in a padded van. As the ambulance attendants dragged her out, she raked her claws through her white-and-black hair and squalled at us — the mothers were peering out the apartment windows.

Look at them, my *neighbours*, she spat in her jagged English. Laughing at me!

She had pulled a red fox-fur coat over her nightgown and slippers.

My mother watched, and cried.

We were both afraid, for different reasons.

I knew, in my heart, I would end up like her.

Stylish and ruined.

Still, I prevail. I had hoped to write a happy ending, like the ones in the only books I can read anymore, books about fat women who modify their appearance, and are loved, in the end, for their lively intelligence and carnality.

But that would be a lie. Life racks back and forth between ups and downs. It is not a single arrow going in one direction or another.

It is hard but, as Muse, the last cab driver to ask, abruptly, for my number, says, What're you gonna fucken do?

I had wanted to engage in an inherently false struggle with the ending of this book, like Anne Sexton did with *Live or Die*.

That book is one miserable poem about addiction and suicide after the other, but it ends with transformative imagery: the notion of writing as an "excitable gift," and Saul Bellow's approval (he replied to a fan letter she sent him and said, "Live or die, but don't poison everything").

Ultimately, she must have waited for a good day — these are the days I say, Thank you, my Redeemer! when I see a robin's egg, or secretly coded license plates like JLOTS, and this moves me to practise the dance interlude in Tom Jones's "Kiss."

These days are so rare, you do not want to be writing and listening to ten gorillas with hammers building "elite and exquisite townhomes!"

You definitely do not want to take a good look at the windowsill beside you.

I mentioned that I let two pigeons roost on my window in the spring and summer, watched them have babies.

They filled the windowsill with shit, then made a nest from it, then the female laid another egg, in December.

I covered up the view.

And, just yesterday, I took a good look. The egg had hatched and grown into a fair-sized bird, then died.

And its mother just sat on it and shit all over it, until it became part of the shit nest.

All night long I could not stop thinking of eating its corpse.

THREE.

Margaux likes the spokes of the sun, orange and yellow.

You feel everything, she says. Like an angel!

I think of someone who hates me hearing this, of their face turning red and they are seeing the word *angel* ease into a glue trap.

Steve put this kind of trap in our bathroom at the Epitome, and cried when he found the headless, exsanguinated mouse our cat had found first.

A little while ago, I walked over to our old place and stood in the foyer, and thought of what it was like to stand there, breathe, and start taking the stairs, two at a time. I wanted to see you and tell you so many things.

The little tree is almost a big tree now, please don't be mad at me anymore.

The painting of three sluggish poppies at Last Temptation, on the grey wall covering Tiger's mural, himself young and lean in a jungle, holding a lion cub. It has been just over a year since I had a drink and I am still a bit anxious and I take in Margaux's pale blue eyes. Later, in the taxi, she rests her head on my shoulder: we are tired from banana cream pie and saffron potatoes. It flares there and stays warm, for a long time after.

Jack and Blaze sleeping side by side in daggers of light. Beside them, half a spider and its legs: they are making me dramatic eyelashes!

The woman in A.S.M. Kobayashi's *Dan Carter*, who keeps calling and calling and finally leaves a message about how happy she is and how good he feels when his body is pressed against her.

The little grave, a stone and plastic iris that Number Four, Bobby Orr, made for a dead sparrow — Frank and I keep going by the building to find Rusty and give him some Epsom salts because of his bad hip, and we notice the grave. Last year, he made snow dogs, with red paper tongues.

The clean, white floor that received you, that took the weight of your great, shaved head and your heavy black glasses, scudding past. I am not feeling well, is what you said.

Michael Jackson felt the air leave his lungs and this good rush, where, finally, there was only love, and love was spelled out big and in gold letters and he laid his head down the back of a black swan, and covered the fire of his black eyes and, curved into a half-moon or a scythe, he cut his way into Heaven at last.

In Heaven, it smells like the Bal à Versailles he applied everywhere;

his crotch just aspirated the scent.

On Valentine's Day, I make the cats a dinner of chicken hearts. Will you be mine? I ask Frank, extending a cookie shaped like a shoe.

My drunk gay student texted me the other day: Lynnnnnn I love you! Come to Sexy Bingo, another wrote. The circuit queen sang, Well I think it would be nice, if I could touch Lynn Crosbie, oh no not everybody, has a body like hers, to me, to the tune of "Faith."

And the one who wants to get into drag said, violently, I want to have assignations with you in fabulous places!

I have my work.

You have your dog, a beautiful girl told me years ago, after Lafitte sailed away.

My father this morning, reporting on their trip to Manhattan. Ah, it snowed a lot, mostly we saw stores. Lynn, what is a psychopath? Because this guy I worked with, this Johnny Appaloosa, he was one. He died! Happiest day of the year so far. This one time, we were waiting by the, what do you call them, the velvet ropes at this big event. The mayor was there, a big deal. And we're three abreast, moving forward, and Johnny Appaloosa reaches behind these red velvet drapes and snags a few sandwiches off the buffet! Sneaky bastard! That's him, in a nutshell.

The nutshell study I want to make for my dad, of the man's cold, dead hand reaching from his coffin for a lady's handbag.

All the small sandwiches, made by birdlike old ladies, that I have eaten at funerals: soft and tasting like delicious paste.

Compliments and small sandwiches: what I like the most.

Lucy, right by where you stayed the last time you were here, I saw a lady in a red cloak, sort of hovering, I saw her today!

It's all right to cry, my father said. Do not try to stop: this is a terrible thing. Someone in my family was murdered, he tells me, and I walk around the block in my bare feet.

Your painting of a little girl, sleeping with a bear, in green light: I thought of you, you said.

The doll is posed right beside me now, its arm with the white gauntlet leading. This is the same doll Blanket undressed and held at the memorial: it's still very hard to understand.

How could this be, that you're not here with me?

My grandmother, in her red velvet dress, pooling around her; my grandfather's deep, slanted eyes, my eyes.

A student, who corners me to talk. Don't you know what happened to me? he says. We sit on a bench in the food court; two girls in front of us lower honey spoons into paper cups. He was hospitalized and broken-hearted, and she still won't take him back. His eyes are brown velvet cupcakes; his lips are red velvet cake; his brown hair flops over his forehead, carelessly. What is the point of living, he asks me, if no one loves you? I surprise and embarrass myself by bursting into tears. He walks me to the corner. I love you, he says. Don't tell anyone.

Lautréamont writes about such feelings, recklessly. Of eating the boy alive, that his innocence makes him sweeter still. *The sanctity of the crime.*

My neighbour Tanya, who is glacial and beautiful, is shouting; a dog is crying and I run over and it is one of her dogs crying; the other has just dropped dead. She sobs, Lynn, what do I do? I tell her where my vet is. They will be gentle with him, I say, and she cries louder, and her boyfriend holds her, slowly turning her away.

This same day, a raccoon, dead on the street, and its paws are so poised and fragile I say to Animal Control, Yes, but can you come faster?

The risqué Polaroids of me and Billy I have inserted into the slots of my new shower curtain, alongside Korean and Indian soap, a sheriff's badge, a periwinkle loofah, and two small purple maracas. Looking back, I can barely make out the relationship between me and this fleshy, toothsome girl, in a bubble bath, on zebra pillows, with a wreath of flowers in her hair. I am glad I got to be young and happy, but it was so long ago.

I see him watching a tape of himself at ten, in a fringed vest and red shirt, singing and dancing. He pours popcorn into his hand from a serrated yellow box. His face is impassive: his black eyes are still and fixed: *I want you back.*

FOUR.

I am looking back at myself, trying to be as dispassionate as Billy in that photograph. I have checked into the Four Seasons to finish this book. I am doing a reasonable impersonation of someone who belongs here. Upgrade to a suite? Why not?

Thanks for your help, Jonquil. Buy yourself something pretty.

I am looking north, from the eighteenth floor, at the city starting to burn in streaks of pale yellow and orange.

The sky is a blue pool, slowly filling with coral. Three grey clouds make a sad face, then rush off.

Quiet as a grave, I told Reservations. I am as jumpy as a cat I once had who always appeared to be having complex Vietnam flashbacks.

And, except for sirens and the oaf upstairs, it is good. I am drowning him out with Handsome Ned.

Who sings about someone who lets him fall in love with her, "in spite of the danger."

He was twenty-nine when he died of a heroin overdose, in the back of the Cameron House, and we were all very sad. He was always smiling, with such genuine sweetness; he sang as though he loved the world.

But twenty-nine seemed old enough then. One of my students called Piper Laurie, after we watched *Carrie*, an "elderly woman."

When you get older, it is all such a blur. Except for this: there are young people and old people. But you are all beautiful! I told a class recently, who said they disliked their lives. Do you think it gets better?

It does. But you have to go back, like an elderly superhero, put on your thick glasses, and look at things clearly.

Then organize your belongings to the best of your ability.

And another day has passed, and I have been upgraded again and the cars are smaller still: Hot Wheels, black sky, Vladimir Horowitz, Schumann's Fantasy in C Major, Op. 17.

On the later records he grunts and exhales noisily as he plays, but he is young here, at Carnegie Hall in a tweed suit, checked shirt, and paisley bow tie.

The CD has scratches from the original record that educes a time when we listened to music as if running our hands over a beloved, deeply scarred body.

I listen, and look at my mail.

A man I dated is married, again, and he just sent out an email about a fundraiser for his child, who has epilepsy, and once had a grand mal seizure at a petting zoo.

Then I get his second email that says, It has come to my attention that I may have suggested my wife also has epilepsy and she does not. I am so sorry for the pain and fear I have caused.

I will get rich writing *Men, and the Strung-out Termagants They Love.*

I liked every woman I met today: some days are like that.

The front-desk clerk said to me, Love, hate. They're both sides of the same stick.

But what is the stick? I asked.

I met Sally, the aesthetician, and Feliciana, the night manager. A cashier with a black pageboy who called me honey baby. A lady in the little pool, smiling and bobbing like a delicious apple.

I had my nails painted purple; I had a massage: the MT played "Bad Romance" and told me stories about odious celebrities and old, lustful men with Kilimanjaro back hair.

I saw Margaux and Leanne, and Max and Simone.

I am slowly putting everything back together, which means holding the sharp, broken pieces and fitting them into an imperfect whole of my own design.

Forgetting, once and for all, Veronica's oriental cruelty; her mouth, a slash of red, a cherry bough drawn in two, severe strokes. Hundreds of paper cranes emerging.

I see my own family, briefly, and we are shaky but strong. As though we are in the middle of a robbery and the gunman has just left, having instructed us to start counting.

And my old friends, in a dream where we are all so happy to see each other and the men have large, elaborately styled hair and the women make me smile like when Margaux swam under the plastic barrier into the outdoor pool and shouted at the cold air, at her breath in the air, visible; like Leanne bringing me a golden coin on a heavy chain, embossed with a chariot and a handsome centurion.

Later, I will throw the chain away, speak less and less to Margaux until she writes me, in letters that seem to ache, Do you still like me?

You are the Mermaid of Ipperwash, I tell her, remembering how she coaxed me into the waves of Lake Huron, whooping as they crashed around us.

Somewhere it is raining and a fine, slender rat is wearing a golden medallion. He sits on a large can of pinto beans, declaiming, My friends we will have our day in the sun!

And I will remember waiting to cross the street, beneath the big silver O in LOVE fused to the art gallery, holding a pot of marigolds. And Lichen was speeding by and he stopped, he stopped traffic.

He called me over and kissed me, and later sent me a single word framed with asterisks:

Beautiful

I think of the time a girl who had a crush on Lichen lost her temper when he withdrew his attention and sent him a crude drawing of a fat naked woman holding a dripping knife, on lined paper.

She is saying FML. There is a brain beside her and a star above her.

He was scared, and I asked for a copy, just in case. Just in case I want to frame and pray to it, I thought.

I was doing so many bad things then, Marlowe writes, of our dalliance. I was vomiting in alleys and rolling in the vomit. I was acting out, my parole officer says.

Marlowe writes, I am saying goodbye this way because my

telephone lies on the mantel beside my wedding photograph.

In this photograph, my wife has a brain beside her, and there is a star above her. Don't be mad, because I am just being honest, he says.

I could say the same to you, I think. To so many of you, even you, elderly chap, who held the door open for me one night as I left work, then bowed!

I don't love you anymore, I think, of all the men up to Marlowe, especially Marlowe and including Lichen. I sound out the words as I walk Frank through the gold light of autumn and my neighbour, a big handsome brute, starts walking like a bear and calling, Baby! Come here, baby!

He is talking to a homeless guy he wants to punch, it turns out.

Maybe I love him, I think.

And the scared dead soul of you.

I have said this out loud. The brute turns and stomps inside; an old man wheeling a flowered cloth suitcase stares at me, then says, That is nice for you, and I cry with joy.

Inside me, the depression and mania cage-fight.

I am breaking glass and making a mosaic of, for example, Otto's letter, sent one year after we stopped speaking, that says, I. DIG. U. Holding Yoko's hand at my grandmother's funeral; she tells me that I shine and I say that I am sorry — this and other darkly coloured fragments replicate the human heart.

Or, breaking glass and the attendant injuries from the smallest pieces, the ones that travel through your skin like the micro-ship in *Fantastic Voyage*, if the ship were hijacked by pirates.

I am a woman throwing a dinner party that is sketchily attended and characterized by small bursts of rage and joy, long periods of nervous silence that I break when I scream, Get out, everyone! Just go!

Then I slide down the wall, snarling, Who needs them? as my dog stares passionately at a plate of cheese he loves more than me.

Have your precious cheese! I sob at the wretched animal.

A long time ago, I had a dream about my beloved first dog, Louis. He was standing near me, there was only a deep line between us, easy to cross, and I knew then that that is all there is.

Milk and honey and Louis, and everyone, everyone.

I do not want anything or anyone back because I already have them. Still, there are certain losses that may make me get there faster, and cross faster.

I woke up ten times last night thinking Francis was with me. Trying to imagine his sweet head on a plush dragon, his Popeye arms and strong, hefty body: when he sleeps he sighs and smells like a Frito pie.

I try to imagine him not there.

An elderly friend has started speaking with God. Often, and at length. God gives him good advice, and a great deal of comfort.

What can I do for you? he asked God plaintively one day.

Love me, God said.

This is all that anyone wants: to love and be loved.

The rest is good and hard, and lives like a stone in this secure moment: the glass ice tongs, Chopin, the road below making a bridal gown's train, the idea of home I hold close like a sleeping, fractious baby.

I hear applause: they are applauding Horowitz and have been for seventy-five years.

I asked to see the owner of L'Atelier Grigorian, which used to be in the suburbs where my parents lived, twenty-eight years ago. He was a terse and elegant man, but after a while he would say hello to me, and I saved money to buy my first art and photography books, and I still have them, and the poetry and music I loved then too; I would walk around the place like it was church.

Why are you whispering? someone once asked, and I could not explain.

I told him some of this today — the owner, who is the same. It was the only place I felt safe, I told him, and he thanked me.

And I thought of the girl I was: no one, according to everyone, and enamored of something too big to understand or explain.

I am standing beside an ice sculpture of a wolf, holding a knife. There is a brain beside me, and above me there is the prelude to a star.

You have come this far, I tell her, and I have, for the most part, kept you safe. I love you, I tell her, I tell God, fearfully, of course, but with my whole heart, where one white sainted speck lies, ferociously guarded, in its strong, blistered hold.

The Four Seasons, Room 2602, 21 Avenue Road, Toronto.
February 20, 2010.

———

I got up early and swam as the snowstorm started, just white specks at first, and wind. I dove under the barrier to the outdoor pool and passed through the white vapours slicing the water. It is His breath, I thought, because I wanted to feel alive, and later, the smell of French vanilla soap and chlorine is succulent and Frankie rolls around with the portly squeaky hippo and this morning we walked a long time. Three men followed us, until I showed them my knife as the storm made cyclones of filth in the parkette.

At home, one cat vomits on its cat toy, and the other scratches, then bites, my arm.

There is my anger, an affliction like lycanthropy.

How blood looks, magnified. Plus one blue-black spore.

I'll get used to this. A loneliness as wretched and sublime as *The Sounds and Songs of the Humpback Whales* with noise-cancelling headphones. As I sit here now, some guy is sawing metal pipe and loading his compact Cat; the workers in the back are making an extension to the townhouses: an elaborate sex dungeon-slash-atrium that is conceptually stunning but hard to listen to.

The whales go, Wawawawawawawawawawawa, hooooooooooo, then chime. Sometimes a gull goes by.

Or Frank will kiss my hand.

On my days off, I get up and farm him and Jack and Blaze, then run repulsive errands, written on sticky papers: "*Get unguent 4 angular cheilitis."

I take pictures of things that are charming or horrible: a million ants swarming a yellow sucker; dolls suspended from wires; a feculent, slanted snowman with a squished construction-cone hat.

And when I am not, despondently, writing "A very nice effort, Bryan!" on a C paper or, more faintly, "kill you," I change my eHarmony profile.

Veronica talked me into joining. You're not an old bag, she said, like Doris Roberts says to Shirley Stoler in *The Honeymoon Killers*.

I was sincere at first. Then monsters from horror movies began pre-emptively rejecting me for "Other" reasons.

"I am pursuing another relationship," one squat, handsome man wrote. "I hope you and your clenched, oily fist will be very happy!" I responded.

Then I changed all of my information and picture, using screen grabs of women from the films of Alan Hamel, and continue to, every day. Today, I am a short, obese "retired exotic dancer." Under "Secrets About Me," I've written "I been in prison." I make reference to my "battery-operated life-partner LOL," "Good BBQ," and my deceased husband, Calvin: "You taught me to LIVE baby I will see you at the Rapture!"

I have been a stringy, rigid Customs agent; a depressive Greeter; and a vulpine, fraudulent "Brane Surgin."

The saddest man in the world ended up pursuing me, which led me to swear off this kind of looking, any kind of looking at all.

That was his name on the site: the Saddest Man in the World. He was a widower, a math teacher with three teenaged children.

He responded to one of my less grotesque personae: "Millie: Former 1950s model and antagonist of the red-headed thorn in my side, Chili. Now spokesperson for women who have had acid thrown in their faces by their envious rivals, causing them to lose so much, including Clicker, the cool photog."

TSMITW wrote, "That must of hurt," and sent me his number.

I called him and throughout the conversation he referred, lugubriously, to his wife's passing. Every time he said "passed," I thought of her eliminating pennies and other hard, shiny objects.

I live by Canada's Wonderland, he told me. But my kids and I never go, he said.

It's so loud, he said. I could hear him wincing. Moments of silence went by. I started a grocery list: Slushies, Cotton Candy, Funnel Cake —

So, do you want to meet? he asked, blowing his nose and sounding like an elephant.

This year's not good for me, I said.

Okay, so I'll see you at Swiss Chalet? he said.

He was on a lot of meds.

I will know you are there, my darling angel, he said.

I wish I had gone, if only to crouch behind him and whisper his name until he dropped his quarter-breast and grabbed the waitress's apron, awe-struck. She came, he would say. She's here!

Maybe she was.

At least you have your ghost! I wanted to snap at Saddest Man. *I was born to be lonely.*

I loved this poem when I was a kid, taught with ill-concealed revulsion by my rigid, matronly English teacher.

Do you remember that poem? I ask my friend Fabian.

He is worried about me, and has taken me out for coffee.

You talk a lot about pills and staggering, he says. Nightgowns.

We are getting old, he says.

Speak for yourself, I say. *I am merely travelling incognito.*

Later, I clean out my basement, getting ready to go, to where, I am not sure. My driving teacher feels I am, after two years of lessons, about a year away from taking the test again.

Last night I dreamed I was driving better than I ever have, to the thrift store I visit so often in my sleep I am certain there is another landscape we all make; that if we dream of each other, we have met, fighting over an antler coat-rack or a Pucci scarf.

And if I fail the test again, I will attack the tester and cover her in honey and fire ants: I have never passed a day without wondering if this is the day I will finally lose my mind.

There will be violence!

Or bliss.

It may be a sweet day, the day everyone looks like Barbapapas, when the skies are waxy streaks of Magic Mint above Inchworm trees and grass, when I turn my face to the Laser Lemon sun.

There *are* sweet days.

I walked in the sun of the false spring, where your tree trembles with hope, where you all move through me like warm vapours, and I bought a pair of narrow, buckled Gucci slides.

To wear some other day, past the couples kissing who sometimes rake my heart, the mothers and their babies, the sisters and friends.

And feel my hair as a circuit of flames, and my hand raised, ready to take Saleem's or Ajax's or Manny's number, setting off, coming home.

William Carlos Williams is dancing naked, in front of a mirror, in the poem. He says he is "grotesque" and "lonely" but he sings, "I am best so!" What does he mean? Mrs. Pineapple asked us.

I had no idea.

I had no idea that one day, it would mean the world to me.

60 Gwynne Avenue, Toronto.
April 14, 2010.

MY BOY

On the fifth day of the flu, I realized I would have to cancel my classes again.

I called a writer I know casually and asked him to fill in for me. I'll pay large! I said.

What's wrong? he said.

That day, I found the mass on Francis's abdomen.

It could be mast cell cancer; it could be a cyst.

But cysts don't bleed like this, my vet said, peering solemnly at me.

I left him there. He was sedated and wearing a leather muzzle.

The vet was holding him awkwardly; Frank looked like he was flying.

When I came back, he kept staring at me. They had shaved him and left a thick, sutured gash.

He is lying beside me now. He wants to eat and play but he can't.

It will be seven days before they will be able to tell me what is happening to him.

I want to stand in the rain that has poured for days; I want to stop people and show them his picture and say, See how they massacred my boy!

Maple, the boy I called Bender, is going to bring me my T-shirt from the Julian Schnabel show, which is Marlon Brando in a black wig, lipstick, and a bare chest, slashed in pale pink and blue. He spent an afternoon shredding and knotting it, he tells me, taking apart the neck and sleeves.

I thank him extravagantly in front of the rest of the class, then kiss him on the mouth.

I won't let you destroy what is sacred to me! I say shrilly, and they lower their heads.

I want you to listen to me and take notes, I say.

As I speak, I am already retreating. I am in a tattoo parlour, having my dog carved into my forearm.

Take beautiful, cursive notes that are annotated with stars, I say. Hold them to your hearts and this is how you will come to love me.

View all that you love as the breath of God, I say faintly, directing them to write in pencil now, softly.

I hear them scratch and rub their papers as I turn inward again, beneath the ink banner filled with his name, in serif, the blue and gold of my skin being bled into a covenant — How I shall honour his diffidence and grandeur, I say.

How brightly he will shine.

I return home to my dog and watch him watching me. In his pain, I see the dog he will be one day, remote and secretive.

I stand in the kitchen crying. The tears are so big, so shapely, it is like my eyes are blowing glass.

I call my mother.

If that dog goes, I am going with him, I say.

I know, she tells me.

I don't love anyone as much as him.

There is the sensation of her small hands again, in my hair.

Or you, I say.

The suspense is killing me.

Please God, let there be good news.

My mother says this to me, and to Francis, and in her voice, beneath the tears and steel, I hear the soft, rustling sound of true love.

ACKNOWLEDGEMENTS

This book was completed in 2009 then overhauled, again and again.

Leanne Delap, *my girl*, read a very early draft and insisted that I continue. I am indebted to her for this and so much more — you found us a home!

Kevin Connolly, David McGimpsey, and Nick Mount read versions of the book and offered many valuable insights. James Crosbie, Jason Camlot, and Janet Stone also read the book early on: I am grateful to them.

To my friend, the heartbreaking painter Margaux Williamson: No, *you* are like an angel. Reid Millard: You pwn the world.

Thanks to my family, to my mother and father in particular. And my dear Janice.

Thanks to Steve Heighton (this was your idea!), Malcolm Ingram (yours too, cubby), Barb Vaclavik, Paule Kelly-Rhéaume, Kristen

Peterson, Danila Botha, Rani Rivera, and my great *Globe, Fashion*, and University of Toronto colleagues. To Ann Marie Peña at the AGO and Alexis Victor at Y&R. And to the rad Lesley G.; to Mark and Peggi and Diego, the Mascot guys, the Magpies, Shopgirls, Cecile, Eric, Sam, Tanya, Quinte, and all my Parkdale friends.

Thanks to Nancy for her photograph of me; to Jamie, for his, and for everything.

Mary Crosbie's funny stories and manuscript *Scary Killy* were a great influence in the early stages, as was William New's *Buzzy*.

Everyone at Anansi is amazing. Thanks, wholeheartedly, to Melanie Little, a great writer and editor nonpareil; Jared Bland, a genuine radical; and Sarah M., a friend to be admired. And to Kate: the whole damn package.

I received a Toronto Arts Council grant, to my shock, and thank this daring agency. Some of the work, which I largely kept to myself, appeared in *Matrix*, *Ditch*, *Driven*, *Court Green*, and *The Walrus*: superstars!

There are a number of references here to songs/lyrics, books, and movies I love, and these are listed, in chronological order, as follows: "The Wretched Life of a Lonely Heart," The Pretenders ("Back on the Chain Gang"); "Goo Goo Muck," The Cramps; Dr. Ananda Chakrabarty's 2009 OCAD lecture on *The Kama Sutra* (in "Sixteen Bites"); "More Dead Than Alive," The Velvet Underground's "Waiting for My Man"; "Dead Souls," Joy Division; *King of the Hill* (Cotton Hill says "a stink for the ages"); "Blood on the Gizmo," Charley Horse; The Crystals, "And Then He Kissed Me"; "Scènes d'un rêve casanier," MOCCA exhibit by David Hoffos; "I Close My

Eyes," Kansas ("Dust in the Wind"); "I'm Pretty Like Drugs," Queen Adreena; "Alcohol, Addiction, Mania," Avital Ronell; "Ray of Light," Madonna; "And the Whirlwind Is in the Thorn Tree," Johnny Cash ("When the Man Comes Around"); "Train I Ride," Elvis Presley (who also said, "I walk catlike!" to his fiancée, Ginger Alden); "With Legs Incomparable" (line from *Viva Las Vegas*, about Ann-Margret's character, Rusty); "I'll Keep Holding On," The Jackson 5 ("I'll Be There"); "The Glory of Love," The Velvet Underground; "And Crave the Love You Threw Away," Hank Williams ("Your Cheating Heart"); "Only You and You Can't Hear Me," Elton John ("Tiny Dancer"); "As the Smitten Tree Gives Birth to Its Fungus" (unknown textbook about lichen); "Save the Broken Things in My Life," Attack in Black.

Additionally, Blanche DuBois is briefly quoted twice ("magic" and God appearing, "so quickly!"), as is the police report of Kenneth Halliwell's murder of Joe Orton ("a deliberate form of frenzy"), Eddie Murphy is the source of the phrase "sexual chocolate"; the songs "Gypsy," "Human Nature," and "Movin' Out (Anthony's Song)" are glanced at; and the line "That don't confront me" is my brother's hilarious misprision, from "One Bourbon, One Scotch, One Beer" in which George Thorogood says, or is supposed to say, "That don't concern me." Franz Kafka's *Blue Octavo Notebooks* is cited, as is John Berryman via Saul Bellow ("We are unregenerate"). The song "Head Games" is swiped at, and the song "She's Not There" and the film *Full Metal Jacket*'s hooker ("Any-ting you want!"). Rambo, of course, screams that he was called "Baby-killer" after his service in Vietnam. "How could this be?" Michael Jackson sings, in "You Are Not Alone." "I know I am someone!" he shouts, in "Wanna Be Startin' Something." Handsome Ned sang of loving someone "in spite of the danger" (may he rest in peace). And it is Vito Corleone, who asks the funeral director, of his murdered son, Santino (in *The Godfather*) to see how "they massacred my boy."

I have attempted to cite my sources/inspirations and to seek permissions where they are warranted. Whatever I have missed is my terrible error. I am sad never to have mentioned "Some Velvet Morning," Scott Walker, Big Daddy Kane, Sidney Sheldon, or David Gest's memoir, *Simply the Gest*.

I wish to thank, above all, my dog Francis, who is my best friend and a very good boy.